The first time he saw her . . .

He'd peered through a window from the outside of the cabin. Courting frostbite to play Peeping Tom, he'd stood there for nearly an hour.

She'd been curled up in this very same chair, reading a book. The flames crackling in the brick hearth had nothing on that curly mop of hers. Childish hair but a ballerina's body. Long, graceful limbs. Narrow hips. Small breasts.

She was built for a gentleman's bed. Instantly he'd imagined touching that slim, silky female body with his big hands. A moment later she'd looked up as she turned a page, and lamplight fell over her face. Smooth, white skin. Butterscotch eyes. Full, rosy lips.

He'd already gotten hard, watching her, but seeing her face made him groan. She might be put together like a porcelain statuette, but that mouth of hers could bring a man to his knees in three seconds.

DREAM
MOUNTAIN

GENA HALE

AN ONYX BOOK

ONYX
Published by New American Library, a division of
Penguin Putnam Inc., 375 Hudson Street,
New York, New York 10014, U.S.A.
Penguin Books Ltd, 27 Wrights Lane,
London W8 5TZ, England
Penguin Books Australia Ltd, Ringwood,
Victoria, Australia
Penguin Books Canada Ltd, 10 Alcorn Avenue,
Toronto, Ontario, Canada M4V 3B2
Penguin Books (N.Z.) Ltd, 182–190 Wairau Road,
Auckland 10, New Zealand

Penguin Books Ltd, Registered Offices:
Harmondsworth, Middlesex, England

First published by Onyx, an imprint of New American Library,
a division of Penguin Putnam Inc.

First Printing, October 2001
10 9 8 7 6 5 4 3 2 1

For my friend Joanne Sears—
who taught me it is possible
to touch another heart with words alone.
Thank you for your wisdom, support, and love,
and for bringing such joy to my life.

ACKNOWLEDGMENTS

My thanks to Chris Hughes, Marilyn Jordan,
Jill Knowles, and Carol Stephenson,
for your invaluable help with "the scene";
and the Stillwater Mining Company
for giving me a virtual look at the real world
of hardrock mining.

CHAPTER ONE

That damn bear was digging through her garbage again.

Through the frosty kitchen window, Delaney Arlen watched the bulky silhouette hunched over her garbage cans. She wouldn't have spotted him, if not for the full moon. Despite the fact it was midnight, and snowing hard, the pale light made everything outside plain as day.

And it was plain to see that damn bear was going to scatter trash from one end of the yard to the other. *Again*.

"That does it."

She'd just cleaned up the latest mess this morning. That was when she'd figured out the wind hadn't knocked the cans over. Wind didn't leave short black hairs and deep tracks in the snow. *Bears* did.

"Not this time." Laney pulled on her parka, then grabbed the shotgun from the rack over the door frame. "Bad enough I'm stuck on this stupid mountain until Uncle Sean comes back—if he ever does—or someone clears the roads to Denver, and why do I get the feeling that might be next spring? No, I think I've got enough problems without having to pick up after you, Mr. Bear. Time for you to find a new hobby."

She was talking to herself again. Well, who could blame her? Stuck up here alone, no electricity since yesterday, thanks to the latest blizzard. The pile of firewood was disappearing fast. Her cell phone lay on the floor next to the wall where she'd thrown it, completely useless because she was too far out of range.

And *this* place. Laney had never built fires, or cooked on a hundred-year-old stove, or chopped wood. She was a city girl, born and bred, and she'd been very happy *not* knowing how to do all that stuff.

You're a dead man, Uncle Sean.

It was her own fault for getting into this mess. If Laney hadn't been so upset about other things, she'd never have fallen for Sean's story. She'd never have come up here with her uncle, only to be abandoned.

For the last four days, when she wasn't thinking up ways to slowly torture her uncle or worrying about her other problems, Laney had been forced to deal with the realities of rustic mountain living. Cooking on the cranky, wood-burning stove. Keeping the pipes from freezing. Swearing at herself for being a trusting idiot.

Now this. Cleaning up yet again after Oscar the bear was, absolutely, the *last* straw.

She checked the load in the shotgun, pumped the slide, then pulled the door open. Icy wind and whirling snow slapped her face and stole her breath. Too furious to care, Laney stomped outside, where she had to slog through the foot-deep drifts to get to the side of the cabin.

"I should have loaded some real shells; I sure feel like shooting something. Lucky for you, Mr. Bear, all I'm packing is rock salt. That should convince you I am not a woman to mess with." Wouldn't it?

Her uncle's voice came back to her. *Never shoot an animal, darlin', unless you intend to kill it.*

Laney winced. Although Uncle Sean had taught her how to shoot from an early age, she'd never actually shot anything but range targets. She had trouble swatting flies. Even if she could get up the nerve to do it, what would she do with the carcass? Make it into a casserole?

Ragout of bear meat, yum, yum.

The falling snow made it hard to see, and that slowed her down. Her stomach knotted as it hit her— she was out here, by herself, with a real, live, hungry *bear.* That didn't make much sense when she thought about it. Oscar should have been curled up in his den, happily snoozing through the rest of Christmas.

What if it isn't a bear?

It's not Bigfoot, for God's sake, Laney, get a grip. She lifted the shotgun, wiped the snowflakes from her eyes, and yelled, "Hey! You! Oscar! Get out of there! Go home!"

Fifty yards away, the bear straightened, and the garbage can fell over. Trash spilled everywhere. The wind, of course, began its inevitable distribution process.

"Oh, for crying out loud—thanks. Thanks *a lot.*"

The bear shifted to the left, then started lumbering toward her, still on its hind legs.

Was it going to attack her? This wasn't good. She gripped the shotgun tighter.

"What are you doing? Don't you see I'm armed here? This is a *shotgun,* pal. Go on, go hibernate or something. Don't make me shoot you, because I will. I'll do it. Do you hear me?"

The bear kept coming straight at her.

For a moment she was too scared to breathe. Then

she remembered how much she enjoyed breathing, and put her finger on the trigger.

"Come on, give me a break here. I don't want to hurt you. Last chance. You don't really want to be a rug, do you?"

If she had to shoot it, the load of rock salt wouldn't kill it. She hoped. Still, she hesitated. Then, with less than ten feet between them, she took aim.

"Please. Just go away!"

He kept coming.

"Oh, shit." Laney pulled the trigger.

A roar followed the shotgun's blast. The recoil made her stagger backward. The stench of gunpowder stung her numb, cold nose. Laney watched as the bear tottered to one side, then fell face-first with a *whomp* into the snow. He made one last sound, then didn't move again.

No bear in the world made a noise like that.

"Oh. My. God."

She tucked the shotgun under her arm, and fought her way through the drifts to get to him. When she reached the big, dirty pile of fur, she saw blood on the snow.

"Oh, God. Oh, dear God. Tell me you're not dead. You can't be dead. It was only salt."

Laney knelt down in the foot-deep snow beside the hide. It slid under her shaking hand, as though separating from the body beneath it. It *wasn't* attached. She tugged at the fur, pulled it away, and stared.

"You can't be. This isn't happening."

She checked for a pulse. As soon as she touched him, a strange sensation shot up her arm. Where did that come from? The flesh beneath the thick black hair felt firm and warm. There it was, she thought, pressing against the heavy beat. Slow, but regular. He was alive.

She looked at his face, sat back on her haunches, and wondered what the hell she was going to do with him.

Laney hadn't killed the bear.

She'd wounded Bigfoot.

Seventy miles away in Denver, Laney's uncle Sean sat in a nearly deserted all-night diner, hunched over what might have been a bowl of chili, or bean soup. He wasn't sure which. From what he could see beneath the quarter-inch layer of melted processed cheese, it could have been either—or both.

"You never put beans in chili," Laney had told him once, when he'd spent the summer working as a short-order cook at her place. "Especially around Texans. No, the beans go on the side—and none of that ground beef, either. Best quality, chopped sirloin only."

"What are you going to do? Fire your own uncle for putting beans in the pot?"

Laney had grinned. "No, I turn you over to my night manager, Robert. He's from Houston. He also thinks hanging is too good for cooks who pollute perfectly good chili with beans."

"Hey."

Sean jumped.

A brassy-haired waitress, whose lipstick had rubbed off on her front teeth, stood by the table's edge. "You going to eat that, Irish, or let it get frostbite?"

He ran a hand over his thick gray hair, scattering a few snowflakes that hadn't melted yet. "To be honest, darlin', I was thinking about soaking my head in it."

"Poor thing, you gotta be half frozen." Like most women, she appreciated his verbal and physical charms at once. She reached out to pat his broad shoulder with one plump hand. "Why don't I make you

some hot chocolate? Nothing better to defrost your in-
sides on a miserable night like this."

She'd probably top it off with miniature marshmal-
lows, too. "No, thanks, I'll stick with the coffee." Sean
couldn't resist giving her the once-over and adding,
"Watching a beautiful thing like you is enough to
warm me to my toes. Unless you'd rather . . ." He gave
his thigh a couple of suggestive pats.

"Behave yourself." She giggled like a young girl
and slapped his arm. "Go on and eat it now. Lester
puts enough hot sauce in that chili to melt an iceberg."

"All right, darlin'"—he waggled his bushy gray
brows at her—"but you be sure to let me know if you
change your mind."

The short-order cook yelled for the waitress, who
winked at Sean before hurrying back behind the long
counter to pick up another tray of plates.

The Irishman's smile faded just as quickly. He toyed
with his spoon, silently cursing Kalen Grady, Charles
Richmond, the weather, and his luck.

*Is she all right? Of course she's all right. Why wouldn't
she be all right?*

He'd intended to go back for her after one night, of
course. Two at the most. Plenty of time for him to
check in with Richmond here, then return to Dream
Mountain to see how the shutdown of the mine was
going. He'd even felt good about it.

True, putting her in the Denver safe house might
have been more prudent. But Sean had felt better
knowing that she was on his home turf, hidden from
anyone who didn't know of her existence. Besides, this
way he hadn't had to come up right away with a convincing explanation for the situation, leaving him
more time for his other problem. His and Laney's
Neal.

But time was running out.

He'd checked the weather, confident the storm would blow through and he'd get her off the ridge as soon as it cleared. The weather cooperated. The only problem was, he'd never considered he'd be needed in Denver longer than a day.

Thanks to Richmond's penchant for high-priced women and French restaurants, his niece had now been stranded for five nights, not two. She had no idea of what her uncle did for a living. Worse, Sean had no way of knowing when he could get back and explain things.

She'll be all right. Delaney's a survivor.

The Chinese had moved up the deadline on getting the first shipment of ore, and had transferred the first of their payments as incentive for Richmond. Richmond in turn had stepped up the plan to make it look like they were shutting down the Dream Mountain mine so he could smuggle the ore out. Now confident of success, Richmond's goons might let things at the site get sloppy. Sean didn't dare leave the operation until Richmond actually began transporting the ore to the Chinese ships. Once that started, Sean's services would no longer be required.

No, Laney would be just fine. She'd be mad as a demon at him, undoubtedly, but otherwise fine. He'd make it up to her when this was all over. Sean picked up his bill and left a generous tip for the waitress, who gave him a disappointed pout on his way out.

The car phone was ringing when he got behind the wheel. He stripped off a glove and picked it up. "Yes?"

"Where are you?" a smooth voice asked.

"Denver. Listen, Kalen, I've been trying to get hold of you for nearly a week. I have to get out of here."

"Why?"

"Laney's still up there, in my cabin on Nightmare Ridge. Alone, I might add."

"I doubt it. Bigfoot has probably found her by now."

"What?" Sean's jaw dropped. "You mean he's *alive*?"

"Alive and causing all kinds of trouble for us."

"You shit son of a bitch." His tattered temper finally gave way. "That's why you said she'd be safer up there. Jesus, you *wanted* her there. Was there ever any threat against her?"

Kalen's voice chilled. "Settle down, Irish. Just do the job. She's safe enough."

"Oh, sure, safe as a baby with a handful of razors, with that big bastard around." Sean swore violently as he remembered what he'd told Laney about Bigfoot. "What were you thinking, man? She's a bystander, a *civilian*, for God's sake. Send in someone and get her out."

"I can't do that, Irish. We need Laney right where she is. He won't hurt her."

"You don't know that." Sean eyed the heavy drifts outside. "Fine, then. I'm giving it another day, then I go back for her."

"How? On a snowmobile?" Kalen scoffed. "There's a new storm heading in from the north. You wouldn't get five miles. Don't worry, she's not going anywhere."

"She doesn't know who she's dealing with," Sean said, and held the receiver cradled against his shoulder while he rubbed some feeling back into his numb hand. "She doesn't know *anything*, damn it. What's she going to do with him?"

"Knowing your niece?" Kalen chuckled. "She'll

probably fix him dinner, tuck him in, and tell him a bedtime story."

"She's got a good heart. That's what you were counting on, wasn't it?" Sean was tempted to tear the phone loose and throw it through the windshield. "I can't believe I let you play me like this."

"Let's talk about your other niece."

His feet weren't the only part of him that was big.

"Mister, you weigh a ton." It took time and a lot of wrestling, but eventually Laney rolled the unconscious man onto the sled she used to cart firewood from the shed to the house. Years of handling delivery crates and heavy pots had given her better-than-average upper-body strength, so she was fairly strong.

Or at least she thought she was. She pulled on the rope and groaned.

"Holy Toledo. Make that two tons. I'm going to rupture something for sure." She paused and looked down at the bearded, snowy face. He had to weigh two twenty-five, minimum. "Sides of beef have nothing on you, pal."

The man in bear's clothing didn't reply. He was still out cold.

Laney figured it would take her a good month to get him into the cabin by pulling, and tried pushing the sled from the back instead. It moved, but not far. She imagined the sled was carrying her uncle and she was shoving him toward the edge of a cliff. There, that was better.

Getting him up the porch ramp and into the cabin was even harder.

"As soon as I get back," she said, huffing with the strain of working the sled through the door, "I'm joining that gym around the corner. I swear it. I'll wear spandex. I'll drink carrot juice. I'll bench-press things. Whatever it takes to get me some muscles. Serious muscles. And you know what, Bigfoot? By the time I'm done, you're going to look downright anorexic next to me."

Bigfoot didn't comment.

After she'd kicked the door shut and pushed the sled close to the fireplace, she pulled off her snowy parka and threw it aside. Then, panting and soaking wet from her exertions, she rolled Bigfoot off the sled and onto the woven rag rug by the hearth.

He landed with a thump, then didn't move.

"Sorry. You're still alive, right?" Her heart pounded as she knelt over him to check his pulse. "Oh, good. I can't imagine trying to explain this to the police. I mean, would you believe me if I told you I thought you were a bear? Probably not. Now that I think about it, you just go right ahead and stay unconscious."

The sight of his face still shocked her. Not that she could see much of it. A thick, ice-coated beard covered most of the bottom half. His lips were colorless. More hair fell in a dull, frozen tangle over his forehead. He had black eyelashes, sharp cheekbones, and a long, high-bridged nose. The skin around his eyes was so tanned it was copper in hue. As she dried off his face, she talked to him. "So what were you doing, running around the Rocky Mountains in a bearskin? In a blizzard, no less? Are you one of those weekend warrior types? Proving your manhood by braving the elements? Or are you the guy Uncle Sean told me about?"

Maybe Uncle Sean wasn't lying just to get me up here. She recalled their conversation after they'd left the police station.

"Want to take a drive?" the big Irishman had said.

"I've got to run up to the cabin, see if Bigfoot's been there."

"Bigfoot?" Laney laughed. "Very funny, Uncle Sean." She saw his expression and stopped. "You can't be serious."

"Not *that* Bigfoot. This one's a homeless man who's been living up on the ridge. Has been, for a couple of months. The locals took to calling him that because he's a shy one."

Predictably her sour amusement had turned to horror. "Living on the ridge? This time of year? He'll freeze to death!"

"Right, which is why I'd like to go and unlock the cabin. Poor bastard needs the shelter." Sean had looked thoughtfully at her. "If he's there already, why, then, you can have a go at saving him, like you did all those other homeless fellows."

The memory of men laughing in the dark made Laney rub her wrists. She could still feel the duct tape they'd used on her, even now. "I don't do that kind of work anymore, Uncle Sean."

"Then, come along and keep me company. You never know. We might even find Neal hiding up there."

Knowing how much Neal hated isolation, snow, and nature in general, she didn't place much faith in that. "All right. I'll go with you."

That had been five days ago.

She pushed the hide away—from the smell, that would have to be the first thing to go—and studied what was underneath. There certainly was a lot to look at.

Bigfoot wore a torn plaid shirt, filthy denim jeans, and well-worn hiking boots. Through the rents in the shirt, she could see a glimpse of his red thermal undershirt. Laney sucked in a breath as she carefully touched his chest, and felt the dampness.

His undershirt wasn't red.

"Sweet Mary, no."

She unbuttoned and yanked the flannel shirt open, and pulled down the bloodstained thermal fabric. The rock salt had done quite a number on his chest; he was bleeding from dozens of small cratered wounds. She'd have to get him warmed up, then take the clothes off him, and clean them before—

Two big hands grabbed her by the arms, and dragged her down on top of the bloody chest.

"You."

Laney forgot to breathe. Bigfoot had the most beautiful, chilling eyes she'd ever seen. Cold, deep gray, the kind found in glacier caves, or shadows on steel. Frightening. Potentially lethal.

He was really strong, too, holding her in a grip that just missed being painful. Laney decided she was in much more trouble now than she'd been facing down what she thought was a bear.

Talk to him, idiot, she thought. *You shot him. He's going to be a little upset about that.*

Laney gulped against her dry throat. "Um, hi there."

"You shot me," he said. Bigfoot's voice was as deep as his hands were powerful.

See?

"Uh-huh." She tried not to lean on his injured chest, but the way he held her made it impossible. "But I can explain. I saw you standing over the garbage cans from the window, and I've been picking up trash every morning, and I thought you were Bi—a bear. Sorry." She winced as his fingers tightened on her arms. Steel vises had nothing on this guy's hands. And his chest felt like the marble board she used to roll out pastry. "I only meant to shoot over your head and scare you off, and then you started coming at me and I thought I was a goner for sure, because I really did think you were a bear, and then—"

"How bad?"

"Uh, not too bad. All I had loaded in the gun was rock salt." She put a hand on the floor to steady herself. "I'm very sorry. I've never shot a bear or anyone else, for that matter. I'm afraid I got most of your chest."

He said something vile, but his grip eased. "You got a first-aid kit?"

"I'm sure there's one around here somewhere. I think I saw one in the chest over there—"

He pushed her away. "Bring it here."

Laney sat back and crouched there beside him for a moment, scared and relieved at the same time. Then he tried to sit up, and she lunged to stop him with both hands.

"Whoa, hold on there." She gripped the top of his shoulders. More unyielding muscle. "Don't even think about it. You're bleeding and you'll end up passing out or something."

Sweat and melting snow had saturated his short beard and the long hair hanging in his eyes. He might not actually *be* Bigfoot, but the resemblance was unnerving.

Through the hair, one eye glared. "Get the damn kit."

"As soon as I know you're going to stay put."

He made a low, rumbling sound, then lowered his head and relaxed. Laney got up and kept an eye on him as she went to the chest of drawers and found the kit. He had his head turned and was watching her, too.

What does he look like, minus the beard?

She returned to his side and opened the small case on the floor by his elbow. "What's your name?"

Playing the tough guy, he ignored her and reached for the kit. Then he groaned through white lips, and his arm dropped.

Laney tried again. "It can't be Big—um, Running Bear."

Bigfoot didn't like her joke. She could tell from the way he snarled. "Why the hell did you think I was a bear?"

Laney had been feeling terrible, up until that point. Now she recalled how she felt just before she'd pulled the trigger. "I don't know. Maybe because you were wrapped from head to toe in a *bear*skin, and didn't say a word?"

A muscle under his right eye twitched. "You like shooting bears?"

"No. You *like* rooting through people's garbage cans?" As soon as she said that, Laney felt ashamed of herself. It wasn't his fault he was hungry; she didn't need to taunt him about it. "Look, I'm sorry. The only bears I've ever seen were at the zoo when I was a kid, so it was an honest mistake. Okay?"

He grunted.

Laney took out what she'd need to treat his wounds, but knew she'd have to get the rock salt cleaned out of them first. She could try to do it here, or get him into the bathroom. He didn't look the type to sit still while she used tweezers. That would take forever. Besides, he was in real pain, and the wounds wouldn't stop burning until she got the salt out.

"Okay." She eyed the distance to the bathroom, then gave him an encouraging smile. "How about we take a little walk?"

"Why?"

"The best way to do this is in the bathroom."

At once he tried to sit up, and Laney slipped her hand beneath his shoulders to help. He elbowed her arm away. "I can do it."

"Sure." Men, always trying to prove they were invincible. Laney got to her feet, folded her arms, and silently counted. Bigfoot had gotten to his knees by the time she reached eleven, then he cursed and nearly fell over. She gave him a dulcet smile. "Change your mind?"

He gave her another of those damn-you looks. "Give me a hand."

Moving Nightmare Ridge with a soup ladle would have been easier. Laney planted her feet, grabbed his hands, and pulled. The man stumbled forward, caught her in his arms, and held on as he got his balance back.

He wasn't big. He was *huge*. Maybe six foot six, a good foot taller than Laney, who was no midget. If he fell on her, she was going to be squashed like a bug.

He made a growling sound. "Let go."

"I'm not holding on to you," Laney said, her face smashed into his chest. She kept still, afraid that any sudden move might send him crashing to the oak floor. He smelled even worse than he looked, and her face was getting smeared with his blood, so it was a struggle. "Let me move to your side, and we'll do this *without* suffocating me, okay?"

He hauled her around, put one long arm across her shoulders, and stumbled forward. "Go."

Laney kept him balanced and bore the brunt of his weight as they crossed the hundred feet to the bathroom. It took some time. Bigfoot's legs were shaky, his gait uneven. He didn't complain, though. A breath hissed through his teeth when Laney's shoulder accidentally bumped his chest, but otherwise he never made a sound.

A *real* tough guy.

"Here we are." Laney helped him over the threshold, then pointed to the toilet. "Sit down there, and I'll—"

"Turn the shower on," he said, and slowly peeled off his shirt and the bloody thermal wear beneath it.

"Not a good idea." She patted the edge of the sink. "I can wash the salt out if you'll—"

"Turn the damn shower on, Red." He met her eyes in the wall mirror. "I haven't had a bath in days."

Days? Her brows drew together. *Weeks* was more like it. Couldn't he let her finish a sentence? And who was he calling *Red*?

Wait a minute, Laney thought. *Don't be a snot.* The man had been digging through her garbage for food. Survival was, understandably, much more important than cleanliness. It wasn't like he could take a bath in a lake in the middle of winter. Plus, *Red* was better than some of the other things he could have called her.

"Okay." She took a deep breath. "Hold on to the sink, and I'll start the shower."

Once Laney got the water running as warm as possible, she turned back to him. He'd already worked his jeans halfway down his thighs, and was struggling with the old combat boots he wore. The boots were ancient. The thighs were definitely *not*.

Stop thinking about that, right this instant.

"Wait. You'll trip." She knelt before him and worked first one, then the other boot from his feet. The thick, dingy socks beneath were as pungent as the rest of him. Something touched her hair, and she looked up.

"You're hurt."

"Huh?"

Bigfoot started running the fingers of one hand over her face, searching for something. "You've got blood on your face."

"It's yours, not mine." She touched her cheek, and made a face when her fingers came away stained red. "It came from your chest, you know, when you almost fell on me."

"Right." The odd expression became a scowl as his hand left her face. "Hurry up." She stripped off the socks, then reached to help him with his pants. "I'll do it." He pushed her away. "Get the first-aid kit, and some dry clothes for me to wear."

The word "please" evidently ranked low on Tough Guy's necessity list, Laney thought, then saw his jeans hit the floor. She hurried out of the bathroom.

Luckily, her uncle was a big man, and had left some clothes behind on his last trip. She went to the bedroom and raided the closet. In a neat stack she put a pair of khaki slacks, a fisherman's knit sweater, and a fresh pair of flannels. However, no shoes were to be had, except for her own, and his big toe wouldn't fit in those. Until his boots dried out, he'd have to make do with a clean pair of socks. She took the clothes, got the first-aid kit, and went back to the bathroom.

Bigfoot was already naked and standing in the shower, his head directly under the spray. Since there was no curtain, Laney got an excellent view of the most well-developed masculine body she'd ever seen.

Whoa. Not Tough Guy, she thought as she whirled around and pressed a hand against her pounding heart. More like To Die For Guy.

She put the pile of clean clothes on the toilet, the first-aid kit on the sink, then focused on a crack in the linoleum. "Is there anything else you need?"

"Yeah." A wet hand grabbed her wrist from behind. First he jerked her forward, then put his arm around her waist and lifted her into the tub.

"Bigfoot!" Laney stumbled backward, which put her head directly under the showerhead. Water streamed over her, blinding her, making her sputter.

He tugged her forward and pushed the wet curls out of her face. "What did you call me?"

She wiped the water from her eyes, and immediately regretted it. Bigfoot might be dirty and smelly, but every inch of him was covered with solid muscle. Wide shoulders stretched above a deep, powerful chest, which tapered down to a waist that was more washboard than stomach.

If he was starving, she was a Dominican nun.

More muscles flexed as he moved a step closer, all corrugated copper skin under curling black hair. Her gaze reached the white tan line just below his flat navel before Laney whipped her head back up.

No need to stare at everything.

He repeated his question.

"Um, Bigfoot." She tried out her best adorable smile on him. "Just a nickname. Like Red."

"I don't like it." He pushed her back under the spray. "Wash the blood off your face."

Laney scrubbed her face with her hands, then reemerged and wiped her eyes with one sodden sleeve.

"Scrub out my chest."

"Would you please—" Laney stopped as she focused on him again. He'd propped one hand against the tile wall, and from the way his arm was locked, it was all that was holding him up. She'd have to help him. "Okay. Here we go."

The water was only lukewarm now, and from the

scant amount she'd judged to be left in the tank, she'd have to hurry. *I can do this.* Laney took the shower brush from its hook, applied some soap, and moved closer to get at his chest. Seeing the wounds this close made her cringe. The shotgun blast had nailed most of his upper torso.

"Oh, Jesus. I'm so sorry." Still wincing, she gently rubbed the bristles over the small, bloody holes.

"Harder."

She bit her lower lip. "I don't want to hurt you."

"A little late for that." He was leaning heavily against his arm now, and his face was white. "Move it."

Laney went back to work. His chest hair brushed her knuckles, and she absently wondered why some women preferred men's bodies to be nearly hairless. They had no idea of what they were missing.

Stop drooling over his pecs, Laney. The man can barely stand. Get it over with.

She had to stand on her toes a few times, but eventually she'd scrubbed out most of the tiny wounds. The last were on top of his shoulder, and she braced herself against him to reach them. That was when she felt something hard nudge her stomach. She looked down.

If his build was impressive, his erection was downright monumental.

What would Neal say in this situation? Laney wondered. Something like, *guess you're glad to see me, big fella.* Too bad she couldn't do the same. But that would require nerve, and all hers were shot.

"Yeah, been awhile since I've done that, too." Bigfoot sounded disgusted. "Don't stand there gawking, Red. Finish up."

Laney silently cursed her uncle to burn in the lake

of fire in Hell everlasting, then completed the work
with the brush. Might as well do the rest of him, she
thought, and traded the brush for her bottle of shampoo.

"Bend down here for a minute," she said as she
poured a generous amount onto her palm.

He let her shampoo his hair and beard, then ducked
his head under the spray to rinse it. While he did that,
Laney lathered a washcloth and edged around him to
get at his back. She reached around to do his neck and
arms, and worked her way down to his waist.

I can do this. Laney was glad he couldn't see her face.
*He's hurt, he can barely stand upright, so it's not like he
could do it himself.*

She jumped when he said in a quiet way, "I'd do it
myself, if I could."

Something passed between them in that moment.
Physical trust—she'd help him, he wouldn't take advantage.

"No problem."

By the time Laney had finished washing him, they
were both pale and shaky. She stepped out of the tub
first to get the towels. Carefully she helped him step
out, dry off, and dress. She was reaching for the tube
of antibiotic cream when he caught her wrist again.

"You're cold," he said. "Get out of those wet
clothes. I can do the rest."

It was true, she was clenching her teeth to keep
them from chattering. "Take it easy, will you? I don't
think I can drag you out of here by myself."

When Laney came out of the bedroom a short time
later, she found Bigfoot sitting in the armchair closest
to the fire. He had pulled on the thermal shirt but not
the sweater, and was using one of the towels to rub his

hair dry. From the look on his face, he was exhausted and in a considerable amount of pain.

"You're a fast dresser. Here, let me do that." She took the towel and rubbed it over the shaggy hair. It wasn't black, but dark brown, and very straight. Surreptitiously she checked for head lice, but found none. "Your hair is really thick, isn't it? So's mine. It takes forever to comb out. Sometimes I get so frustrated I think about shaving my head and just wearing a wig for the rest of my life. I tried straightening it once, when I was in high school, but that was a total disaster. I looked like—"

He tilted his head back. "What are you doing up here on the ridge?"

Oh, boy. There was no way she could tell him about her crazy uncle or Neal. He'd think she was completely nuts. "Shooting strange men full of rock salt. And you?"

He snorted. "Getting shot by trigger-happy redheads."

"Then, we were meant to meet. That's fate or karma or something. Not that I believe in that kind of thing— Father Patrick would have a heart attack if I did. He's the priest at my church, Our Lady of Hope. Father Pat's still mad about the bishop making him perform masses in English instead of Latin, so you can imagine how he feels about all that New Age stuff—"

He gave her another look. The shut-up one.

"Right." She bit her tongue and tried to smooth his damp, snarled hair. That only made it look worse. He must not have found any combs or brushes when he was out rummaging through people's garbage cans. Poor man. Big as he was, he must have been desperate to resort to that. It hurt to think of him being alone and cold and hungry.

"There." She gave up on his hair. "Relax now. I'll make you something to eat."

"Yeah." He sat back in the chair. "Thanks."

While the woman was in the kitchen, he relaxed his guard. The pain he accepted as his due. It wasn't the first time he'd been shot, anyway.

He should have seen it coming. When he'd spotted her out in the storm, his first instinct had been to confront her rather than run. In spite of the shotgun she'd pointed at him. After all, there was the possibility that she was exactly who she appeared to be. And whether she was or she wasn't, she certainly wouldn't shoot him out in the open.

He'd neglected to take into account the low visibility caused by the storm. That, combined with the old hide he'd scavenged from the caves and wrapped around himself, had apparently convinced her to think he really was a bear. She'd yelled at him, but the wind made it impossible to hear what she'd said.

He'd started walking toward her, trying to catch the words, and then she'd shot him.

He savored the warmth of the fire for a few moments. Thanks to her, he'd been stuck in the cave for days. Nearly a week of freezing his ass off. Getting his chest peppered hadn't improved his mood.

Good thing Little Miss Chatterbox had only loaded the shotgun with rock salt. If she'd shot him at that range using standard cartridges, what was left of him would have been smeared over several yards of snow. He'd destroyed all his identification months ago.

Kathy would have never known the truth.

The trip to the bathroom had been informative. With one glance he'd seen the door to the back bedroom was shut, and the small scrap of paper he'd wedged at the top was still in place. His gear was safe, for the time being.

Or was it all part of the game?

The first time he'd seen her had been three days ago, when he'd peered through a window from the outside of the cabin. Courting frostbite to play Peeping Tom, he'd stood there for nearly an hour.

She'd been curled up in this very same chair, reading a book. The flames crackling in the brick hearth had nothing on that curly mop of hers. Childish hair, but a ballerina's body. Long, graceful limbs. Narrow hips. Small breasts.

She was built for a gentleman's bed. Instantly he'd imagined touching that slim, silky female body with his big hands. A moment later she'd looked up as she turned a page, and lamplight fell over her face. Smooth white skin. Butterscotch eyes. Full, rosy lips.

He'd already gotten hard, watching her, but seeing her face made him groan. She might be put together like a porcelain statuette, but that mouth of hers could bring a man to his knees in three seconds.

For a split second he'd wondered if she was one of Richmond's women. No, the bastard preferred sleek, skilled blondes, and wouldn't waste his time with a sweet young thing—even one with a mouth designed for maximum performance.

The girl had shifted in the chair, rested her cheek against one palm, and sighed. The innocent, faintly troubled expression was the tip-off.

She was either bait, or a player.

He silently acknowledged Richmond's shrewdness. She wasn't beautiful, not with that young face and Orphan Annie hair. Nor was she put together to tempt a discriminating man—too small and fresh. But she was vulnerable, and she was alone. It had been nearly six months since he'd gone near, much less touched, a woman.

So Richmond had thrown him a tender little morsel to lure him in. You didn't bait a trap better than that.

She couldn't belong to the owner's family, he knew that. The Irishman had spent every summer on the mountain for the last twenty years, but never made mention of a daughter. No sign of a wedding ring or husband. She was too old to be a granddaughter; the old man's son was only in his early thirties. Even if she was related, there was no way in hell her family would permit her to stay on Nightmare Ridge alone, with no way out. Not this time of year.

He had even gone so far as to scout for an abandoned or broken-down vehicle. There wasn't a car within a five-mile radius of the cabin. Besides, how would she have known how to get here?

He'd nearly walked in on her four days ago, when she'd first appeared. Coming back from his daily scouting expedition, he'd gotten within two hundred yards of the cabin before smelling the wood smoke. He hadn't lit many fires in the cabin, knowing the odor would give away his own presence.

Now he looked around the interior of the cabin. She kept things tidy. The garbage she'd thrown away had told him little about her, except that she didn't waste food and had already cleaned everything inside the cabin at least once.

Was she a player? If she was, why bother to drag him inside and treat his wounds? Had she meant to disable him then interrogate him? The Florence Nightingale act could be a ploy, to throw him off guard. Looking into those soft, caramel-colored eyes, he'd almost fallen for it.

She didn't act like a player, but none of them ever

did. He'd been down that route before, knew now he couldn't trust anyone. Least of all a friendly, compassionate woman who showed up helpless and alone in the middle of a snowstorm.

He'd play along. Little Red would eventually show her hand. Richmond wasn't known for his patience. Given the recent activity at Dream Mountain, time was running out. Richmond had a specific schedule to meet. She couldn't afford to wait too long before making a move on him.

That was the final problem: when she did, he suspected he'd end up killing her, too.

Laney ladled the chicken stew she'd made that morning into a big bowl. She added a handful of her homemade rolls, a slab of butter, and a tall glass of orange juice to the tray, then carried it out to the living room.

Thank the Lord my blasted uncle keeps enough stuff in the pantry and freezer to sustain an army. Bigfoot's going to need plenty of feeding.

Her unexpected houseguest was leaning back in the chair, eyes closed, his chest rising and falling slowly. Worn out, she thought, and carefully set the tray down beside him. Before she could retreat, his nose twitched, those unfriendly eyes opened, and he sat up with a jerk.

"Just me," she said as she pushed the side table closer. God, he was jittery. "Do you like New Brunswick stew? It's got chicken and vegetables in it."

"Doesn't matter. Just as long as it's hot." He looked at the food she'd prepared, then fingered the folded napkin she'd tucked under the spoon.

It must have been a long time since he'd had a decent meal, Laney thought, her heart aching for him.

"Drink as much of this as you can." She tapped the rim of the glass. "It'll help with the blood loss. At least, I think it does. They always made me drink orange juice whenever I donate blood. It's supposed to ward off infections, too. I read this article that said we never get enough vitamin C—"

"Here." Bigfoot held out a spoonful for her. Surprised, Laney took a step back. "I can't tell how hot it is, my mouth still feels numb. Taste it for me."

"Oh. Right." She leaned forward and sampled the stew. He watched her mouth, and self-consciously she chewed and swallowed. "It's just right. Try it."

He picked up the bowl in his hands and began to eat. A moment later he stopped and eyed her again.

Laney grinned. She'd seen that look before, many times. "Good?"

Bigfoot only grunted and wolfed down the rest.

Watching him eat gave her the usual sense of satisfaction. Her mother had taught Laney to cook as soon as she'd been tall enough to reach a stove. Lucky for Neal, who otherwise might have had to live on breakfast cereal and pizza and Happy Meals.

Laney had taken to cooking like nothing else. She began reading cookbooks, watching Julia Child and Martha Stewart on television, and swapping recipes with neighbors. Eventually the pleasure of preparing good food had become her vocation. "So what's your name?"

He bit cautiously into a roll, chewed, and swallowed before he answered. "Why?"

Lord, he was suspicious. "No reason, unless you've changed your mind and *like* me calling you Bigfoot."

After giving her another surly look, he ate the rest of the roll in two bites, drank half the juice, then sat back. He'd cleared the tray in less than five minutes.

Laney frowned. "Look, if it's a problem—"

"Joe."

"—you don't have to tell . . . oh. Okay." She got up to take the tray, stopped in mid-motion, and held out her hand. "Hi, Joe. I'm Delaney Arlen. Everyone calls me Laney."

For a full thirty seconds he completely ignored her outstretched palm and simply stared at her.

"Awful, right? But that's what you get when you give your kid two last names. I had a really rough time of it when I was a teenager. You know, when they put up my name, D. Arlen, well, of course all the boys had to make fun of it. There was this one little dweeb, Craig Learman, who drove me crazy my whole freshman year. He used to follow me to algebra class calling me Oh, My Darlen—you know, like in that Clementine song? Sometimes he'd sing the whole song, too. It was so embarrassing."

He hadn't taken her hand yet, which made her stop rambling. How long had it been since someone had shown him a gesture of friendship? Months? Years? Laney could have wept. No wonder he was so withdrawn. At last Joe took her hand in his. His flesh felt rough and warm.

Too warm.

Laney pressed her other hand to the side of his face, only to find his fingers wrapped around the same wrist a second later.

"What are you doing?"

"Settle down." She shook her arm, trying to dislodge Joe's grip, and slid her fingers up under the tangle of black hair to his brow. He wasn't just warm, he was *hot*. "You've got a fever. Damn." She swung away to head for the kitchen. "I can't remember if I threw some aspirin in my purse. I usually carry some because of my back. I get these awful muscle spasms when I—" She came up short when he retained his hold on her. "Hey. Let go."

"I don't want any pills."

Her jaw dropped. "Huh?"

Joe yanked on her arm, nearly making her topple over on top of him. "No pills."

What was this about?

"Look. Joe." Laney tried to sound calm. What she really felt like doing was thumping him. "You have a fever. If you get really sick, there's no way I can get you to a hospital. I mean, can you see me, carrying you down the mountain? No way. I practically blew a kidney out just dragging you in here. Come on, it's only some aspirin. It'll help."

His grip relaxed, and Laney cautiously eased her hand free. She had to remember that Joe, though injured and evidently ill, was still a lot stronger than she was. Laney suddenly realized how much trouble she was in—alone, in the middle of nowhere, with a complete stranger.

A very large, very strong, very *paranoid* complete stranger.

CHAPTER TWO

Jillian Hunter left Charles Richmond's empty office and walked to hers. She wished she could type up her resignation. Scream. Throw something.

I'll never get through this without having a total nervous breakdown.

She had good reason to be angry. Although they'd torn down the drifter drill assembly and removed it piece by piece from stope nine more than a month ago, the parts to rebuild its damaged pneumatic centralizer hadn't been ordered until yesterday. She'd finally found the invoice on Richmond's desk, along with a stack of other, unpaid bills.

They were on COD with everyone, so the supplier wouldn't ship the parts until the invoice was paid. Even if Richmond approved a check to go out today, the drifter wouldn't be ready to sell for another week, maybe two.

Bad enough they'd have to wait until all the stope sill cuts had been backfilled with waste rock and sand before they could sell the LHD units. And whose men had wrecked the centralizer? Not Jill's.

They're not your men anymore. This isn't your mine. It belongs to Richmond Corporation.

There wasn't a damn thing she could do about that.

Jill had believed her father had spent the last thirty years building up Hunter Hardrock Mining. Until Charles Richmond had set her straight. Learning how deeply Big Ben Hunter had gone into debt to keep the operation going—among other things—had horrified Jill.

Dad, why didn't you tell me about the money?

She'd already put the house she'd lived in most of her life on the market. Yet even if she got her asking price, it wouldn't be enough. The only way to satisfy the loans and Richmond Corporation was to shut down the mine and sell everything, lock, stock, and barrel.

Richmond made sure I had no choice.

Before his death, Big Ben Hunter hadn't known Charles Richmond would go back on his promises and shut down the Dream Mountain mine. Jill's father had arranged the buyout with the specific understanding that his employees would be kept on the payroll once the new owner took possession. Understanding that had never been put into writing.

"Mr. Richmond wants to upgrade the operation," her father had assured Jill. "He'll take care of everything."

A week later, Ben had suffered a massive heart attack and died alone in his office.

After the funeral, Richmond had come to the house and spoken privately with Jill. She'd been stunned by the amount of debt her father had amassed, trying to keep Dream Mountain going. Richmond quietly but firmly refused to invest any further in the operation.

"Your father was unable to make this operation profitable, Ms. Hunter. I seriously doubt I could do any better."

That had made her angry. "They didn't name this

place Dream Mountain on a whim, Mr. Richmond,"
she said. "Samples taken thirty years ago prove the ore
bed extends for a minimum of twenty miles. We can
keep this mine going, I know we can."

"Ben made similar assurances. However, his
records proved otherwise. As it is, I already stand to
lose a substantial amount of my investment. I will not
waste any more of my money attempting to find your
father's 'dream,' Ms. Hunter."

Jill had sat down and buried her damp face in her
hands. "I can't believe this is happening."

"There, now." He'd patted her shoulder with the
kind of false sympathy that made her want to shriek.
"I'm afraid we were both deceived. You understand
I'm only doing what I have to."

Jill didn't understand. Mining wasn't like the stock
market; sometimes it took months to hit a paying vein.
Anyone coming in to the business should have known
that. Richmond was simply too eager to close down
Hunter Hardrock and sell it off to the highest bidder.
Though she had no evidence, something was wrong,
and she was going to find out what it was.

That had required some strategy and a major ad-
justment in her attitude. Namely, that she go back to
work the very next day and pretend to be both meek
and apologetic.

"I'd like to stay on, if I could, Mr. Richmond. I'd feel
better if I could help make up for . . ." She wasn't
going to condemn her dead father's actions. Part of
what he'd done had been for her. ". . . everything."

"Of course." Charles had given her one of his small,
chilly smiles. That day he'd been visiting the site, but
somehow his hand-tailored Italian suit never got dirty.
"Your knowledge will be invaluable."

Her knowledge. What a crock. All those years Ben

had spent encouraging Jill to pursue her dream of becoming a mine engineer. After she'd graduated with honors, her father had hired her on the spot.

Now? All she was permitted to do was type, keep the coffeemaker going, and get the filing done. A mining engineer playing secretary. Richmond's idea of a woman's place—or a tasteless joke.

Jill had no choice but to continue playing a role she despised. The helpful little typist, eager to wait hand and foot on Richmond and his crew. Sometimes it made her want to throw up.

Thank God Dad is dead, Jill thought. If he'd seen what she'd been reduced to, Ben would have pulled his service revolver from his desk and started shooting anything in a three-piece suit that moved. Starting with Chuck the Jerk.

She opened the door to the tiny corner office Richmond had banished her to. The sight of the man sitting behind her desk made her come to an abrupt stop.

"Mr. Pagent?" She pushed some blonde hair that had escaped her ponytail away from her eyes. *Be nice. Sound like an airhead.* "Can I help you with something?"

"I'm going over the last of the monthly production reports," Matt Pagent said, not looking at her.

He was *supposed* to be doing his job as foreman and supervising the teardown crew on day shift. The lazy hayshaker. Jill glanced around the top of her desk. From the looks of things, he'd gone through every folder. Of course she couldn't say anything about that.

"Did you need anything else?"

"The quota sheets from last quarter."

Jill pulled the appropriate file from her cabinet and handed it to him.

"Thanks." He put on the gold-rimmed glasses he wore to read and scanned the first report.

"Excuse me, Mr. Pagent, but do you know where Mr. Richmond is?"

"Is there a problem?" Pagent got up and came around the desk.

Jill had to resist the urge to back away. It wasn't his size—they were about the same height. He wasn't as big as most of the miners who'd worked for Jill's father. In fact, she couldn't figure out what it was about Pagent that bothered her so much.

The eyes, she decided, as he came closer. Behind the glasses he wore, they were a mild hazel, but with far too much hiding behind them. His close-clipped brown hair and trim mustache gave the impression that he'd just gotten out of the military—or prison.

She was pretty sure Matt Pagent had never been in the military.

Jill took two full steps back in spite of herself. "I really need to speak with him, it's important."

He eyed the foot and a half of carpet she'd put between them. He always seemed amused by her reluctance to get close to him. "I'd be glad to relay a message for you."

His knowing smile made Jill clench her fists. "Thank you, I appreciate it, but I'd rather talk to him myself."

Since Richmond had begun the process of closing down Hunter Hardrock Mining, Jill had frequently aired her concerns to Pagent. She suspected few messages, if any, ever reached Richmond.

Pagent sat down on one of the chairs scattered in front of her desk. "Mr. Richmond isn't coming back from Denver for another week."

Jill gnawed at her lip. That was too long. "Is there a number I can reach him at?"

"Tell me what's wrong, Jillian." Pagent leaned back in the chair and watched her steadily. "You can trust me, you know."

About as much as a snake-oil salesman during an epidemic.

"The parts for the drifter haven't come in, because the bill hasn't been paid. We can't sell it if it doesn't work. No one has removed the jacklegs and stopers on level three, either." Her throat hurt, and she swallowed. "Even used, we can get a good price for those at auction."

"I'll take care of it."

Sure he would. And she'd give up engineering to become *Cosmopolitan*'s next supermodel. Jill tried another tactic. "There's a blizzard headed in from Utah. A bad one."

"Is there?" One dark eyebrow arched. "I'm glad you let me know. We'll have to rent a snowplow to keep the roads clear."

That did it. "We should have waited until spring to do this. My father never—" Jill choked on the words. *You're not being an airhead, Jillian.* She had to get him out of here. No, she'd leave, before she took a swing at him, got herself fired, and ruined everything. "Never mind. Excuse me."

Jill felt better as soon as she left. Until she turned the corner. Until she looked back at her office. Matt Pagent stood in her doorway, watching her go.

He wasn't smiling anymore.

That night the cables of the skip carrying the men down into the mine made a distinct whine as it descended four hundred feet to the lower stopes. The graveyard teardown shift coming down changed their places with the men coming off afternoon duty. Out of habit, they nodded and greeted each other.

"Jerry, Pat, harya?"

None of them liked working in the winter. "Cold 'n starved."

"How's the plug going?"

One of the men spit over the side of the skip. The others only shook their heads. They'd been backfilling the old shafts for most of the week, and the job would be finished all too soon. A couple had talked about putting in some extra hours and trying to strike a new vein, to keep the few men left from hitting the unemployment lines. Jill Hunter had promised to help, but not even Big Ben's daughter could pull a rabbit out of this played-out hat.

Endless yards of electric light had been strung along the shafts and stopes. They were the only means of illuminating the artificial tunnels of the Dream Mountain mine. Without them, darkness would fill the man-made cavities. Darkness so complete that a man couldn't see a hand an inch from his face.

Oggie Butler and Webb Upton traded their places with another pair and walked down the crosscut to level number seven. Though no more than average height, both men had to stoop over as they made their way along the tunnel. Years of doing the same had molded the men's bodies so that even aboveground they remained hunched and round-shouldered.

"Og." Webb nudged his partner with an elbow and nodded at a trio standing at one side of the shaft, watching the men come and go. "More new faces."

Oggie didn't bother to look at them as he and his partner trudged by. Richmond had laid off all the crew chiefs in the first week, and the hayshakers he'd brought with him knew squat about hardrock mining. Lately it seemed like the stopes were crawling with them. They watched and murmured to each other and made wise-ass remarks about the age and intelligence of the crew.

Maybe, Oggie thought, a support would buckle. Then he'd dig out an airhole and ask them what they thought of the old farts and their shovels.

They reached their slots in the bedrock and picked up the job where it had been left off by the previous shift. Topside the temperature was a mean 10 degrees and dropping; here inside the stope the air was damp but considerably warmer. Above them, a web of chain link kept chunks of rock loosened by vibration from falling down on their heads.

Webb blew his nose in his bandanna. Years of working around high-speed pneumatic drill rigs and a thousand different types of dust made allergy attacks common among the men. He eyed the pitted face of the wall with habitual gloom. "Never thought I'd be plugging Dream Mountain."

Oggie had the cold comfort of his pension and Medicare to look forward to. His wife was already fretting about how to pay for her expensive medications once he was laid off. "Let's get on with it."

Before Richmond had bought Hunter Hardrock, the two men would have been busy working an existing vein, or locating the next nickel deposit. Now they had the joyless task of packing the productive shafts with endless trams of granite rock fill.

The stope lights unexpectedly began to flicker, like bulbs on a Christmas tree. For several moments the shadows grew deeper, until the single-bulb battery light from Og's helmet seemed as powerful as the sun itself.

In the shafts around them, the rest of the crew automatically stopped working. Voices fell silent. The mine itself seemed to hold its breath.

At last the lights stopped winking out and glowed steady.

Webb swore softly. "Damn generators."

Oggie didn't comment. The generators had never been a problem before Richmond had taken over.

"We should be shooting ten 'fore this one," his partner said as he shoveled the useless rock from the tram cart, then paused to cough.

"Not me." Oggie didn't like ten. Working down there gave him the willies.

"Look." After taking a cautious glance around, Webb pulled a walnut-sized chunk of dark ore from his pocket. "Found this in that fellow Tremayne's locker."

"Hmmm." Oggie tilted his head to shine his helmet light on the rock, and turned it over in his hands. "Nickel. So?"

"Feel it, Og."

The old man rubbed the surface of the metal with his fingers. It felt unusually slick, almost wet. "Ain't nickel. Ain't silver, either."

He brought it closer to his eye. Whatever it was, it had a pretty, almost rosy shine to it. And in all his years underground, he'd never seen the like. Made him want to throw the chunk of ore down that bottomless shaft they'd found in ten.

"What the devil you doing messing in a dead man's stuff, Webb?"

"Just looking around. So what do you think? Should I show it to Miss Jill?"

"If you do, don't tell her where you got it." Oggie tossed the rock back to his partner. Nothing about

Tremayne's death seemed right, but he wasn't about to get involved with the fools topside. He'd finish this job, then find another. One that would hopefully cover the cost of living and starving in the state of Colorado. "Come on. Let's plug this mother up."

Joe eventually accepted the aspirin, but only after Laney had swallowed one he'd handed her from the bottle first. He refused to sleep in her uncle's bed, too.

His demands hadn't bothered her. Let him sleep where he wanted to—she certainly had no desire to spend the night on the hard puncheon floor. And she needed the aspirin. Dealing with him had given her a headache of epic proportions.

Laney piled together as many spare blankets as she could find in front of the fireplace for him, and added one of the pillows from Sean's bed. Then she got to stand and watch Joe remake the makeshift bed, using only one quilt for the floor, and two to cover himself.

"Guess you're used to roughing it, huh?" Laney picked up the discarded blankets. "I've been camping a few times, but I never liked sleeping in a tent. I like walls. Brick walls, wood walls, cement block walls, whatever. Just something between me and all the bugs and frogs and snakes and spiders out there—"

He gave her that look again.

She put the blankets away and came back to find Joe stretched out before the fire. His bloodshot eyes were still unblinking, still watching her. "Do you need anything else?"

"No."

"Well, good night, then."

Laney didn't lock the bedroom door, even though an inner voice suggested that might be wise, under the circumstances. She'd have to get up to check on Joe in the middle of the night anyway, and she refused to treat him like some kind of criminal. She had a responsibility to him—she'd shot him, hadn't she?

Besides, the man was in no condition to do anything but sleep.

She changed into her pajamas and set the windup alarm clock to go off in three hours. She needed to keep an eye on Joe's fever; if it spiked before the morning, she'd have to talk him into taking more aspirin.

He'll probably give me grief about that, too. That man was born to be contrary, you can tell by looking at him.

She curled up under her aunt's wedding-ring quilt and huddled against the cold sheets. She hadn't bothered to light a fire in the bedroom, and it took a long time to warm them up with her own body heat. Even when she finally felt cozy, she couldn't get to sleep.

Something was wrong.

Laney lay awake, trying to figure out what was bothering her. It wasn't the silence of the cabin—she'd gotten used to that. The wind moaning outside usually didn't make her tense. Certainly Joe being there was unsettling. But it wasn't him, there was something else . . .

Something she'd forgotten to do, maybe?

She ticked off items in her head. She'd cleaned up the kitchen and bathroom. Turned off the stove. Left water trickling in all the sinks. Kept a couple of blankets out by the fireplace, in case Joe got cold. Washed the dishes. Stored the rest of the stew in the freezer chest. Put away the first-aid kit. Hung up her parka in the utility room to dry. Put away the shotgun . . .

Laney sat straight up and jumped out of bed, nearly falling flat on her face in the process.

Mother of God, she'd forgotten about the *shotgun.*

She'd left it out there, leaning against one wall by the door. Not more than twenty feet from where Joe was sleeping. *If* he was sleeping. Immediately she sat back down on the bed. Why was she panicking? Joe probably hadn't even noticed it.

But what if he *had*?

It wasn't loaded, but he'd find the ammunition in no time. Her uncle kept the cartridges on a shelf in the utility room, in plain view. Boxes of them.

"He's too sick to go looking for shotgun shells." Even as she said that, she got up and turned on the small battery lamp on the wall. The freezing night air made her push her feet quickly into her slippers and grab her robe.

She'd simply go get the shotgun and hang it back up on the rack. Check on his fever. Stop imagining him shooting her in the head.

The main room of the cabin was cold and silent. Laney's eyes went to the huddled form on the floor, then to the fireplace. She'd used plenty of the firewood to build it up before she'd gone to bed. Surely it hadn't burned out by now. No, not even an ember glowed. The dark made it hard to see, so she tiptoed over to the wall by the front door.

Laney crouched down and felt around for it. The shotgun wasn't there. She stood and reached for the rack above the door. Empty.

Don't jump to conclusions.

She turned, and tiptoed over to Joe. He was buried under the blankets. Perhaps he'd tucked the shotgun under the covers with him. She'd have to check. But what if she woke him up and he tried to wrestle with her over it?

Please, dear Lord, don't let me get my face blown off doing this.

Laney got down on her hands and knees and felt cold air. Coming in from a small gap at the bottom of the front door, she saw, locating the source. No wonder he was hunched under the covers like that. And him with a fever.

Get the shotgun, Laney. Worry about the draft later.

Gently she pushed her fingers into the tangle of blankets, feeling for the outline of the gun barrel.

"Hold it." The business end of her uncle's shotgun pressed against the back of her neck. "Don't move."

She didn't. She felt like an idiot for not seeing what he'd done. The way he'd piled the extra blankets under the topmost cover, making it look like he was sleeping beneath it.

"Are you—are you having trouble sleeping?" Her voice squeaked on the last word. "I'm really sorry I didn't know about this awful draft. You must feel like an icicle. Why don't I go and make you some hot cocoa or milk? If you don't mind reconstituted milk, that is, because—"

"Get up."

If he'd found the shotgun, he'd found the cartridges. She carefully got up from her crouched position, moving as slowly as she could. Her heartbeat, on the other hand, was accelerating like a blender set on puree.

One part of her brain went off. *I can't do this again, not again!*

Another sent soothing signals. *Don't make any unnecessary moves. Stay calm. You've got to reason with him. You can't do that if you're having screaming hysterics.*

"Joe." What could she say that would make him feel safe? "I was worried about you."

"I'll bet you were."

"You're not going to hurt me." She deliberately made that a statement. "I'm your friend, remember?"

"Like hell you are." The shotgun nudged her. "Get back to the bedroom."

"I don't think I can do that right now." It was true. The memory of another harsh voice kept her paralyzed.

. . . just because you got a hard-on . . .

"Get moving."

Laney couldn't bat an eyelash. "That's going to be a problem. You see, I think I'm having an anxiety attack. Well, I don't think I am, I *know* I am, and—"

She heard Joe pump the slide. "Walk."

He wasn't the type of man to make empty threats— he'd certainly shoot her. Probably wanted to.

She could have an anxiety attack later.

"Okay. I'm walking."

Laney forced her legs to move, one step at a time. She had to think of a way out of this. A way that wouldn't get her beaten, raped, or killed. Or all of the above.

Another frightening memory came back. *What if they don't find her?*

He pushed her into her bedroom and toward the bed, then slammed the door shut. Laney jumped at the sound. She was out of alternatives. Out of opportunities. Slowly she turned around to face him and held out her open hands.

"Tell me what's wrong, Joe." Laney kept her voice soft and nonthreatening. She'd worked with dozens of combat-scarred veterans for the last five years at the homeless shelter. She knew how easy it was to spook them. "You don't need the gun. I'm not going to hurt you."

"You're good, lady. Damn good." White teeth

flashed for a moment. "On the bed." When she didn't move, he pointed the shotgun directly at her heart. "Now."

He was injured, feverish. Surely that would make him slow to react. Laney pressed one hand to her mouth and stumbled forward into a half crouch. "I think . . . I'm going to . . . be sick . . ."

When she lunged for the door, a number of things happened.

Joe's hands caught her before she could get around him. The shotgun dropped to the floor. A hard shoulder collided with her abdomen. For a second she flew through the air. Pain exploded over her body as she landed with Joe's full weight on top of her.

Once all these things were done, all Laney could do was wheeze in air and wonder how many of her ribs had survived still intact.

"Try that again," he said, his breath rushing against her ear, "you'll be sorry."

She was already sorry. Very sorry her sympathy for him had gotten her into this situation. She didn't bother to tell Joe that.

He had to be a full-blown lunatic.

He rolled off her. "Get up."

When she didn't, Joe jerked her upright along with him. Another hard shove sent her sprawling backward on the bed. She tried to crawl away, but he was already leaning over her, his big hands pinning her against the mattress.

Talk, Laney. At least you can do that this time. Your life depends on it. "Joe, listen—"

"Who are you?"

"Don't you remember?" Maybe his condition included some sort of short-term cognitive problem.

"I'm Laney. Delaney Arlen. I accidentally shot you because I thought you were a bear, and—"

"Who are you working for? Richmond? The Chinese? All part of the orbiter project?"

The *orbiter project*? He really *was* crazy as a loon. "Um, no. Actually, I'm self-employed."

"Is that what you call it? Why did you come here? Who sent you?"

"Wait." Telling him the truth would only make things worse. She needed to give him an explanation he'd believe. How else would she have gotten stranded in the mountains?

A breakdown.

"Look, I was driving through the mountains, and my car broke down. I remembered this cabin from a vacation I took around here last year, and figured it was closer than trying to walk back to Denver. So here I am. I just didn't tell you because I didn't want to get into trouble for breaking in."

"Where's the car?"

"About two miles down the road." To back up the lie, she added, "A red Ford Escort. You can't miss it."

"No." He sounded odd. "Guess I wouldn't."

A moment of silence passed, then Joe's hands clamped around her neck.

"I'll be about two hours," Charles Richmond said as his car stopped in front of the Chinese restaurant. He despised having to frequent the Golden Dragon, but he had no choice. "Wait here."

Deep in the heart of the Asian quarter, the Golden Dragon's only value was the anonymity it provided for its patrons. The restaurant belonged to one of Fai Tung's minor relations, one who knew how to keep his mouth shut and his dining room clear until Shandian business was completed.

Richmond's upper lip curled as he looked at the tattered banners drooping from the front pagoda facade above the entrance. The door was locked; he had to knock and wait to be admitted. A smiling waiter appeared, greeting him with a flurry of Chinese and a half-dozen eager bows. Richmond pushed past him without a word.

The faint smell of ancient, repeatedly used cooking oil permeated the place. Gaudy paper lanterns hung from the water-stained ceiling tiles by mere threads. Strips of duct tape had been used to repair tears in most of the red vinyl booth seats.

Richmond momentarily toyed with the thought of placing an anonymous phone call to the health department. Perhaps after the deal was finalized. For now, he'd simply have to endure the rat hole. He knew better than to reveal his disgust for his surroundings as he approached Fai Tung and his associates. Instead, he stopped before the table and performed an elegant, if shallow, bow.

"Mr. Fai." Richmond nodded to the six men stationed like an honor guard behind the short, plump businessman. "Gentlemen."

"Ah, Charles." Fai Tung did not return the bow, but turned his head and spoke in rapid, dialectical Chinese. Abruptly five of the six men silently vanished, leaving Fai with the last and largest standing at the back of his chair. He pointed a pudgy finger at the seat across from him. "Sit down, please. I have taken the liberty of ordering for you. Where is the lovely Miss Beck today?"

His mistress wouldn't be caught dead in this part of town. "She decided to go shopping."

"A pity." Fai made a show of disappointment as the waiter brought a huge tray of covered platters. "Come, sit down, and share my meal with me."

The last thing Richmond wanted to do was eat, but he took the chair and picked at the food. Fai Tung, on the other hand, ate with visible gusto. His chopsticks never stilled until the platters were empty and the same nervous waiter cleared the table.

Over a tiny cup of green tea, Fai smiled with a gourmand's satisfaction. He had very small, very white teeth. "You have good news for me, my friend?"

"Yes. Analysis confirmed the previous levels." An analysis that had never been performed, of course, but Fai didn't need to know that.

"I am eager to hear the results."

Richmond nearly sipped from his cup, until he saw the faint imprint of lipstick on the rim. Abruptly he set the tea aside. "The vein is very high grade, nearly seventy-five percent pure. The cutoff grade was only twenty-three percent. We know we have a proven reserve of forty thousand tons, minimum. More than enough for your government's orbiter project."

"Excellent." Fai clapped his hands together twice. The owner of the restaurant instantly appeared, and he ordered a bottle of champagne opened. "We must celebrate our very good luck, Charles."

Luck, Richmond thought, had nothing to do with it. Getting the initial sample from Hunter had been like winning the lottery—ten times in a row. Ben hadn't even realized what his men had found, only that it was different and needed extensive analysis.

Richmond had flown down personally to meet with the owner, and given him the falsified report. He remembered the way defeat had filled the old man's eyes as he tossed the test results away from him.

"This will shut us down for good, then," Ben had said, then suddenly erupted into fury. "Hell, I can't do this to my men. The local economy is in the toilet already. This mine"—he stared out the dust-filmed window at the entrance to the main access shaft—"it's all they've got left, most of them."

Richmond remembered being pleased by the despair and desperation in Hunter's voice. After all, he'd gone to great lengths to put it there. "I have a proposition for you, Ben."

A proposition that, in the end, had required a murder, he thought. The sound of Fai's smug tone dragged Richmond back to the present.

"We have only to arrange the first of the shipments." One of his men poured more tea for Fai Tung. "I will send some of my men back with you to assist with the transportation."

What he meant was, to keep an eye on the operation. "That isn't necessary, Mr. Fai, I assure you."

"Regretfully, I cannot accept your assurances, Charles." The cheerful smile faded. "My superiors are most anxious to avoid any further damage to my government's space program." He didn't specify the recent debacle over the SOAR technology, but Richmond suspected that was the cause. "They are also very disturbed that Tremayne had access to the mine for nearly a month before he was killed."

"He didn't have time to do anything," Richmond said. "Delaney made sure of that."

Another near disaster, barely averted. He'd considered using persuasion to keep the geologist quiet—citing the enormous implications of such a find, the media, and the possibility of the locals descending on the mine in hordes. In the end it had been simpler to have Delaney arrange an accident. Richmond frowned slightly as he recalled the spontaneous avalanche that had eliminated the need to finish Delaney's plan. A very convenient avalanche at that. Perhaps he should have had his men search until the body had been recovered.

"Nevertheless, I must insist." Fai lifted his flute and toasted Richmond. "To our profitable venture, Charles."

Richmond nodded but didn't drink. "There is one more item to discuss. Hunter's daughter."

Thin brows rose. "Yes?"

"She's been a nuisance." Richmond templed his fingers over his half-filled plate. "I thought about firing her, but she'd probably go to the media with some nonsense about keeping the mine open."

"Then there is only one solution, Charles." Fai gave him a benevolent smile. "Have your Delaney kill her, too."

Little Red looked terrified. The light from the battery lamp displayed all the evidence. Her pupils dilated until the iris was only a rim of amber. The edge of her teeth pressed into her lower lip. Her heartbeat pulsed frantically in the hollow of her throat. She'd even stopped babbling.

A red Ford Escort. Two miles down the road.

He was startled by the sudden urge to look for the car—a car he knew didn't exist. Christ, she was lying to his face, the same way Susan had, and he *still* wanted to believe her.

He grabbed Laney by the throat. He wanted to shake some sense into her, make her see that she couldn't bullshit him any longer. Her skin felt like cool satin.

Her skin . . .

Muscles in his arms bunched as an unexpected, ferocious need surged through him. The body under his was yielding, feminine, frightened. It called to him. Pulled at him. Put thoughts in his head. Like using his mouth on her throat, instead of his hands.

He got hard, just thinking about all the other places he could use his mouth on her.

"Please, Joe." Laney's voice dropped to a whisper. "Please let me go. I promise I'm not going to hurt you. Look at me, do I look like I could hurt anybody? You've got to believe me."

She sounded terrified, but it had to be a performance. Another move to throw him off balance. She probably practiced making her teeth chatter like that.

Next thing you know, she'll be breaking out the tears.

Disgusted with himself, he grabbed Laney's legs and flipped her over on her side. She didn't give in but kept struggling beneath him. His own weakness made the task difficult; straddling her torso with his heavy legs proved to be the only way he could immobilize her. While she lay gasping between his thighs, he jerked her arms behind her back and pinned her wrists together.

"No!" Laney went ballistic. "Don't do this to me again, please!"

Again? "Hold still." With one hand he groped in his pocket for the panty hose he'd taken from the bathroom.

"Don't tie me up."

He tore the hose in half and used one leg to bind her wrists.

"I won't fight you. I promise. I'll do whatever you want." She was sobbing now. "Please. Just don't tie me up, I can't stand it."

There were the tears, he thought. Right on cue. Little Red could have given Susan lessons.

He ignored the pleading and concentrated on making the knots tight. Once he'd taken care of her hands, he bent down and used the other half of the panty hose to tie her left ankle to his right.

There. She wouldn't be able to move without waking him up.

The sound of Laney's muffled weeping scraped over him like barbed claws. He clenched his teeth. Damn, she'd gotten under his skin already. That would have to stop. Now.

After her leg was bound, he bent down, clamped his hand over her mouth, and brought his face close to hers.

She must have been practicing crying, too. Her face was wet, nose pink, and little helpless sounds burst against his palm. Tears beaded on her eyelashes, around eyes that had become wide coins of black-shot gold.

How long had it taken her to perfect this bullshit act? How many men had she killed, using it?

"If you don't shut up," he said, dragging the words out, "I'll gag you. Understand me?"

Red curls bounced as she nodded frantically. He pulled his hand away. At last he could let down his guard. He was in bad shape now. Fever burned behind his eyes. The night air numbed him to the bone. It took the last dregs of his strength to lug the heavy quilt from the bottom of the bed and pull it over both of them.

With a groan he let his head fall back in the space where a pillow should have been. She'd brought it out to the living room, he recalled. Another thoughtful little gesture to make him feel comfortable. To make him believe her cover.

Laney's long, slim body shook beside him, and absently he pulled her closer. She was twisted, her upper torso on her left side, her arms bound behind her, her hip and leg were straight beside his. She groaned.

Let her be uncomfortable. He was too damn tired and sick to manage anything else. He had to sleep. She had to stay where she was. Little Red would just have to endure.

"Joe?"

Didn't the woman ever shut up? "Go to sleep."

She went to whispering again. "Joe, what did I do wrong? Why are you afraid of me?"

Afraid of her. Christ. He had a good hundred pounds on her. Then it hit him.

He *was* afraid of her. Afraid of letting her get under his guard. Afraid of giving in to the needs brought on by months of being alone. Afraid of taking the warmth she offered. He could lose himself in a woman like Laney.

But she worked for Richmond, and he'd rather screw a snake first.

"Game over, Red. Go to sleep."

CHAPTER THREE

A shadow detached itself from the corner of the
wall. It moved silently over to the armchair where
Jill Hunter had fallen asleep, and picked up the remote
that had fallen from her hand. One long finger caressed the button that would turn off the crackling sta-
tic of the off-air station.

He'd leave it on, Pagent decided, and put the remote back on the armchair by Jill's right hand. The
sound would cover any noise he might make while he
searched the house.

She'd started packing, he saw, in anticipation of
selling the house. Half-filled cardboard boxes lined
one wall. Hopefully she wouldn't have gotten in to her
father's office yet, or this would be harder than he'd
thought.

Pagent knew better than to linger, but for a moment
stood and watched her sleep anyway. Jill lay curled up
in the chair, huddled beneath a crocheted afghan. Her
face was absolutely serene. From the slight movements beneath her eyelids, he knew she was dreaming. She had bright blue eyes, the kind that burned
when she looked at someone.

What do you dream about, Jillian?

Pagent already knew most of the details of her life.

Her mother had died when Jill was a young teenager, and her father had started taking her to the mine soon after that. She'd gone on to get an engineering degree from Virginia Polytech, then come back to Colorado to work for her father as the company mining engineer.

Then Ben had sold out, died, and Richmond had forced her to sell her home and her legacy.

Pagent still couldn't figure out why she'd gone along with Richmond. Jill could have fought him. She could have gotten a position with any comparable company in the region, taken out loans, gone to court.

Instead, she'd given up her career to spend her days typing, making coffee, and watching her father's company being sold off, piece by piece. Was it shame over the debts? Some way to redeem her father's name? Or something else?

Pagent turned and walked carefully across the old hardwood floor. Tonight he'd have to go through everything in the old man's study, see if he could turn up any of Tremayne's original surveys. He let himself into the dark room and locked himself in. Then he went over and turned on the desk light.

A dozen photos of Jill looked up at him. Jill taking her first steps. Jill in a miner's helmet. Jill in a bikini. Jill smiling.

Matt began pulling out the desk drawers. Ben had done his own books—a fact that had delighted Charles—and had known the value of organization. Files and receipts were alphabetized, and Pagent had gone through half of them when he heard the first sound.

She must have woken up.

He crossed the room, stood at the door for a moment to listen for her footsteps, then released the lock and darted back to the desk. He'd just switched off the light and ducked under the space between the drawers when Jill walked in.

The overhead light snapped on. There was a pause, silence, then Jill approached the desk.

Would he have to deal with her tonight?

She made an odd, wounded sound.

"Dad." She picked up something from the desk. "I miss you." A sniff, then a sob. "I miss you so much."

Whatever she had picked up fell from her hand with a clatter. Or was thrown. Pagent couldn't tell which.

"I won't do this. I won't."

She ran from the desk, knocking into something before she turned the light off and slammed the door.

He waited until there was only the barely perceptible sound of her weeping from the back of the house, then got out. On the desk, a frame lay on its side where she'd dropped it. It was, Pagent saw, a recent photograph of Jill, not smiling, standing with her arm around her father. It had been taken on the day Richmond had closed the deal with Ben to take over the business. The same day Pagent had met Jill, in fact.

A very interesting photograph. Because standing beside Jill was his own, unsmiling image.

Delaney was silent after that, though she didn't go to sleep. Drained as he was, neither could the man lying beside her. He knew what waited for him as soon as he closed his eyes.

That last, nightmarish scene at his place. He'd known from the moment he'd walked in the ransacked apartment that his time was up. Susan had confirmed it when she stepped out of the shadows.

"I want those surveys, Gareth."

"Why, Susan?"

"Don't try to stall me, lover, it's so tiresome." The .22 she held pointed at his chest jerked as she gestured with it. "Get the surveys and bring them to me."

He lied without blinking. "They're at my office on Dream Mountain, locked up in my desk."

"Excellent. I'll get them in the morning." She came closer, a sneer spreading across her lovely face. "I told Charles he didn't need to use his contract killer. Poor Delaney is going to be *so* disappointed."

So Richmond knew everything. "Did you sleep with me for Charles, too?"

"Oh, yes. A nice little bonus for me, I have to say."

She aimed for his heart. "Say good-bye, lover."

Joe had thrown himself at her, trying to wrestle the gun from her hand, but she'd worked it down between them.

The weapon had fired. Susan's eyes had gone wide, then she'd collapsed. He'd knelt in the spreading pool of blood, pressing his hand over the chest wound, trying to resuscitate her. Nothing had worked.

Susan died, still clutching his arms.

In the end he'd had no choice. He left her to go back to the mine and collect the samples. Once he'd gotten them, he'd go to the police and turn himself in.

Somehow he didn't think his claim of self-defense would convince anyone.

Once more he relived those final hours. Climbing into the skip. Lowering himself down the shaft. Crawling past the barricade into stope ten. Discovering his cache was gone. Swearing under his breath. Punching more ore from the wide, exposed vein, using only his hands and a pickax.

All the while knowing time was running out.

It had taken too long. Richmond had been waiting up top for him, along with two men who identified themselves as federal agents. Joe's pockets had bulged with ore samples, but Richmond hadn't said a word. He'd only smiled, turned, and walked away.

They'd found Susan.

He knew something was wrong after they'd slapped the cuffs on him but didn't bother to read him his rights. He'd muttered something about it, and one of the agents had laughed.

"Where you're going pal, you won't need an attorney."

A few minutes later he was being escorted up the mountain. Probably to a remote spot where his body could be buried or tossed off one of the sheer cliffs into a deep ravine.

"Where's Irish?" one of his escorts said along the way.

"I'm not waiting," the other replied. "Let's get it over with."

Richmond's bogus agents would have been successful, too, had it not been for the avalanche. Hundreds of tons of rock came down the mountain, an unstoppable stone river of death. Richmond now thought he was dead, his body buried under fifty feet of rubble.

Kathy. It must be tearing her apart, thinking she'd lost him, that she was all alone in the world now. He closed his eyes, summoning her beautiful face, wondering if he'd ever see it again.

It was close to dawn when Red spoke to him again. "Joe."

"What?"

"Your fever is getting worse."

She was right. He could feel the ache of it deep in his limbs now, burning him up, draining the last of his strength. "Go to sleep." He fumbled in his pocket for the bottle of aspirin he'd taken from her purse. Then he swore.

She tensed. "What?"

"Shut up." He had no intention of telling her that his hands were shaking so much that he couldn't open the childproof cap.

Laney propped herself up enough to watch what he was doing. "Let me help you."

He snorted.

"Untie my hands, and I'll open it for you."

"Forget it." He let the bottle fall between them, and sank back on the mattress. It was getting hard to breathe; she'd built the fireplace up too much. He should have doused it. Then he remembered he had doused it and they were in her bedroom now.

Fever was making him hot, making it hard to think straight. How bad was it?

Laney wiggled against him, and he turned bleary eyes to see her face pressed against the space between them. "What the hell are you doing?"

She straightened. The aspirin bottle was in her mouth. "*Ol ih,*" she said around the cap.

Joe reached to take the plastic bottle away from her, but she was quick. Pills went everywhere.

She spit the cap out of her mouth. "There, got it."

He would have thanked her, but he couldn't keep his eyes open another second.

From there he drifted in and out of consciousness. A real shame she was a player. How had she gotten involved with Richmond? Had to be the innocent look. Who'd suspect a pretty little airhead like her?

And that mop of hers. He hadn't been able to keep his hands off those silly curls. He hadn't liked seeing the blood on her face, though. He'd looked for a wound, until she'd told him it was his—

"Joe."

The way she said that distracted him. Every time. The way her lips pouted on the "j," and rounded on the "oe." Would they look like that, if she was kneeling in front of him while he guided her soft mouth to his—

"Joe. You've got to wake up now."

She sounded scared, so scared it made him fight his way back to consciousness. She needed him. Had Richmond come after them? He'd kill that spineless bastard before he'd let Richmond touch her. No, that wasn't how it was . . . she worked for Richmond. . . .

He felt soft lips brush against his mouth.

That cleared his head a little. Richmond. A trap. She'd shot him. Why the hell was she kissing him? Couldn't she give it up?

It took some effort, but he turned his face away from her. "No."

"Open your mouth."

He made a disgusted sound. Open his mouth. Sure. *Next thing you know she'll be telling you to make her job easier and pull the trigger yourself.*

"I'm going to put an aspirin in your mouth."

He wouldn't do it. She'd have to find another way to kill him. Then he felt her rest her cheek against his. Something wet plopped on his nose.

She was crying again.

"Joe." Why was she doing this? Contract killers didn't weep and beg. Could she really do it on cue? "Come on. I can't get my hands loose. Help me out here."

The fever was spreading over him, sinking into his bones, burning away the anger. Determined to stay conscious, he focused on Laney. Her tears felt so cool on his skin. The touch of her lips soothed the fiery ache in his head. Even her breath felt like a delicate caress. He could practically taste her scent.

Some nights, when he'd been hiding alone in the cave, Joe had thought about what he missed. A bed that wasn't made out of rock. Two hours under a hot shower. Good scotch. A steak the size of Nebraska. But what he'd wanted most was a woman. The sound of a woman's voice, the feel of a woman in his arms, the smell of a woman filling his head.

Now here she was, wrapped up like a present. Joe knew he couldn't hold on to consciousness much longer. He also knew he'd do anything to get a taste of her mouth. Even chew on the end of a shotgun, if necessary.

As if reading his mind, Laney's mouth pressed over his, light and hesitant. Her tongue coaxed his teeth apart, and something dropped into the back of his mouth. Reflexively he swallowed it, then opened his eyes when she lifted her head.

"Okay." She took a breath. "Let's try that again."

Damn right they'd try it again. He wanted her mouth, wanted to grab her and hold her still so he could get at it, but the image of her face doubled. Shadows crowded in on his field of vision. Frustration made him snarl.

"Kiss me."

"Wait." She wriggled down, then worked herself back up against his side. "Here." Her nose bumped his chin. "Joe. Open up for me."

She tried to do the same thing as before, her lips on his, her tongue slipping in, the pill dropping in the back of his mouth. He tried to spit it out, choked, and swallowed it instead.

Why was she doing this? Screw her pills. He might

not make it through the night, but he was going to take what he needed. Her. Now.

Joe grabbed a handful of hair at the back of Laney's head. As he worked his fingers deep into the silky curls, he tugged her back down. He could feel her astonished jerk of reaction as he returned the favor and opened her mouth with his tongue. She tasted as good as a peach stolen from a summer grove.

If you're going to kill me, Red, this is the way I want to go.

He cradled her face between his hands, and poured all his hunger into the kiss. She was very still, not fighting him, not trying to stop him at all. He felt her body change, felt the deep trembling and slow relaxation. All the signs were there. She needed him, too.

Without taking his mouth from hers, Joe pulled her on top of him.

Sean took the first opportunity to go back for Laney, although it had meant a dangerous trip along the only road still open into Nightmare Ridge. He knew he was compromising his position—possibly his life—but this time he'd put his family first.

And he would, too, as soon as he checked in at the mine and took care of a little business.

Pagent had somehow kept the pass clear, Sean saw as he drove up the twisting road to the cluster of buildings perched on the side of Dream Mountain. He wasn't surprised. Richmond's lieutenant was an efficient man. He'd probably gone and rented a snowplow to do it himself before going into work.

Sean drove his rented utility vehicle past the ruins of the old camp. Frost and snow had softened the ugly piles of rotted wood and collapsed shacks. The new site, built next to the Grey Lady mine, abandoned back in 1899, had produced steady amounts of nickel, zinc, molybdenum, and trona for the last decade. Would have gone on with production for another twenty years, too, had it not been for the vein discovered in stope ten.

That mother lode had made all the difference.

He'd have to get down there, see how far they'd progressed. The deadline on the job was approaching fast, and it was time to tie up the last of the loose ends. Sean would begin the process of cleaning house, and getting the operation ready to begin final production.

He pulled up outside the main office, making note of the two cars parked outside. There weren't any others. Richmond had let most of the administrative staff go, leaving only a skeleton crew to maintain the legitimate business front. Once inside, he followed the sound of typing back to Richmond's secretary's office.

"Morning, Miss Hunter," Sean said from the door.

"Good morning." She didn't stop working or turn around, but waved toward the coffeemaker in the corner. "I just made a fresh pot, help yourself."

"Thank you, ma'am." He poured himself some and sat down beside her desk, warming his hands on the sides of the Styrofoam cup. "Slow day today?"

"Uh-huh." Light blue eyes shifted in his direction. "The weather has kept everyone else in town. What are you doing here?"

Sean grinned. "I'm not one to let a little snow keep me twiddling my thumbs."

Jill's neat blonde ponytail bounced as she shook her head. "That attitude will get you nothing but trouble, Mr.—"

"Call me Sean." He rested an elbow on her desk and looked at the form she was typing. "What's this, now? Mr. Richmond has you doing the payroll, too?"

"The payroll clerk was laid off last week." Jill ripped the completed report from the typewriter and tossed it aside before she loaded in a new blank form. "*Someone* has to do it."

And Ms. Hunter's none too pleased to be that someone. "Is Mr. Pagent in today?"

"I haven't seen him. He should be downside with the crew, but"—her slim shoulders shrugged—"he could be anywhere."

And undoubtedly was. Richmond's man had eyes in the back of his damned head. "I'll go hunt him down."

"You do that."

The snap in her tone caught his attention. Now, what was going on here? Sean gave her a sharp look, but she never missed a keystroke. Surely Pagent hadn't started in on Hunter's daughter. Or was it the other way around? Sean had noticed the way she watched the foreman when she thought no one was looking.

Sean was tempted to warn her to stay away from Pagent, but that would serve no purpose. In fact, it might work to his advantage to report his suspicions to Richmond, who would use the excuse to fire the girl on the spot.

"Well, I best be getting my own self in gear. Have a good day, Ms. Hunter."

"Thanks." Jill adjusted the form in her typewriter.

He left her office and quietly made sure no one else was around the business trailer. Then Sean slipped into Richmond's office and closed the door.

Laney rolled off Joe's chest, and landed on her bound arms. Not even the stabbing pain in her muscles made her move for a full minute. Beside her, the big man breathed slow and deep.

Thank God he'd finally passed out.

I have to stop shaking, she thought. *Have to.*

She'd only gotten two aspirin down him before he'd fallen unconscious. Maybe that would be enough to keep his fever under control until she found a way to get loose. With a halfhearted tug, she tested her bonds again. No luck. Sick as he was, it hadn't taken him more than two minutes to completely incapacitate her. The knots were tight, yet permitted enough circulation to her foot and hands. Joe might be a paranoid schizophrenic, but he certainly knew how to tie up a woman.

What else does he know how to do?

"Oh, cut it out, Arlen." Laney curled over on her other side. "You've got major problems to deal with here."

She was tied up, nearly helpless, and the only person who could help her was unconscious. And thought she was trying to kill him to boot. If she lived through this, Laney knew one thing. Uncle Sean was getting one of two things: surgery, or a memorial marker. Maybe both.

Why did he grab me like that?

Joe's reaction to her putting the aspirin in his mouth had been totally out of left field. First he'd accused her of trying to poison him. Or kiss him. Then he'd started kissing her.

Okay, so he can kiss like nobody's business. He's delirious. That's all it was.

Laney looked over at him. Joe knew how to use a weapon, survive a blizzard, and restrain a prisoner. Who was he? A soldier? He was too young to be a Vietnam veteran. Could he have been in the Gulf War? That might explain his irrational behavior.

Laney tried to remember everything the shelter counselors had taught her about shell-shocked veterans and how they adjusted after returning from a war zone. They went through terrible ordeals sometimes, especially the ones who'd been on the front lines.

Before the holdup, Laney had taught cooking classes at the shelter. Her work had been part of the veterans' reintegration program, and she'd enjoyed it immensely. Only learning that three of her former students had been responsible for that night of terror had compelled her to abandon her volunteer work.

They were drug addicts, looking for easy money. Joe doesn't have any needle marks. He's not one of them. He's a soldier.

She'd shot him, unintentionally, of course. But maybe that had been what pushed him over the edge. Could that be all there was to this? Would Joe eventually snap out of it? Or would he attack her again?

Would you fight him?

Laney closed her eyes tightly as the phantom sensation of his hungry mouth on hers returned. He'd tasted of the orange juice she'd given him to drink, and his mouth had been hot from the fever. She'd meant to pull away, to stop him. Only the way he'd taken her mouth had shocked her. She'd never been kissed like *that.* Ever. Her scalp still tingled where he'd curled his fist in her hair. Her lips felt tender and swollen. And the way she'd gone limp, like she was a boneless fillet, just before he'd pulled her on top of him and—

"Stop it."

The man was hurt, feverish, and obviously mentally ill. Not only was she responsible for part of his condition, *she* was the only one who could help *him.* And she wasn't going to get that done lying here daydreaming about his incredibly talented mouth and to-die-for body.

The leg first. Their ankles were bound together under the quilt; she had to get that off and get at the knots. Laney sat up, and used her head to nudge the quilt out of the way. By the time she'd uncovered their legs, Joe was muttering and frowning in his sleep. She went still, waited for him to wake, then exhaled as he fell silent.

I really need to join that gym, Laney thought as she bent over and stretched her upper torso toward their feet. *Maybe a yoga class?*

The muscles of her back and neck strained as she got her face down by the knotted panty hose around her ankle. Almost there, just another couple of inches— there. Delicately she tugged at the knot with her teeth.

The nylon tightened at first, until she found the right bulge and pulled at it. Slowly, her body straining with the effort, she unpicked the knot and slipped her ankle free. Now she could get off the bed.

Carefully Laney inched away from Joe. The last thing she wanted to do now was wake him up. She immediately went still when he flopped over in her direction, his face only a few inches from hers. Gradually his breathing deepened again, and she was able to get her legs off the mattress without disturbing him further.

Her feet touched the floor. With a muffled grunt she levered herself back and up onto her legs. Behind her, Joe turned again and muttered something that sounded like "aspirin."

Don't wake up, Laney chanted in her head as she backed away from the bed. *Not yet, not yet.* Her gaze never left his face as she headed for the door. *Where is the shotgun?* There it was, on the floor. Getting it would be her second priority. First she had to free her hands.

Opening the door required some concentrated backward fumbling, but at last she turned the knob. The loud squeak of the old hinges made her catch her breath. Joe didn't move. Quietly Laney eased her way out and into the hallway.

She didn't waste time but went immediately to the kitchen. What could she use to cut the panty hose off? Her eyes moved around the counters and spotted the wooden chopping block where she'd put the dish rack. Had she left the knives in it? She had.

Another five minutes passed as she turned her back to the chopping block, grabbed one of the vegetable knives with her cramped fingers, and jammed the sharp tip into the wooden surface. Now all she had to do was work her bonds against the blade.

It wasn't a piece of cake. Laney hissed several times as the sharp edge cut her wrists, and finally forced herself to slow down. She wouldn't help either of them by slicing open an artery and bleeding to death in the kitchen. The sound of the last nylon loops shredding apart made her sigh with relief.

She yanked her wrists apart. At once cramps knotted in both arms. She rubbed her hands over the painful muscles and staggered over to sit down. Blood trickled down her arms and dripped onto the floor, before she checked her wrists.

Couple of good nicks, but nothing serious. She'd done more harm to herself during a busy evening back home. And the pain in her arms was nothing compared to—

No. Laney pushed aside the memory. *I'm not going to think about that.*

It was morning already. Dawn sent a finger of sunlight through the window, making the knives in the dish rack glitter. She'd better take one with her when she went back for the shotgun, just in case. A jug of drinking water from the pantry, too, for Joe's fever. She paused long enough to tie a pair of dishcloths around her wrists as temporary bandages, then took what she needed back to the bedroom.

Joe had thrown off the quilt, and lay shaking uncontrollably. Laney forgot about the shotgun and the knife she dropped on the floor as she rushed to his side.

"Oh, no." She dragged the quilt back over him.

He opened his eyes at the sound of her voice. "Kathy?"

Who was *Kathy*?

"Yes, I'm here." Maybe if Joe thought she was this Kathy, he wouldn't go crazy on her again. Laney poured some water into a glass and sat down beside him. "Can you sit up and drink some of this for me?"

"Not dead," Joe told her, and shook his head.

"No, you're not dead." Laney tugged him into a half-sitting position and held the glass to his lips. "Drink this, it'll make you feel better. Come on, do it for good old Kathy."

He swallowed half of the water, choked, then collapsed back on the bed. "Too hot."

Laney pressed a hand to his forehead, and nearly spilled the water all over him. It was like touching the side of an oven. If she didn't get him cooled down, right now, he could go into convulsions.

"Mr. Richmond, we've got a problem."

Charles pulled free of the slim arms around his neck and rose naked from the bed. The beautiful blonde woman he left behind made a plaintive sound of protest. He ignored her and walked through the suite to the next room before he spoke into his cell phone.

"What problem?"

"Two guys showed up an hour ago. Chinese guys. They look like professional muscle. One of them wants me to take them down to see the vein; said you knew about it."

"Yes." Fai Tung worked quickly, Richmond thought, and went to the bar. He poured two inches of bourbon into a glass, then took a sip. "Show them whatever they want to see."

"They want to talk to you, too, sir."

He picked up his watch from the elegant desk where he'd dropped it and checked the time. "I'll be down on the next flight out. Did you find Tremayne's surveys?"

"No, sir. We searched through everything, but all that turned up were some notes he'd written about an underground aquifer."

"Destroy them."

Richmond clicked the phone off and contemplated his drink. Had he underestimated Shandian's capacity for stratagem?

"Charles." His mistress appeared in the doorway, the satin sheet from the bed wrapped around her. Diane Beck's face and body had graced the covers of a hundred fashion magazines before she'd retired and put her assets to more lucrative uses. "Come back to bed."

Enticing as Diane was, Richmond no longer had the time or inclination to indulge her. He finished his drink, and shook his head.

"I have work to do, Diane." Absently he reached for his jacket, extracted his wallet. "Here." He tossed several large bills on the glass table. "You can spend the rest of the weekend amusing yourself."

"I was under the impression we were going to spend the whole weekend amusing each other."

Diane sauntered over to him, her hips swaying with a perfect runaway gait. The sheet slid down, low enough to display her surgically perfected breasts.

She definitely earned every penny. "Were you?"

"Naturally." One long-nailed hand stroked down the front of her body. "I was looking forward to it, Charles."

Charles doubted Diane preferred his company to the delights of spending his money. "I have to go back and deal with something at the mine." He took his briefs and trousers from the back of the chair and stepped into them.

"Take me with you. I've helped you with these . . . projects . . . before, haven't I?"

"So you have." He considered it for a moment. "This one will have you bored to tears, I'm afraid."

Diane halted, and allowed the sheet to slither to the floor. "*You* won't."

Richmond paused long enough to appreciate the full impact of her display. "You'll need to be ready to leave in an hour."

The ex-model smiled her delight as she came over and pressed herself against him. "I don't need an entire hour for *packing*."

It took some coaxing and maneuvering, but Laney finally got two more aspirin down Joe, along with almost a full glass of water. Then she hurried to the bathroom and retrieved some washcloths. After soaking them in a basin of tepid water, she started wetting down his brow, neck, and chest.

It wasn't enough; the fever seemed to get worse. She set the cloths aside and stripped him down to the skin. The intimacy of undressing and bathing him was as unnerving as it had been the first time, in the shower.

Mother of God, Laney, he's a homeless, helpless soul in need. You have to focus on that. Not on his . . . She glanced

down at the damp cloth she'd just spread over his
groin. . . . *charms*.

Neal would have smirked and said something like,
that sure as hell isn't charm-sized, babe.

"This . . . would be . . . a lot easier . . . with a . . . pal-
let jack." At last Laney rolled Joe onto his side to get at
his back. "Whew. There is just too little of me, Bigfoot,
and too much of you."

Joe muttered something under his breath and rolled
back over, trapping Laney's hands under him. Her face
ended up in his neck.

"Hey, pal, this is hard enough without you fighting
me."

His eyes opened for a moment. "Susan?"

"Right. Susan." Laney's teeth clenched. "What happened to Kathy?"

"How could you do this to me?"

She rolled her eyes. "How could you do this to poor
old Kathy?"

His hands clutched her, jerked her down to him.
Hostility made his expression hard and frightening. "I
trusted you, you lying bitch."

No, not hostility. Pain. What had this woman done
to him? "Joe. I'm not Susan."

She sighed her relief as he frowned, then let go of
her. Confusion made him reach out, touch her hair.
Slowly his arm sagged, and his eyes closed.
"Sorry . . . Kathy . . ."

Kathy again. Well, he seemed to like her more than
Susan. "Yes, it's Kathy. You're safe here, Joe." She blot-
ted his face with the washcloth. "Everything will be
okay now."

"Safe . . . okay . . . now . . ."

Laney spent the rest of that morning and the next
three days fighting Joe's fever. Hours blurred as she

bathed his big, hot body, coaxed him into taking in medicine and liquids, and kept him as clean and comfortable as was possible.

Sometimes Joe seemed halfway lucid as he looked at her, but when she spoke to him, his delirious replies made no sense. He called her Kathy, Susan, and during one dark night when his temperature soared, his mother.

She felt like a mother with a new baby. One that weighed over two hundred pounds.

Like a new mother, Laney learned to sleep when Joe did, in short naps. She'd given up trying to sleep on the sofa—every sound he made sent her running for the bedroom—and made do with a quilt on the floor beside the bed.

She made him drink, diluting crushed aspirin in water when he refused to swallow the pills. She poured quarts of her homemade chicken broth in him, wet him down whenever his fever spiked, and prayed that would be enough to get him through this.

Near dawn on the fourth day, she was so tired she couldn't think straight. Feeling distinctly light-headed, Laney finished spooning the last of the broth into Joe and slid down to sit on the floor beside the bed.

Luckily his fever had broken at last. She should change the sheets; the sweat that had poured down his face and chest had soaked them.

I'll take care of it in a minute.

She leaned back to rest her lolling head against the edge of the mattress.

Kathy had come to him in a dream. They were sitting in the middle of a desert, and she'd bent over him, tenderly sponging off his hot face.

"Am I dead?" he asked her, not entirely sure he wanted an answer.

No, you're not dead, Joe.

Why was she calling him Joe? He frowned. And why was her hair so short?

Drink this for me.

"Why did you cut your hair?"

She'd smiled and touched the bright curls. *Why, don't you like the new me?*

"I liked it better long."

Chauvinist. Come on, now, drink up.

"Okay." He swallowed water from the cup she held to his mouth. "Why am I so hot?"

I don't know. Maybe because you look like Hercules?

The fever seemed to drag him along an endless bed of fiery coals, with periodic rest stops that only left him even more disoriented and confused.

Lift your head for me, Joe. That's it.

"Kath, what are you doing here?"

Taking care of you, Bigfoot. You're really sick.

"Bigfoot. Very funny." His damn malaria must have flared up again. "How long?"

Three days. No, don't take the cloth off your head. Your fever's gone back up again. We need to get it back down now.

"What are we doing in the desert?"

Is that where we are? She sounded wry. *Here. Take these.*

Joe grimaced as he forced the aspirin down, then drank again for her. "You look tired, honey."

You have no idea. Don't worry, I'll get some sleep when you're back on your feet. Lie down now.

The dream had stretched out, until he felt the darkness thin and heard the sound of the wind. Something light touched Joe's face, and he opened his eyes.

He wasn't in the desert.

Above him, chinking made uneven gray lines between weathered logs. The sound of someone breathing slowly made him turn his head. The sheets under his cheek and the quilt over his chest felt damp. A washcloth in the same condition slid off his brow as he sat up.

The girl. Joe whipped his head from right to left. She was gone. He pulled the quilt off and rolled over, preparing to swing his legs to the floor. And stopped just short of stepping on top of a curly redhead.

Laney sat propped against the side of the bed, a shallow bowl of water by her hip, a cloth still clutched in one hand. The shadows under her closed eyes were so deep they looked like bruises.

She made a small sound. Snoring. She was snoring.

The fever. The aspirin. Kathy. Suddenly the dream made sense.

How the hell had she gotten loose?

He watched her as he slid off the bed, careful not to wake her up. Why had she come back? He saw the shotgun, still sitting where he'd dropped it in the middle of the floor. She hadn't touched it, hadn't hidden it.

The weapon was in his hands when he turned back to wake her. Then he saw the bloodstained rags on the table, and swore.

Laney's lashes fluttered open. She stared at him, puzzled for a second, then she gaped.

"Joe!"

"Hello, Red." He knelt down beside her and grabbed her arm. "Start talking."

CHAPTER FOUR

It was nearly shift end when Webb saw the men. He stopped, stared, then nudged his partner.

"Og. Lookit."

Oggie positioned the last tram of waste ore on the conveyor, and eyed the stope. Even if they'd tried dragging their feet, they couldn't make the work last another week, and that had him worried. "I'm busy."

Webb's elbow hit the same spot. "Og, *look.*"

The old man swore, wiped the sweat from his upper lip on his sleeve, then turned around. At the other end of the stope, the shift crew chief and two Asian men in dark suits stood in the skiff as it dropped down the main shaft. Just before their heads disappeared, the chief glanced his way.

"Damn." Oggie turned instantly back to the wall, but knew it was too late. Kerass had seen him watching.

Webb parked his shovel with a thump. "What is he bringing those two Japs into the mine for?"

"Chinese." Oggie had worked with enough Asians over the years to recognize the subtle differences between the two nationalities. "I don't know."

"He's taking them down to ten, I'll wager."

Oggie glanced on either side of them before leaning

close. "Your mouth is going to get us both canned, you nosey old fart."

Webb chuckled without mirth. "That's gonna happen, with or without my mouth, buddy."

"Maybe worse than canned." Oggie remembered the quick frown on the crew chief's face.

His suspicions were confirmed an hour later, when the crew chief appeared and called down the stope, "Listen up. I've got a couple of announcements to make."

The miners' voices died away as Richmond's dayshift crew chief Kerass strutted down the center of the level. Several exchanged stricken glances when Kerass produced a familiar clipboard.

"The following employees are to report to personnel to pick up their checks at the end of the shift." Kerass began to read the first name on the list, when one of the younger men tossed his shovel across the shaft. The steel tool collided with rock, creating a loud clang that echoed through the mine.

Oggie clapped a big, scarred hand on the younger man's shoulder. "No call to be getting excited, Jimmy."

"This is bullshit." Jim had a pregnant wife at home and a heavy mortgage. "Ben promised us—"

"Ben Hunter? Didn't you hear? He's dead." Kerass's perpetually wet lips stretched into an oily grin. "And your name just went to the top of the list, Deaton."

This time Oggie grabbed Jim Deaton by the arms. "Hold on, boy. Don't give him the satisfaction."

"Kiss ass bastard." Jim spat at the crew chief's feet, wrenched out of Oggie's hands, and stalked away to the skip.

Kerass didn't bat an eyelash, but kept grinning and reading off names. Another third of the crew dropped their equipment and headed for the shaft.

Webb and Oggie stood silently waiting to hear their own names. When they weren't called, Oggie closed his eyes for a silent prayer of thanksgiving.

"I'm going to need a couple of you men to get started down on nine," Kerass said, and looked down the diminished row of men. His gaze stopped and lingered on Oggie. "Butler. You're a good *company* man. You and your pal Upton get another couple weeks. Congratulations." The crew chief jerked a thumb back toward the skip. "Shake a leg."

Webb would have groused the entire length of the shaft, if not for the expression on his partner's face. Oggie wasn't a fearless man, no miner was, but it took a lot to scare him. Right now he looked ready to puke.

"Og?" Webb glanced over the side of the skip into the seemingly endless black hole beneath it. Sometimes the realization that millions of tons of rock were above rather than below you cropped up unexpectedly, even in the most experienced men. "You want to catch some daylight?"

Oggie ignored the question and rounded on Webb. "They see you fooling with that rock hound's gear?" Webb shook his head. "You sure?"

"Yeah." Webb frowned. Oggie had ten years on him, and he'd never seen him so rattled. "What's wrong with you?"

Oggie only shook his head and turned back to peer down into the hole.

Five levels above, Kerass and two of Richmond's hired hands walked away from the last of the day-shift crew and entered the crosscut. They kept their voices down to a bare murmur as the crew chief passed along their latest instructions.

"Ten's almost prepped for the heavy equipment,"

Kerass said. "Transport will be rolling in as soon as we shut down, so be ready."

"Why'd you send those two old geezers down to start on nine?" one of the men wanted to know. "Can't do anything with them bird-dogging us."

"They're our insurance." Kerass chuckled. "Anything goes wrong, we blast out nine, then have the regular crew dig 'em out from the east shaft. It'll keep them tied up and out of our hair until we can get the rest of the gear down."

"Blow out the stope?" One of the men shuddered. "Man, that's cold."

"They're trouble." Another gestured toward the surface. "Saw one of them snooping around in Tremayne's stuff."

The crew chief lost his grin. "I thought I told you to get rid of that crap." When the man started making excuses, he waved a hand. "Do it later."

"What about the old guys?" One of them asked Kerass. "We just let them watch us move the drifter down into ten?"

"Doesn't matter what they see. They aren't getting out of there alive."

"Kerass." A man stepped out of the shadows, startling the four men.

"What are you doing down here?" The crew chief folded his thick arms and regarded the mine foreman with a bland smile. "Figured you were scared of the dark, or something."

The man's cool eyes never flickered. "You've got a big mouth, Kerass. What's going on here?"

"Briefing the guys on what to do," Kerass said. "Just like you told me to, Mr. Pagent."

* * *

The daze of being dragged from sleep cleared instantly. Laney's gaze darted from Joe's bearded face to the shotgun sitting three feet away.

How could she have been so stupid?

"You'd never make it," Joe said, reading her mind perfectly.

"I know." Her parched throat ached, and when she shifted her weight she winced. "Can I get up? This floor is about as comfortable as a rock."

"Stay put." Joe let go of her arm and stood with some effort. The first thing he did was retrieve the shotgun and check the chambers. The second thing he did was point it at Laney's head. "Okay. Now get up. Nice and slow."

She got up. All she could manage was nice and slow—every muscle in her body screamed. If she hadn't known better, Laney could swear Joe had beaten her with a blunt object while she'd slept. A gasp left her as her spine straightened.

"What's wrong?"

"Nothing. I love to sleep sitting up on the floor."

Four days of watching over him had nearly exhausted her. She felt exceedingly stiff from the hours she'd spent kneeling beside the bed. Her position had aggravated her old back problem, too. Even her bottom was numb. For a moment she felt so wretched, she almost wished Joe *would* shoot her. A glance at his face made Laney forget about her own discomfort. He was too pale, the glitter in his eyes too bright. "You're still running a fever, aren't you? You need—"

"Hold it." Under the beard, Joe's mouth stretched to a hard line. "On the bed."

Not again. Reluctantly Laney sat down on the edge of the mattress. The only good thing about this situation was the panty hose were shredded beyond repair.

Then she remembered the economy pack she'd thrown in her suitcase. Scratch nothing to tie her up with off the list.

Joe's harsh voice intruded on her thoughts. "What happened last night?"

"You slept through it. In fact, you've been sick in this bed for four days. Running a high temperature most of the time, but I got some washcloths and water and bathed you, and of course the aspirin helped—"

"*Four days?*"

She frowned. "Don't you remember?"

"What happened while I was out?"

"Let's see." She planted her hands on the mattress, inadvertently drawing his attention to her makeshift bandages. "Before you became delirious, you held me at gunpoint, tore apart my panty hose, tied me up, and"—she wasn't going to remind him of how she'd gotten the aspirin down his throat the first time— "passed out. I got loose. I've been taking care of you ever since." She stared at the floor. "I must have passed out myself last night, when your fever broke."

"What's wrong with your wrists?"

"My wrists?" She went blank for a moment, then rolled her eyes. "Oh. Right. I nicked myself when I cut the panty hose off. I stuck a knife in the chopping block, and then rubbed my wrists against it, and, of course, I couldn't see what I was doing, so—"

"Show me."

Laney started to refuse, but the end of the shotgun jerked. With a sigh she unwound the gauze around her wrists, grimacing as she peeled the cotton loops away. Two of the scabbed-over gashes started bleeding again. At the same time, a very natural need made itself known.

"Look, Joe, I need to use the bathroom." Laney used

one of the bloodstained dishcloths to blot the blood from her cuts.

"Up." Joe stepped away from the door. "Walk."

Laney got to her feet and walked slowly out of the room to the bathroom, with Joe right behind her. He refused to let her close the door or turn his back while she took care of the basic functions.

As an experience, she thought, it was embarrassing in the extreme. Until he made her stand against one wall while he took care of *his* necessities. Laney quickly averted her gaze, telling herself her face was not as red as it felt.

"All right." Joe said. "Clean them up."

She whipped her head around in time to see him zip up his pants. "I beg your pardon?"

"Those cuts on your wrists." He jutted his chin toward the sink. "Wash them."

Why was he worried about her wrists? She edged around him and bent over the sink. The icy water felt good against her skin. She washed the fresh blood away, then held them up for his inspection.

"Swab them with peroxide while you're at it."

"Why?" Laney felt grumpy and would have sold her soul for a cup of coffee. She'd snatched a sandwich or two, but hadn't had a decent meal in days. Her stomach rumbled in agreement. "Let them get infected. You'll save yourself a shell."

That earned her a frosty look. "Do it."

Laney took the bottle of peroxide from the cabinet, and poured a little over the cuts to disinfect them. She couldn't help hissing as the antiseptic stung the raw spots. After she pressed both wrists against a hand towel to dry them, Laney held them up again for his inspection. "There. Satisfied?"

He backed out of the doorway. "Kitchen."

"Tell me," Laney said as she brushed by him and trudged down the hall. "Do you have something against multiple-word sentences? Because if you do, you should really tell me now. Is it a religious thing, or just the strong, silent-type-of-guy deal?"

Joe didn't answer her. In the kitchen Laney saw the mess she'd left on the counter and floor, and without thinking reached to clean it up.

"No." The shotgun pressed into the small of her back at once. "Get away from the knives."

That was enough. She hadn't had her coffee. Her back hurt. The ingrate hadn't even had the decency to say thank you for sitting up with him for the past three nights. "Get real! If I'd wanted to kill you, I'd have done it the first day!"

Joe's eyes narrowed. "Sounds like you were tempted."

"You have *no* idea how much." Laney crossed her arms and regarded him. "So what now?"

Joe sat down at the kitchen table. "Make me some breakfast."

"*Make me some breakfast?* Just like that?" She snorted. "Go chop a hole in the lake, and jump in it."

A corner of his mouth curled into his beard. "I know you can cook like nobody's business, Red."

"It is my business. I own a restaurant."

"Whatever." Joe got comfortable and swung an arm toward the stove. "Just do it."

She planted her hands on her hips. "Why should I?"

Joe dangled a piece of the panty hose that was still intact. "If you don't, you get tied to the chair and *I* make breakfast. And I'm no chef, Red."

"Honestly." Laney went to the cabinet and threw the door open. "After everything I've done for you." She yanked out the copper-bottomed skillet and slammed it on top of the stove.

Joe made a sound that could have been a rusty chuckle. "There is that."

"Yeah, there *is*." Laney opened a loaf of bread. "I dragged your sorry, oversized butt out of the snow—"

"You shot me first," Joe said.

"*That* was an accident." She grabbed the last of the fresh eggs from the cold pantry. "Plus I fed you, washed you, cleaned your wounds—"

"Wounds you inflicted."

"Took care of you, gave you medicine for your fever—" Laney's voice broke off. No reason to bring that up.

"Yeah, I remember," Joe said. The growl in his voice mellowed to a purr. "You'd make a hell of a nurse, Red."

Stupid, how she'd walked right into that one, she thought, then realized the stove was cold. She bent to open the lower door, then slammed it shut a second later. "I need to get some firewood."

"No, you don't."

"Okay. If you want the last of the stew, it's in the freezer. The ice pick is in the second drawer, over there."

"Isn't there anything else?"

"I would have baked you a cake, Joe, but I've been a little *busy*."

He shook his head. "Just make anything that doesn't need cooking."

"Well, then. What would you like with your raw eggs? Raw bacon, or raw sausage?"

Joe's mouth thinned. "Fine, smart-ass. Get your wood and build the fire. But make it small."

It took time to lay fresh wood and kindling and get

the stove heated. By the time she had the skillet oiled, Laney didn't want to cook in it, she wanted to throw it at him.

Her voice was tight when she asked, "How many eggs?"

"Six."

"By the way"—she nodded toward the diminished woodpile—"we're going to need more firewood soon."

"Right."

"I'll hold the shotgun while you chop."

"Just make the eggs, Red."

He was watching her. Laney could feel his gaze boring into her shoulder blades. She started cracking shells against the side of the skillet, and amused herself by pretending they were miniatures of Joe's head.

"So where's your restaurant?"

"The Denver Federal Penitentiary. A little cafe on death row. I have to serve some fast meals sometimes, but the customers never come back to complain." She turned the bacon. "Ever had reservations there?"

"No." One of his brows rose. "That where you learned to do it? Prison?"

"Oh, sure." She snorted. "For your information, Julia Child taught me. So did Martha Stewart and Betty Crocker."

"Must have been some cooking school."

"Yeah. It's called life." She was in no mood to tell him the story of hers. "Do you like fry bread?"

"Navajo?"

"English toast. Quick-fried in the bacon drippings."

"Yeah, throw a couple of slices in."

Preparing a meal quickly was her business, so Laney had the hot food on the table in front of him a few minutes later.

He pointed to the other chair. "Get a plate and sit."

She shrugged. "I'm not hungry."

"It's not a suggestion."

She got a plate and sat. "I live for the day when you make one."

Joe had no choice but to stay in the cabin and wait for Richmond to come looking for his little hired hit woman.

He watched Laney clean up after breakfast. A hit woman. No way. Too many things about her that didn't add up. The way she'd taken care of him when he was sick. The scatterbrained chatter. The fact she hadn't tried to kill him when she'd had ample time and opportunity. Could he be wrong about her?

I told Charles he didn't need to use his contract killer. Poor Delaney is going to be so disappointed.

The way she slammed around the dishes, he could go along with that. If Susan had said Bob or John, that would be one thing. But how many people could be named Delaney?

He wasn't wrong about her. He'd learned that much from Susan. She'd taken care of him, too—in and out of bed. She'd convinced him of her love. And she'd kept up the pretense for months.

Little Red had only bluffed her way through a few days. With enough time, she'd slip up.

He went to the windows to have a look outside. The blizzard had blown through, but had left behind a good foot or more of new snow. No tracks, no sign of life anywhere. "How did you get into this business?" he heard himself ask.

She looked sideways at him. "I don't like starving."

"There are other ways to make a living."

"What's wrong with cooking? I like it, and I'm good at it."

"Cooking." That wasn't all she was good at. "Right."

For the rest of the day, he held on to the shotgun and kept Laney in plain sight, while he stayed away from the windows and tried to figure out what Richmond's next move would be.

She stayed on the sofa, alternately reading and napping. Joe sat in the armchair to watch her, and found himself nodding off more than a few times.

Once, when she woke up and stretched, the book fell to the floor with a thump.

He jerked out of a doze and brought the shotgun up.

"Sorry, Bigfoot." She picked it up. "False alarm. I didn't mean to startle you."

She'd done more than that. "What are you reading?"

A is for Apple." She held up the cookbook for him to see. "Do you want to hear how I make the perfect two-crust pie? A half-teaspoon of nutmeg, a little wine, and then you flour the bottom crust before you—"

Here she goes again. "Why do you read cookbooks?"

"Gee, I don't know." She gave him an ironic look. "I got bored with *A Dozen Ways to Kill Large Men Using Ordinary Household Items.*"

He fought back an involuntary laugh. "Cute, Red. And knock it off with the Bigfoot."

"Sure thing, Fathead."

She dropped back down on the sofa and started thumbing through pages until she found her place and started reading again. "How about baked apples? Do you like them? I don't like raisins in mine. Not that we have any raisins here I could use, of course, but I was thinking about making some stuffed with a little pineapple chutney . . ."

A week passed. Joe had expected to have his hands full keeping Little Red out of his hair, but he discovered she was content to spend her time reading, messing around in the kitchen, and keeping the cabin tidy.

He found he liked watching her. Especially when she worked in the kitchen. She'd had some kind of training, judging by the efficient way she handled preparing their meals. Plus she made even something as simple as whisking eggs together look graceful.

Her cooperating didn't mean she accepted the situation. No, she made a point to express her displeasure with it, each and every single day.

"I think using the bathroom by myself is a basic human right." "Wouldn't you be more comfortable sleeping *without* tying us up together? I know I would." "If I was going to kill you, I'd use something a lot bigger than a paring knife, you know" were some of her complaints.

This evening, however, she began showing all the signs of classic cabin fever.

"All I want to do is take a walk. You know, outside? In the fresh air?"

And somehow signal Richmond? "No."

"You can come with me. Five minutes. That's all I want. Just five minutes to walk around the cabin and look at the trees and try to clear these cobwebs out of my brain."

Or maybe she had a cache of weapons stashed outside. "No."

"Look, I haven't made a fuss about this aversion you have to fireplaces. Or the fact you make me douse the stove every time I'm done using it. Or the cold showers. Or the way you've been tying me to the—*restraining* me every night when we go to sleep."

"Yes, you have."

"Okay. I admit, I have fussed. A little. I'm the hostage, I'm entitled. But I'm telling you, Joe, if I stay inside this cabin for one more minute, I'm going to start screaming, and I promise, no, I *swear* I won't stop."

Joe gave her the once-over. "Nice try. Do it, and I'll gag you."

Laney gave a long, loud groan of frustration and stalked back to the bathroom. He'd let her have that much privacy, but only after he'd searched the small room and removed anything she might use to disable him.

She reemerged with a bottle he hadn't seen before.

"What's that?"

"Cyanide."

He gave her a dark look.

Laney sighed. "My sleeping pills."

Joe got up and took the bottle from her. "You don't need these."

"Well, we're running low on cyanide, so, yes, I do. Do you mind?" She held out her hand. "If I'm ever going to get any sleep tonight, I need to take one."

He shook one out, examined it closely, then handed it to her. "I want to see you swallow it."

"Far be it from me to deny you your voyeuristic pleasures." She stalked off into the kitchen.

After Joe watched her take the pill, he set the shotgun on the counter and read the label on the bottle. He didn't like the idea of her having to use drugs in order to sleep. "This is pretty heavy stuff. How long have you been taking it?"

"Six months, but only when I really need it. Like the times I get held at gunpoint." A strange look passed over her face, one he'd seen before, usually when he was tying her up. Then she fell silent.

Laney never shut up. "What are you thinking about?"

She gazed blankly at him. "Nothing."

"Something's bugging you, Red. Spit it out."

"I just—" She sighed. "I just get claustrophobic sometimes. Like I can't breathe, you know. I've been stuck in here so long, I feel like the walls are starting to close in on me. That's all."

It wasn't. He could sense it. He moved in, tossing the bottle of pills in his hand. "Feeling a little guilty, are you?"

"Guilty?" Her eyebrows arched. "About what?"

"This job Richmond hired you for. Hard to have a conscience, in your line of work. Isn't it?"

"Yeah, No Morals Arlen, that's me." She got angry. "I buy day-old bread and pass it off as fresh. I cut milk with water and reuse cooking oil until it turns black. I scrape the extra icing off doughnuts and save it to frost my cakes. Oh, and there's that terrible habit I have of trying to kill people I've never met before in my life, especially the ones I have to nurse back to health first."

He thought of Susan. Lovely, lying Susan. "Women like you don't have morals to begin with." Joe pocketed the bottle and picked up the shotgun. "I'm tired. Time for bed."

They'd established a routine between them. He let Laney have fifteen minutes for a cold water wash in the bathroom, then he tied her up on the bed and took his own icy shower. Since they'd been hit by two more storms, the electricity still hadn't been restored. He figured it would be a long time before either of them had a hot bath again.

She emerged a short time later from the bathroom, pink and shivering. "I'm going to have to do some laundry soon. There are only so many times I can wear the same pair of jeans."

"Maybe tomorrow." He jerked his head toward the bedroom. "You know the drill. Let's go."

Laney silently climbed onto the bed and held her hands out in front of her. Joe bound them with a strip of toweling, then she put her legs together and he did the same with her ankles.

All the while, he noticed the same, vague revulsion flit in and out of her gaze.

"Stay put." He took the shotgun into the bathroom with him.

As he took a rapid shower, Joe thought again about how quiet she'd gotten. Laney only got antsy when he tied her up. Why?

He didn't like her being quiet, either. Maybe he'd gotten used to her normal chatter. She certainly brought up the strangest topics. One day she'd done nothing but wonder out loud what it would be like to be in a war. Another time she talked about how tragic it was to be homeless and out of work. Then there was that whole thing about mental illness and the amazing strides doctors were making in finding effective treatments for delusional people.

Joe listened to every word, but didn't say much himself. He knew little about the military, and even less about the homeless or the mentally disturbed. He was too busy watching her lively face as she babbled. Then there were those intense looks she kept shooting at him.

Tonight she'd decided to start on the topic of war again, as soon as he walked back in the bedroom.

"I was too young to remember Vietnam, but my mom said it was terrible. Lots of the guys she went to school with died over there. Like her best friend's brother. It was a real tragedy."

He grunted a "yeah," stowed the shotgun under the bed, then stretched out beside her.

Laney held out her hands so he could tie them, as he

did every night, to one of his. "I know people don't think the Gulf War was as bad, but there were terrible things that happened over there, too." She gave him that significant look, inviting him to comment. When he didn't, she sighed. "Those poor men. Stuck out in the desert, with all those chemical weapons and STUD missiles—"

"SCUD."

"I beg your pardon?"

"*SCUD* missiles."

"Oh. Oh, right. All those *SCUD* missiles landing around them. It must have been a real nightmare. I mean, can you imagine, defending your country in the middle of Kuwait with tanks shooting at you and planes diving at you and then those bombs raining down on your head all night?"

"Uh-huh." Joe closed his eyes and hoped the sleeping pill he'd let her take would kick in soon.

"Joe?"

"What?"

"Do you think young men should be forced to serve in a war? You know, the way all those reservists were sent over to the Middle East, during Desert Storm?"

"They joined the reserves. They knew it was a possibility, Red."

"I don't know. If someone had to go over there, you know, a reservist, and didn't want to, and then something terrible happened to them, it might really wreck their life, don't you think?"

He yawned. "Yeah. I guess."

"They'd need help, right?"

"Go to sleep, Red."

Sean knew having Charles Richmond at the Dream Mountain site would make it difficult for him to slip away and get Laney off the ridge. When Fai's men arrived, difficult abruptly became impossible.

He couldn't afford to leave the mine while the Chinese were there. Not for a moment.

Richmond wasn't any happier about Fai's watchdogs. "I want you to keep a man on them, Irish. Twenty-four-seven."

Sean assigned Kerass the babysitting job, then got back to finalizing the arrangements for transport of the ore. Luckily, he was in Richmond's office going over the schedule when the crew chief reported in about a new problem.

"They've been scouting around the camp," Kerass said over the radio. "One of my guys mentioned something about spotting smoke while they were out on Nightmare Ridge. Thought I'd have a look." The crew chief paused. "Seems there's a woman living in that cabin."

Sean dropped the doctored shipping manifests he'd been stacking, swore, then spoke into the radio. "You've been out in the snow too long, boyo. That cabin's been empty for months."

"Well, it isn't now," Kerass snapped back.

Richmond gazed at him. "What's a woman doing out on the ridge?"

Sean knelt down to pick up the manifests. Icy sweat trickled down his spine. *Dear God, Laney.* "Maybe she's a tourist who got stranded." He put the paperwork back on Richmond's desk, then called over the radio, "Is she alone, Kerass?"

"Far as I could see, boss. Don't know how she got there. No car parked outside or broken down on the road."

Sean kept his expression bland as he cursed inwardly. Kerass had done his job a little *too* well. But at least he had the comfort of knowing Bigfoot hadn't gotten to her. Yet. "Could be a local girl, checking on the place," he said to his employer.

"I doubt it. Not even these yocals are crazy enough to stay on the ridge in the dead of winter." Richmond sat back and looked thoughtful. "If there's no car, that means someone dropped her off."

Sean thought fast. "Then she could be another of Fai's deputies."

"Perhaps." Richmond casually took the hand-held radio from Sean and spoke into it. "Describe her to me, Kerass."

"Just a woman, Mr. Richmond. White, mid-twenties, redhead, skinny."

Richmond frowned. "Find out who she is, what she's doing there, and report back to me."

Sean waited until Kerass signed off. "She can't be involved, Charles. It's some sort of coincidence, that's all."

"We can't afford to assume anything, not now." Richmond turned to gaze at the site through the window. "Fai and the tong may not have much use for women, but the federal government has no problem employing female agents."

Sean shuffled the transport schedules into a neater pile. "And if she's a fed?"

"Then you'll have to take care of her, Irish."

The redhead alone on the ridge was preparing to spend her eighth day of captivity going quietly out of her mind.

Laney had tried to humor Joe and go along with what he wanted, but she was tired and scared and ready to go home now. He never let her have a moment of privacy, except for the scant few minutes she spent in the bathroom. To add insult to injury, he made her wait on him, hand and foot, while he ducked around doors and stooped down to avoid windows.

This secret-agent fantasy of his was really getting old.

This morning he told her to cook breakfast for him. Again. She took what she needed from the cold pantry and left the door open to make another trip for the syrup.

"I'd like to do some laundry today, okay?"

"No."

That was almost all he ever said: no. Somehow it was the last straw. Laney dropped the box of waffle mix on the counter and folded her arms. "Okay. I'm going back to bed. *You* cook your own breakfast."

He raised the shotgun. "Don't get mouthy with me."

"I mean it."

He pumped the slide. "So do I."

"I swear, you are the *stupidest* man I have ever known." Angrily she took out the old-fashioned waffle iron and set it on the stove to heat. "It isn't a crime to want clean clothes, you know. Besides, how could I 'assassinate' you by doing laundry? Do you think I'm going to spike your orange juice with Tide? Beat you to death with a clothes basket? Strangle you with a wet hand towel?"

"Don't give me any ideas."

"Oh, honestly, would you just give it a rest?" She looked over her shoulder at him, then turned back to the window. And froze. Her eyes went wide as she stared.

What the hell is Uncle Sean doing out there? And who is he with? And why are they carrying rifles?

Joe noticed. "What? What is it?"

She couldn't let him start shooting at them. "Nothing. Just a deer." She had to find a way to warn them about Joe.

She never got her chance. A moment later Joe jerked her away from the window and shoved her up against the counter. He held her there, one hand around her neck, and looked through the frosted glass. Then he turned his head and got in her face.

"Funny-looking deer. They friends of yours?"

"My friends don't carry guns." Laney wheezed in a breath as his hand tightened around her throat. "Guess they must be yours."

He hauled her over to the cold pantry and thrust her inside. "Not a sound."

"No, Joe, please—"

He slammed the door shut, locking her inside.

Joe recognized both men from the mine, and stepped away from the window. The sounds coming from the cold pantry made him drag his hand through his hair.

"Christ, doesn't she ever shut up?" He went over and yanked the door open. A second later he found his arms full of a hysterical, weeping woman.

"Thank you, thank you." She curled over, sobbing and cringing like he'd beaten her.

Why was she so damn scared? Joe gave her a small shake. "Stop it. What's the matter with you?"

"I'm just, I'm just . . ." She'd been crying so hard she had the hiccups.

"Settle down," he said. She nodded, and he eased his hands away from her arms. "Stay there."

Joe moved over to peer around the edge of the window, and saw the men walking toward the front of the house. Were there others, covering the back? Probably not, or they'd never let themselves be seen out in the open like that. He'd have to move fast, they'd be at the front door in thirty seconds.

"Out the back," he told Laney.

She was knuckling the tears from her face, and looked up, confused. "What?"

He shoved her toward the utility room. "Go."

"But—"

"*Now.*"

"This is crazy."

In the utility room, Joe thrust his boots into a pair of snowshoes and snatched two jackets hanging by the door. One he threw to her.

She handed it back to him. "I can't—"

He didn't have time to debate it, so he clamped his free hand over Laney's mouth, at the same time pinning her to his side with his arm, and dragged her out through the door.

Outside the wind was bitterly cold, and the hard crust on the snow crunched underfoot. He didn't stop to pull on their jackets, but headed for the trees as quickly as the snowshoes allowed. Under his arm, Laney floundered and stumbled. Probably on purpose. He held on and hauled her along with him. He looked back a few times, but evidently the men were already in the cabin and hadn't heard them go.

A muffled shriek exploded against his palm, then Laney bit him.

"Shit." Joe got his fingers loose but didn't let go of her. She stopped yelling and tried to squirm out from under his arm. With a quick jerk he pulled her up off her feet and carried her full weight.

Once they were deep in the timber, Joe stopped, let go of her mouth, and set her back down. "Don't scream, or I'll knock you out."

She took a deep, shuddering breath. "Joe. We've got to go back."

"Not now." He pulled on one of the jackets, then forced her into the other. As he pulled the hood over her head, Joe checked back over his shoulder. "Maybe tomorrow."

"Joe." Her voice sounded low, soothing. The same way it had been, he remembered, in his desert dream. "Joe, I can't trek through the woods like this."

She was cold. He could feel the violent vibration of her body as it tried to generate heat. "The coat will keep you warm."

"That's not my problem." She pointed at the ground.

Joe glanced down. Laney didn't have any snowshoes on. Or any kind of shoes at all. Both of her bare feet were covered with snow.

He exploded with illogical rage. "Goddamn it! Why didn't you say something?"

"I tried! I even *bit* you!"

"Next time, bite *harder.*"

Laney paused, took a deep breath. "Joe, please, be reasonable. I can't go running around like this."

He bent down, encircled her knees with an arm, and lifted her over his shoulder. "Hold on."

She clutched at his back. "This is what you call reasonable?"

"Shut up."

It took time to carry her through the maze of pine trees and snowdrifts. Joe was careful to backtrack several times and confuse his trail as much as possible. Laney held on and thankfully didn't struggle. By the time he reached the entrance to the hidden cavern, he was tired and sweating.

He set her down, moved aside the woven-brush

covering he'd made to conceal the entrance, and nodded toward the small gap that uncovered in the rocks.
"In there."

"What's in there?"

He pushed her forward. "Go."

Laney edged into the gap while Joe shadowed her.
Her subsequent halt and gasp didn't surprise him.
He'd had the same reaction the day he'd found the cav-
ern.

"Keep moving, Red."

The narrow passage opened to an enormous natural
vault with a convex ceiling. Stalactites of various
lengths and thickness hung like stone icicles everywhere. Vent holes formed during an ancient volcanic
period allowed much needed light and oxygen into the
chamber. Solid shafts of sunlight poured into the cavern at several points, highlighting the glittery quartz
crystals embedded in the smooth, glaciated rock walls.

"It's beautiful," Laney said, looking all around.

"It's a cave. Sit." He pointed to a flat boulder and
went to the cache of supplies he'd hidden before leaving the cave the last time. He didn't notice Laney following him, and reacted instinctively when she
touched his shoulder.

"What's that—" She broke off as he turned and
caught her wrists in his hands. "Hey!"

"Don't come up behind me." Joe pushed her away.
"Ever."

"Okay, okay." She rubbed her arms where he'd
grabbed her. A pile of dirty fur caught her eye. "I see
you collect bearskins. Is that a hobby, fetish, or some
kind of personal fashion statement? Or did someone
steal your Teddy when you were a kid?"

"Bears used the cave to hibernate. They come here to
die, too."

"How pleasant. Can we go now?" Joe shook his head. "I don't think the bears are going to like us being here. And I for one don't want to argue with them about it."

"Relax. Nothing has lived in this cave for a couple of decades."

"No wonder that thing I shot you in was so . . . fragrant." Laney eyed the cave walls. "Are you sure it's safe to stay in here? Some of those rocks up there look a little rickety to me."

"It's Precambrian gneiss."

"I'm sure pre-whatever is nice, but is it safe?"

"*Gneiss.*" He spelled it for her. "Basement rock, about two billion years old. Don't worry, Red. You're safer here than in a bomb shelter."

"If you say so. What's all that stuff?" She gestured to his supply packs.

"Food, blankets, some clothes."

"This is where you've been *living*? In here?"

"Yeah. Home sweet home." Since she'd arrived, anyway. He'd stolen a pair of extra boots from the site, and handed them to her with a pair of his cleanest socks. "Put these on." When she wrinkled her nose, he said, "Don't be picky, Red. It's seventy miles to the nearest Laundromat."

"I know. It's just . . ." She slipped one foot into the sock, then hesitated. "Do you have any Band-Aids?"

"Why?"

"I should cover this up." She extended her right foot, and Joe saw the blood seeping between the small toes. He caught her heel in his palm and eased her foot up. A long, jagged gash ran across the ball of her foot.

It made him furious. He tugged her foot closer to examine the wound. "When did you do this?"

"I didn't. You did, hauling me barefoot through the woods. Remember when I bit you?"

"I remember." Her toes were white, he saw, and although the skin wasn't stiff it was still cool to the touch. "I'll take care of it." He hesitated, then added, "Sorry."

"You didn't know." She studied his expression. "Why are you angry? It's *my* foot."

"Can you feel my hands?"

"Yes." She yelped as he began roughly massaging her injured foot. "I feel them, I feel them, cut it out!"

"You're half frozen." Joe ignored the knot of guilt in his gut as he worked to improve circulation. "Do you feel sleepy?"

"Sleepy, no. Homicidal, yes." She realized what she'd said, and red curls escaped her hood as she ducked her head. "No, I'm not tired."

Good. She didn't have hypothermia on top of it. "Why weren't you wearing your shoes in the cabin?"

"I forgot to put them on." She gave him a thin smile. "Shotguns in my face as soon as I wake up make me absentminded. So does being kidnapped and dragged to a bear cave. Ow, come on, now, that *really* hurts!"

The pain was an excellent sign—Joe suspected she'd just missed getting frostbitten. When her toes were pink and the cut was bleeding freely, he reached back for the pack he'd filched from the site infirmary.

He doused the cut with rubbing alcohol, making Laney nearly jump a foot off the rock. "Joe!"

"Hold still, Red." He held on to her ankle and cleaned the gash thoroughly. "Give me that other sock." He rolled it over the clean gauze and set her foot down. "Here." He wrapped a blanket around her.

"You're a sadist, did you know that?" Her teeth began chattering with cold and reaction. "You could have warned me, that alcohol really burns. I bet you're enjoying every minute of this, aren't you?"

Joe sighed. "Come here." He sat down, pulled her onto his lap, and braced his back against the stone. "Sit still, Red."

He held her, rubbing his hands over her to warm her up. After a few moments she snuggled closer, tucking her head under his chin. Both of her hands worked in under his jacket and spread out over his chest. Her breath tickled his neck when she spoke.

"Joe, how do you know all that stuff?"

"What stuff?"

"That nice, excuse me, *gneiss* stuff."

Hadn't they briefed her? "Didn't Richmond tell you? I'm a geologist."

"Who's Richmond?"

"Never mind." Joe thumped his head back against the stone wall. "They won't find us here."

He felt Laney's head turn as she looked around them. "How long have you been hiding out in this cave?"

Forever. "Couple of months."

"Better you than me. I've only been stuck in the cabin for a couple of days, and it's driving me bonkers." She laughed at herself. "And to think, I used to dream about getting out of the city and buying an A-frame cabin up here. You know, return to nature, that kind of thing? Boy, was I living in a dreamworld. I never knew it was this *cold*. I'd have spent the rest of my days hiding under an electric blanket."

She couldn't be a contract killer, Joe thought for the ten thousandth time. Not with a laugh like that. And why would she spend four days taking care of him if she'd been sent to kill him? Could she be just what she appeared to be? A beautiful, golden-eyed chatterbox who was driving *him* crazy?

Joe pushed back her hood and caught some of her curls in his fingers. Her hair felt like down, so fine and silky that he wanted to bury his face in it.

Laney lifted her head, and her mouth brushed his chin on the way. "Joe?"

"Hmmm?" He fingered one of the red corkscrew curls, idly winding it around his thumb. In the diffused light, her eyes were pure gold. "You've got pretty eyes."

"Thanks." The edge of a thin, sharp blade touched his neck. "I've also got a knife. Now, let go of me."

Kerass searched the entire cabin while Sean dealt with the padlock on the door to the spare bedroom. He found exactly what he'd thought he would.

"She must have gone for a walk, the silly bitch," Kerass said as he appeared in the doorway. "What's this?"

"Camping gear, from the looks of it." Sean closed the backpack and tossed it back in the small closet. "Did you check the back?"

"Yeah, there were some snowshoe prints. Maybe she went to get more wood."

"We'll have to wait, then. Come on, let's see if there's coffee to be had."

In the kitchen, Kerass sat down at the table, and frowned at the twin place settings. "Two plates. She's got someone with her."

"Could be." Sean made up the old-fashioned percolator, then built up the fire in the stove. "What did you find in the other bedroom?"

Kerass shrugged. "Bed's been slept in. Appears one of them was sick. And I found these." He took a hand-

ful of rags and torn panty hose from his jacket and displayed them for Sean. "There's blood on them. Some
on the floor, too."

Sean willed himself not to react to the sight of all
those stains. What had that bastard done to his niece?
"Not much. Maybe she cut herself shaving."

"Yeah." Kerass regarded the plates again. "Or he
did."

"Why assume it's a man?" Sean asked.

"Makes more sense than two broads." The crew
chief settled back in his chair. "Where did you take
Richmond while you were in Denver?"

Sean gave the other man an amused smile.
"Around." And wondered if the man he was after had
indeed come down and hurt his niece. No matter what
the stakes, if Tremayne had put his hands on her, Sean
would personally take him apart. Piece by bloody
piece. "You'd better call this in to Pagent."

"Yeah, right." Kerass pulled a hand-held radio out
of his jacket pocket and spoke into it. "Crew chief to Pagent, over."

Pagent's voice replied after a few seconds. "What is
it, Kerass?"

"We're at the cabin now. No sign of the girl, but it
looks like she may have taken a walk. She's not alone,
either. We're going to wait for her, over."

"Negative. We need you both back at the site. Immediately, over."

CHAPTER FIVE

Laney had spotted the penknife from the moment he'd shoved her on the rock. Joe had taken all the knives from the kitchen back at the cabin and hidden them somewhere. If she could just get the small blade, she might have a chance to escape. She moved carefully into position, distracted him by yelling when he poured the alcohol over her foot, and scooped it up.

It had been hard to wait, to lull Joe into a sense of false security. Harder to keep the small knife palmed until she could get close enough to use it. Now that she had it against his throat, all Laney wanted to do was throw it as hard and as far away from her as she could.

I can't hurt him. Not after what he's been through.

Neal would have smacked her for thinking that. *You can't even defend yourself without feeling sorry for the other guy, you mush-hearted idiot.*

Unblinking gray eyes stared into hers as his arms fell away. Was he scared? No. Joe never looked scared. But now he seemed almost . . . disappointed.

Slowly Laney slid off his lap and got on her feet. She forced herself to keep the blade pressed against his neck the entire time.

"Please, do exactly what I tell you," Laney said,

"and everything will be fine. I promise. Just don't make any sudden moves, and listen to me."

A muscle twitched along his jaw. "Give me the knife, Red."

"I don't think so. Come on now, get up."

Laney realized that was a mistake when Joe pushed himself up. He towered over her. She put as much space between them as she could while still holding the knife at his throat.

"Here's the plan: you and I are going to walk back to the cabin, and talk this out." Her hand trembled, but she locked her arm and made herself go on. "All you have to do is cooperate, and you won't get hurt. Okay?"

"No."

Laney hadn't counted on a refusal. "What?"

"I'm not going." His hand flashed out, seized her wrist, and pressed the knife harder against his neck. "Go on, Red. Do it. Finish the job. That's what you're here for, isn't it? What you've been waiting for?"

Laney stopped breathing when she saw blood trickle down his neck. Automatically she released the knife, which dropped to the floor of the cave. Joe kicked it away, out of her reach.

She reached out and touched the bloody cut on his throat, then stared at her fingers.

Then she hit him on the chest with her fist.

"You lunatic! What were you thinking?" She was so angry she tried to hit him again. "Look at you, you're bleeding! What did you do that for? I could have *really* cut your throat!"

"Not so easy to do, is it?" Joe grabbed her arms and yanked her closer. "Killing a man while you look into his eyes? What do you normally use? A long-distance scope?"

Laney jerked back, but it was already too late. He had his long arms locked around her waist, one hand clamped to the back of her head. The last of the cold left her limbs as an insidious heat began to build inside her.

"*No.*"

"Go on, tell me, Red." He shifted her, tucking her inside his jacket, holding her against him, forcing her face at an angle to his. "How do you do them? Poison? Explosives? What? It can't be close work, you're no good at it."

"I don't know what you're talking about. I don't kill people. I feed them."

"Goddamn you." Joe's fingers tightened in her hair. "I know what you are. *I know.* And still I want to—"

His mouth covered hers.

She wasn't going to let him do this. He'd come at her using every weapon he could think of. Playing on her sympathy for a homeless, hungry man. Making her relive her worst nightmare. Even making her take care of him while he was sick. She wouldn't let him use her. Not like this.

Joe lifted his head for a moment. Touched her lips with his fingertips. Before she realized what he meant to do, his thumb pressed against the seam of her lips.

"Open your mouth."

Laney couldn't pull back, not with his other hand at the back of her skull. Frightened by how much she wanted to do what he asked, she shook her head.

"Open up for me, you deceitful little bitch."

The pressure on her jaw increased until pain forced her to give in to him. His thumb pushed in over her teeth and stroked against the tip of her tongue.

"Good girl."

Laney got out, "You bast—" before he removed his hand and sealed his mouth over hers.

The way he kissed her hurt. He was punishing her, using her mouth without any tenderness. All Laney could do was hold on and hope it would be over soon.

Joe finally wrenched away.

Laney tasted blood as she stared up at him, wounded and numb. He swore. When he tried to kiss her again, she recoiled. "No, don't."

"Laney." He turned her face back to his. "Kiss me."

"Please." Her voice broke. "Please don't do this."

It was hopeless to even try to resist. He was twice her size and ten times as strong. Yet as she cringed under his mouth, waiting for him to start ripping at her clothes, something happened. His hands gentled. He didn't force her lips apart. He made a strange, low sound.

What now?

Joe began using long, slow, persuasive kisses, trying to coax her lips apart. Her skin grew hot and damp where his hands touched her. She could feel the tension in his fingers, the roughness of his palms sliding around her throat.

She let him in, let him taste her, and the stone beneath them seemed to rock as he groaned again.

Oh, he was good at this, too good; it was burning her up, making her press herself into him, her hips moving, her hands digging into the sleeves of his jacket—

I can't let him do this. No matter how good he feels. He's sick, unstable—this is wrong.

If only it didn't feel so right.

"Stop." Laney managed to break off the kiss and ducked her face into his jacket when he tried to take her mouth again. "Joe, stop. We have to stop."

Joe ignored that and moved on to the spot where her jaw curved up. "You're so soft, so pretty." His voice sounded slurred as he bit down gently on the lobe of her ear.

The new ache between her thighs went from unbearable to agonizing. "Joe. We can't."

She went rigid as he buried his face in her curls and breathed deeply.

"God, you even smell beautiful," he said.

A subtle movement of Joe's hand tipped her head back. She felt his thumb press against her lower lip. Separate it from the upper curve. Gently he caressed the small cut his first, brutal kiss had made there.

"You want me, Red?"

"No."

"You're lying." He caught one of her hands, guided it down between their bodies. "Feel how I want you."

The moment her palm slid over his erection, his other hand slipped between her thighs.

His breath teased her ear. "I can feel the heat, Laney. Are you getting wet for me?"

Laney was lost. No man had ever touched her like this, or made her touch him the same way. And she wasn't just wet down there, she was *soaked*. Before she could stop herself, she stroked the length of him with her hand. His fingers urged her thighs apart, then returned the favor.

"Yeah." A rumble of pleasure came from deep inside his chest, and he thrust his hips against her hand. "Harder."

He moved his hand as she stroked him. The sudden give of the fabric at her waist told her what he was doing.

He's going to take off my jeans.

The thought of making love to him didn't frighten

her. It felt too good to be anything but natural and right. But she'd never thought she'd blindly give in to temptation. Not like this. His touch was making her into someone else. Someone who was needy, pliant, out of control.

Worse, she knew she was standing on the edge of something far more dangerous. *Wanting* to be that for him.

She jerked her hand away from him, determined to stop things before it was too late. "Why don't you just use that knife on me and get it over with?"

It was too late, judging by the way he looked at her. "Don't be afraid, baby."

She was afraid. *How can I stop him? Right now he looks ready to gorge himself on me, one bite at a time.*

Joe pulled her slender hips against his. The unexpected intimacy created an explosion of new sensations between her thighs. Exactly where he would fit.

"You like that, Red, don't you?"

"Not particularly." Laney tried to back away. "You don't have to rape me to prove your point."

"It won't be rape, lady," he said against her cheek. His head dipped again. Laney yelped as she felt him gently bite the side of her throat. "Not with you begging me to take you."

He licked the spot he'd just bitten. Like a mountain lion roughly laving a chunk of deer, Laney thought, and her knees began to buckle. In a simultaneous, erotic stroke, he ran both hands down her back again. Fit them beneath the swell of her buttocks. Supported her. Moved her. Rubbed her against him.

I want him.

He lifted his mouth from her skin. Put it next to her ear. Whispered like a lover. "Feel it? This is just for starters. Do you know how good it will be, when I'm inside you?"

"On a cave floor?" She tried to laugh. "My butt will get frostbite."

"You can be on top." His beard tickled as his mouth moved over to hers. "Laney. Let me have you."

She closed her eyes, knew she couldn't pull away. His tenderness made it as impossible as his anger had before. His tongue stroked against hers, filling her head with his taste and textures. It was like being kissed by two different men. One who terrified her. One who made her tremble.

Her eyelids stayed down. Her palms pressed against his chest. She found his shoulders. His hair. A strange, unfamiliar urgency took over. When Joe lifted his head, she whimpered. Her mouth throbbed. Her entire body ached. Laney rested her forehead against his chest. Tried to breathe again. Felt a thousand different needs sizzling through her veins.

Was she panting? Oh, God. She was panting. The strong beat beneath the flannel shirt he wore thudded fast and heavy. So it wasn't only her. Maybe he wasn't panting, but he felt it, too.

"So now we know." Unexpectedly Joe lifted her and set her a foot away from him.

She looked at him, completely bewildered now. "Joe?"

"Appears you're good at something." The crystalline eyes that met hers were as cold as a gravestone. "Want to take another shot at me with the knife?"

"Miss Jill?"

Jill looked up from her computer to see one of the older men standing in her doorway. "Hello, Mr. Upton. What can I do for you?"

"I was wondering if you could take a look at something for me," Webb said, and pulled a crumpled paper bag from his pocket. "Just a rock I found in—on the north slope."

Webb Upton, like many miners, was something of a rock hound. He'd brought specimens he couldn't identify to her before. "Sure." Jill took the bag.

"You hear about the new layoffs?"

Jill stopped unrolling the top of the bag. "What new layoffs?"

"Kerass sent fifteen guys topside yesterday." Webb shook his silver-haired head. "Real shame."

"I didn't know." The bag crackled under Jill's hands as she fought to keep from exploding with rage. "Who—" She broke off when Matt Pagent walked in the office.

"Upton." Pagent nodded to Jill. "You're needed downside."

"Sure thing, Mr. Pagent." Webb beat a hasty retreat.

When the miner had gone, Richmond's foreman went to the filing cabinet across from Jill's desk. "What did he want?"

She didn't want Webb to get into trouble for his hobby, so Jill quietly put the bag in a desk drawer and closed it. "Just stopping by to say hello. What did you need, Mr. Pagent?"

"Gareth Tremayne's personnel file and whatever reports he filed before his death."

"I'll get it for you." She rose, eager to send him back out of the office.

"You're upset."

Wasn't he a genius to figure that out. She stalked over to the row of filing cabinets. "I get that way when fifteen good men lose their jobs." She yanked open the drawer and jerked out a thick folder. "Here's what you needed."

"Thanks." Pagent took the file and set it on the end of her desk. "Jillian, you knew they'd be laid off by the end of the month. The mine is being closed. What's left to be done doesn't justify carrying the payroll."

Jill's rage faded as quickly as it had flared. "They're good men, you know. Worked this range all their lives. Since the processing plant closed down, mining is all they've got. Now they'll be lucky to get a shot at serving up burgers and fries in town. And it's all my fault."

Pagent's eyes narrowed. "How do you figure that?"

"If my father hadn't borrowed all that money, we could keep the mine going." Jill folded her arms over the knot in her stomach and stared miserably out the window. "A couple of the wives called me," she said. "They're scared they'll all end up losing their homes. They probably will, unless the men get some help."

"You're losing your home."

"It's not the same thing," Jill said. "I don't have kids or a husband to support. Dad was the only family I had, and he's gone. I can go and get a job anywhere."

"I'll talk to Charles."

The same thing he'd said the last time, Jill thought bitterly. What was she thinking, pouring her heart out like this? Pagent didn't give a damn about the miners. She went back to her desk and dropped into her chair. "You do that."

"Tremayne's personnel file?"

Jill would have told him to get out of her office, but the phone rang. She picked it up and willed her voice to remain neutral. "Jill Hunter."

"Miss Hunter." Richmond was back. "I need to see you in my office at once."

"Yes, sir." Jill replaced the receiver and turned to

Pagent. "Mr. Richmond wants to see me." She pointed to a filing cabinet. "The other files you need are in there."

For a moment Pagent actually looked startled. Then he gave her another of his cool smiles. "Don't forget to take your steno pad with you."

Jill had no intention of taking anything but the proposal she'd been working on all morning.

A half hour later, she stood in front of Richmond's desk, well into her presentation about reopening the east shaft. Pagent, who had followed her in, sat to one side, occasionally trading looks with the other man.

Jill found the nerve to spread the geological survey map out in front of Richmond, and pointed out ways to keep the mine in operation. "—and if we sink a second adit on the east face, where the old Grey Lady smelter used to be, next spring we can tap—"

"Charles?" A tall, elegant blonde entered the office and gave Jill a dismissive smile before addressing Richmond again. "Sorry to interrupt, darling, but is someone ready to give me the tour?"

"Certainly, Diane. Ms. Hunter will be happy to accompany you. Jill, show Ms. Beck around our operation."

Our operation. Like he had anything to do with it.

"Of course." Frustrated but only too aware she had to keep playing her part, Jill smiled at the beautiful woman. "You'll need a coat, Ms. Beck."

Diane moved to Charles's closet and extracted a stunning fur jacket. "Will this do?"

Russian sable, Jill guessed, and worth more than a miner made in a year. The fact the other woman chose to wear real fur in this day and age disgusted her. "Yes. It will." She turned to Richmond. "I will be able to finish my presentation when we return." It wasn't a question.

Charles gave her a noncommittal nod. "Enjoy yourselves."

Once outside the business trailer, Diane Beck instantly dropped her seductive mask and gazed around with visible distaste. "I am not going down into those dirty holes."

"That's half the tour, Ms. Beck."

"Oh, call me Diane . . . Jane, is it?"

"Jill." Who felt like knocking a few of those perfect teeth out of perfect alignment. "All right, since you don't want a tour of the mine itself, would you rather see the mill?"

"I'd rather be on the Riviera, improving my tan." Diane eyed the surface structures, and wrinkled her nose. "But Charles expects me to do this, I suppose. Let's get it over with."

As they walked to the mill, Jill began automatically reciting the facts. "The present Dream Mountain site was established in 1971, to take advantage of the pre-existing tunnels left behind from the Grey Lady mine, which was abandoned in 1899." She pointed in the direction of the old camp.

Diane covered a yawn with her hand. "Why was it abandoned?"

"At that time, the investors were more interested in gold and silver than nickel and iron." Jill opened the side door to the mill for Diane. Inside, the giant machines were silent, something Jill had never gotten used to. "This is the mill, where the mined ore is transported and processed."

"How disgusting. It's filthy in here."

Jill immediately took offense—her father's mill was immaculate by anyone's standards—then recalled

Diane Beck had no experience with hardrock mining methods. "Actually, it's quite clean, considering we process over two thousand tons of ore through here a day."

Used to. Used to process two thousand a day.

Diane pulled up the collar of her sable and checked the condition of her long nails. "That's it?"

Jill felt like slapping her cosmetic-coated face.

"There's quite a bit more involved." She showed Diane where the mined ore was crushed, then further ground to the consistency of coarse sand. "The end product, or slurry, is blended with various chemical agents and pumped into the segregation unit, where the valuable ore is separated from the waste rock."

"Really." Diane smothered another yawn. "God, this is putting me to sleep."

Jill felt like doing the same thing. "If you're bored, we can go back to the business trailer."

"Could we?" Diane gave her a grateful smirk. "I *am* getting a little cold."

She doubted the blonde's temperature ever rose above tepid. "Sure. Let's go."

On the way back, Diane touched Jill's arm. "Tell me something. Ben Hunter was the one who owned this place before Charles. That's your father, right?"

"Yes." Jill thrust her numb hands in her jacket pockets. "He was my dad."

"Shame." As she walked, Diane removed a lipstick and refreshed the color on her lips. "Pouring all that lovely money back into this filthy business." She paused in the middle of application. "Oh, dear, I forgot. He spent most of that money on *you*, didn't he? Your college tuition, or something like that? You must feel awful."

"Yes." Humiliated, Jill gritted her teeth. How dare

Richmond discuss her father's private finances with this bimbo. "I do."

"Don't sweat it, honey." She rolled down the lipstick, capped and pocketed it. "It's for the best, you know. You're a woman, you don't belong up here. Fix yourself up, buy some new clothes, and you could land yourself a nice situation down in Denver."

Like Diane's? Jill would shoot herself in the head first. "Thanks for the advice."

When they returned to Richmond's office, Diane made some nice noises about how fascinating the operation was, then disappeared to repair the wind damage to her tousled hair.

Richmond absently offered his gratitude, and Jill seized the opportunity to finish her presentation.

"I see," Richmond said when she was done. "Thank you for your suggestions."

Jill straightened, and took the map her employer handed back to her. "So you'll think about it?"

"I will take your advice under consideration."

She was so happy she practically stuttered. "Th-thank you, sir. I know this will mean a lot to—"

"Yes, yes." He waved one of his manicured hands. "I'm sure the new owners will be very interested in looking this over. Thank you."

The new owners. Jill's delight fractured into a million shards. The map crumpled in her hands. "But, Mr. Richmond, I thought—"

"You're not here to think, Jill. You're here to *type.* I need you to prepare these letters for my signature before the end of the day." Richmond opened his briefcase and pulled out a thick folder. "Be sure to make copies of all the inventory sheets, and call the auction house. Let them know Shandian Corporation has a preferential bid on all the equipment. We'll be ready to begin transporting it to their warehouse by the end of the month."

"Yes, Mr. Richmond." Jill blindly took the folder before turning away and heading for the door. Diane brushed past her on the way.

"Thanks for the sight-seeing trip," the blonde said.

Jill couldn't speak. The horrible embarrassment only increased when she carefully closed Richmond's door, and heard the sound of her employer and his mistress laughing.

Joe used Laney's moment of confusion to pick up the knife and shove it in one of his pockets. Then he grabbed her and sat her back down on the rock. "Don't move."

He could feel the weight of her wide, disbelieving gaze as he checked the entrance and then his watch. He swiveled around to see her still gaping at him.

"Why did you do that?" she asked him. Then again, as she rose from the rock and took a step toward him. "Why?"

"You should find another occupation." Joe checked his supplies, and figured he had enough here at the cave to keep them both warm and fed for another week. Then he'd have to hit the camp, or the cabin to restock on food and fuel. "Go sit back down and stop putting weight on that foot."

Rather than obeying his command, Delaney hobbled toward him, and smacked him on the arm.

"What?"

"You . . . you . . ."

"Yeah, you what?"

She kicked him in the leg. "You are a complete *snake*, do you know that? How could you—and when

I—and then you—oh, you are just the most *hateful* man I have ever met!"

With that she limped back to the rock and sat down, pulled her hood over her head, and huddled in her jacket.

Joe considered grabbing her again, but his blood was still up from the last time and he didn't want to touch her. Besides, he'd wanted her to react this way. He suspected she had no idea what she'd just done to him.

He knew. Joe's hands shook as he sorted through one of his packs. He'd known her mouth was soft, from the dim memories of that first night. What he hadn't known was how it would feel, open and vulnerable beneath his. How it would taste while he was wide awake and rational enough to appreciate it.

He'd only wanted to teach her a lesson. Rather than hit her, or turn her over his knee—two thoughts that still held enormous appeal—Joe had kissed her. Kissed her mean, intending to leave her bruised and breathless. She needed to learn what happened to amateurs when they got in too deep.

Instead? She'd all but mowed him down.

He pulled out his supply of powdered eggs, some dried beef, and other packets of dehydrated food. *How the hell had she turned that around on him?* His spider skillet, scoured out with sand, would do for the quick meal. *No woman in memory had ever demolished him like that.* He'd get her to cook it, give her something to do. *If he was going to be stuck in this cave with her for another week, he'd have her.*

"Get over here," he said.

"Go jump off a cliff. A large cliff. A large, remote cliff. In the Himalayas. Have someone film it and send me a copy of the videotape."

"It's not a request." He set the supplies by the small container of sterno he'd lit and started after her. She reacted like a terrified mouse, jolting out of his reach and retreating farther back into the cavern. "Laney!"

She looked around. "Oh, God."

Before Joe could reach her, Laney shrieked and darted back out of the small recess.

"You really are claustrophobic, aren't you?"

She pressed a hand to her chest, her face white. "Give the man a prize."

"Why?" Without thinking he reached toward her. "What happened to make you afraid?"

"You . . . you keep your hands off me!" she yelled, still retreating. She lost her footing a moment later and went down with a thump.

"Damn it." He yanked her up. "I'm not going to hurt you."

Her mutinous gaze scalded him. "Too late."

He marched her over to the fire, and pointed at the skillet. "Cook."

"All right!" She wrenched her arm free. "But I'm only doing this because *I'm* hungry. I wouldn't make *you* chili with beans in it."

"Huh?"

"Never mind."

He took up a position by the cave entrance, telling himself he needed to keep watch. The problem was making himself not watch her. She had some kind of survivalist training, he guessed, judging by her familiarity and swift preparation of the emergency rations. Or she could simply cook. Like nobody's business, his nose told him.

But why the hell hadn't she slit his throat when she'd had the chance?

"It's ready," she said after a few minutes. "Get over here or I'm dumping yours in the fire."

He took the tin plate she offered him and sat down on a nearby ledge. The concoction she'd prepared looked revolting, until he put the first forkful in his mouth and closed his eyes.

She'd even managed to make powdered eggs taste like heaven.

"This is good."

"Thanks." Laney wouldn't look at him. "I hope you choke on it." She finished her own portion before Joe did, and immediately began tidying up.

He didn't stop her until she reached for one of the packs. "Leave it."

"Fine." She dropped the pack, and stalked past him to the entrance of the cave. He considered going after her, but the way she limped told him how sore her foot was. She wasn't walking or running anywhere, for now. "So. How long do you intend on keeping me up here?"

He could tell her that much. "A week."

"A week?" She whirled around, and her voice got shrill. "Are you nuts? Wait." She held up her hand. "I already know the answer to that one. But I can't stay in this cave for a week! There's no bathroom, no kitchen, one pan, and I certainly can't keep cooking over this fire—"

"You have an appointment with someone? Richmond, maybe?"

"Will you stop already with this Richmond guy? I don't know who he is, but when I meet him, I definitely have plans." Absently she rubbed a hand against the small of her back. "I'm going to ask him why you think I work for him, and then I'm going to kick him, really hard, where it hurts the most."

"What's wrong with your back?"

She snorted. "You won't get off it."

"Get used to it, Red, you're staying here." Joe polished off the last of the eggs and set his plate aside. He reached for the jug of meltwater he'd boiled last week, and checked the level. A half gallon. He'd need to make more, he thought, then drank from it.

Laney stood brooding by the entrance, until he came up behind her. Then she literally jumped, landed on her injured foot, and swore lightly. "Don't do that!"

"Here." He handed her the jug. "Have a drink. I'm going out for awhile. Stay out of sight."

Her hands tightened around the plastic container. "You mean you're just going to leave me here? Alone? In a bear cave?"

"There are no bears. I have only one pair of snowshoes." He looked down at her foot. "And you're in no shape to go with me."

"Great." She took a sip from the jug. "Have fun. Hope you get attacked by wolves. A lot of wolves. A wolf pack. A really hungry wolf pack—"

"There aren't any wolves left in Colorado."

"Vultures, then."

"They went south for the winter." He grabbed her chin and forced her to look up at him. "Stay out of trouble, Red. I'll be back in an hour."

His condition made him cautious, and the trek back to the cabin took longer as a result. He saw no sign of Richmond's men, but that meant nothing. Only the double tracks of their footsteps in the snow leading to and from the front of the cabin convinced him it was safe to slip in through the back.

Inside the cabin, nothing moved or made a sound. The smell of fresh coffee lingered, and he found the pot growing cold on the back of the stove. The smell of gunpowder lead him farther in, until he spotted the open door of the spare bedroom.

They'd found his gear.

No matter how crazy, strong, or determined Joe was, Laney had no intentions of spending a week in a cave. So as soon as he disappeared into the woods, she went to work.

"Time to exit the premises."

He'd taken the only pair of snowshoes, but she didn't care. They'd only come half a mile or so, surely she could cover that distance if she wrapped up well enough. She had no idea of what she was going to do once she actually got back to the cabin—short of barricading herself inside one of the bedrooms—but decided she'd figure that out when she got there.

"I'll brain him with the skillet. The big skillet."

Joe had enough clothing to allow her to bundle up well. The spare pair of boots she found, once lined with several pairs of socks, fit her feet better. The gash on her sole was still sore and throbbing, but that wasn't going to hinder her. Not as angry as she was right now.

"Ouch," she said when she put her full weight on it. "Okay, so I'll keep limping."

After a thorough rummage through all of his packs—discovering some very odd items in the process—Laney packed up what she thought she'd need and headed out of the narrow entrance. Outside the air was freezing, and she adjusted her hood so that her face was nearly covered.

"I'd kill for an electric blanket," she muttered, glancing at the bear hide. No, she'd rather freeze than wrap herself up in that smelly thing.

It would be one hell of a long walk. Without the

weight-distributing support of showshoes, Laney would have to break a path into the woods with her feet and legs. The resistance of the hardened icy layers was more than she'd expected, and before she'd gone twenty feet her legs were trembling and aching from the effort. Then there was the ever-present danger of sharp rocks hidden underneath the snow to consider. The boots would protect her feet, but if she slipped and fell—

"I'm chopped liver." Laney wished she could scream, but that might bring Joe running.

As she struggled through the deep drifts, a faint sound made her stop in her tracks. It was something she'd never heard before, something wild and ominous.

It wasn't Joe, that was for sure.

Of course there were no more timber wolves or grizzlies in this part of the country, even a city girl like her knew that, but plenty of black bears and other dangerous predators.

A bobcat, maybe? "Nice kitty, kitty, kitty."

Laney eyed the faint trail left by Joe's snowshoes. She had no weapon, no means to defend herself. Maybe it was better that she wait for another opportunity. She heard the sound again, this time much closer.

"That cave wasn't so bad." She turned around and headed back. "I could live there. A few cushions, some rugs, and it'd be just like home."

At least she'd already broken a path, so she was able to move faster. Her breath rushed in and out of her dry mouth. Her nose felt nearly frozen, and her cut foot was really starting to ache now.

The hair on the back of her neck rose. Something was following her. Something just beyond the timberline. But not for long.

"Oh, God." Would she make it, or would whatever was stalking her intercept her first?

She got her answer when she glanced over her shoulder and saw a tawny blur dart behind a huge aspen. If she hadn't seen pictures in books, she wouldn't have recognized it.

A cougar.

Laney knew the big cats were extremely shy and tended to stay away from human beings. On the other hand, it was the middle of winter, and the cougar was probably hungry.

She needed to get back to the cave *now.*

"Nice kitty," Laney said as she hobbled toward the entrance to the cave. Only a few more yards. "You don't want a stringy thing like me. Go get yourself a big, fat rabbit."

Fear-induced adrenalin gave her the reserve strength to cross the snow and squeeze back into the narrow passage. Once inside, she leaned back against the stone wall, dragging oxygen in with deep relief.

"Who needs a cabin? This is a good cave. I love this cave."

She was safe. But Joe was still out there, and so was the cougar.

No one would blame her for letting Mother Nature take her natural course. Yet no matter what he'd done, she couldn't stand by and do nothing. It wasn't Joe's fault he was unstable. Leaving him to that cougar out there would be like abandoning a toddler in the middle of Nightmare Ridge.

She didn't want to be brave. She wanted to be in Denver. She wanted to be behind the counter at her diner, pouring coffee and joking with her regulars.

Time's running out, Laney. Move it.

"Okay." She checked the interior of the cave. "What do I do, and what can I use to do it?"

She looked around until she found a dried length of wood light enough for her to swing like a baseball bat.

Her brow furrowed. "I don't think the cougar is going to stand there and *let* me brain him."

Even with the natural skylights above, it was getting dark, and hard to see.

"Be nice if he'd left me a damn flashlight," Laney said as she idly swung the wood back and forth. "Even the fire doesn't . . ." Her voice trailed off as she stared at the banked coals.

Fire.

Then she pulled out one of the socks from her borrowed boots and wrapped it around one end of the wood.

"Where is the rest of that stuff?" She hunted around until she found the round aluminum tins of sterno Joe had been using to cook with. "Bingo."

By dipping the sock-wrapped end into the gelatinous pink compound, then lighting it with the matches she'd ferreted out from another pack, Laney was able to fashion a crude torch.

"Good." She held it at arm's length. "I'll probably end up setting myself on fire, but maybe someone will see the smoke."

Laney carried it back to the entrance, and eased out until she could see from all directions. There was no sign of the cougar, but after a few minutes she heard the distant sound of crunching snow.

Joe. She put a hand to her mouth to call him. "Joe! Watch out! There's a cougar nearby!"

He immediately yelled at her. "Get back in the cave!"

"I'm not kidding! Listen!"

The sound of the cougar's roar echoed through the forest, and it was much closer this time. Too close.

"Joe!" Laney watched the trees, trying to see where the big cat was lurking. Joe's dark silhouette appeared farther back, moving toward her and the cave. A moment later she spotted a dark blur behind him. "Joe, run!"

That was when she heard him yell, and ran.

On the other side of the clearing, Joe stood with the shotgun trained on the huge cat, prepared to fire. Laney shrieked when something seemed to drop out of thin air to land on top of him. The shotgun went flying.

Laney slogged toward them, waving the torch. "No! Get off him!"

The cougar, stretched over Joe's back, lifted its head and bellowed at her. Its larger companion started padding through the snow toward Laney.

"Oh, no, you don't!" Laney swept the torch back and forth in front of her, making the first cougar stop and back away, snarling and spitting. The second, smaller cat was clawing at Joe's arms, which he had raised to protect his head. "Hey, you! Want to be a jacket? Get away from him!"

Laney went after the one attacking Joe, nearly smacking the torch into the animal's side before it leapt off Joe and retreated, baring impressive fangs as it yowled. It was barely half the size of the first one.

"Don't hurt it," Joe said, panting the words as he rolled over and grabbed the shotgun. "It's a mother and her cub."

"I don't care what they are," Laney said. "They'd better get a move on or they're going to be kitty kabobs." The two big cats paced restlessly a few yards away as Laney reached Joe and held out her arm.

"Come on, get up, we have to get out of here." She kept the torch between her and the two cougars, never taking her eyes from them.

Joe got up, put an arm around her, and carefully backed away toward the cave, also keeping the shotgun raised and ready. After several seconds the two cats turned and loped off into the timber, away from them.

"Move, now!"

Laney didn't stop for a second. She ran with Joe back to the cave, and only once they were inside did she let the torch drop from her nerveless fingers. "God, that was close."

"Yeah. It was." Joe put the woven covering back in place and swiveled around to glare at her. "I thought I told you to stay put. What the hell were you doing out there?"

"Going for a stroll. I get bored so easily."

"Did you really think you could get away?"

"No."

"You have to be the stupidest woman I've ever met."

"Yeah? Well, the stupidest woman you ever met just saved your ass, pal," she said, and let herself slide down until she was sitting back against the cave wall. "And I haven't the slightest idea why."

But she did know. She'd known it the moment she'd seen that cougar drop down on top of him. And it terrified her.

She'd fallen in love with Bigfoot.

CHAPTER SIX

"Damn it," Jill said under her breath as she tore another botched report from her typewriter, balled it up, and tossed it in the wastebasket. "This is useless."

She opened her desk drawer to take out a new pack of forms, and found the crumpled paper bag Webb Upton had given her. A rock he'd found, she recalled, and opened the bag.

Inside she found a fist-sized chunk of a strange-looking metallic ore, unlike anything she'd seen. It was like silver, except this rock had a strange, ruddy gleam. It was also exceptionally hard.

"Wow." She traced her fingers over the contours, and the lustrous feel of the rock startled her. "Webb, you definitely found something interesting this time."

Jill needed to take a closer look at the specimen, so she headed over to the mill, where the equipment she needed was kept in the ore analysis lab.

She shivered with cold as she walked into the processing mill and made her way around the silent equipment to the analysis room. There she turned on the heaters and removed her jacket.

"Okay." She pulled down a couple of reference manuals from the shelves along one wall and took

them along with the rock to a worktable. "Let's find
out what you are."

After chipping a small sliver from the ore, Jill performed a series of standard tests. The silvery-white
metal proved to have an extraordinarily high melting
point, and got its reddish tint from some very distinctive-
colored salts.

After checking her data against the books, Jill realized what it was, and dropped into a chair.

"This is crazy. It can't be."

She jumped up and took two more slivers from different portions of the specimen, and repeated the tests.

The results were identical to the first series.

Jill weighed the specimen, then packed it into a
sealed container and cleaned up after herself. She left
the mill and returned to her office, still flabbergasted
by what she'd discovered.

She put the bag back in her desk drawer, closed it,
and wondered how Webb Upton had stumbled upon
such a find. It couldn't be in its raw state. What he'd
brought her alone was worth more than twenty-five
thousand dollars.

"Jillian."

"Ah!" Jill jumped in her chair, then pressed a hand
to her thumping heart. "What is it with you hayshakers, always sneaking up behind people?"

"I'm sorry I startled you."

"Uh-huh." She turned to her typewriter and in-
serted a fresh report form.

"Why do you keep calling us that?" Pagent said
from behind her.

Why did his voice feel exactly like a slow caress,
running down the length of her spine? Jill didn't turn
around. "What can I do for you, Mr. Pagent?"

"You can call me Matt." He turned her chair around

and gazed down at her. "And you can answer my question."

"Hayshaker?" She could think of a few other things to call him. "It's miner's slang."

"For what?"

She sniffed. "For you surface slugs."

His jaw set, and through his reading glasses the hazel eyes looked menacing. "I'm not a slug."

"Right. Whatever you say." Jill shrugged, and when she would have turned back to her work, he held on to her chair. *If he doesn't get away from me soon, I'm going to deck him.* "Is there something else, *Mr.* Pagent?"

"Why were you in the mill?"

"I needed to get a reference book."

Pagent glanced at her empty desk. "I don't see any books."

"I couldn't find the one I needed." She made a mental note to take the ore home with her. No need to leave it lying around for Richmond or Pagent to find. "I'll check with Mr. Richmond, see if it's in his office. Excuse me, I have to get this report finished."

"Let me know if you can't find the book," Pagent said.

She kept typing until he left her office, then stopped long enough to release a grateful sigh.

It can't be. Not pure. Where the hell did Webb Upton find it?

Jill thought back to the day he'd brought it to her. He'd found it on the north slope, he'd said. But that was preposterous. A chunk that size, worth a thousand dollars an ounce, just sitting out in the open?

I have to get him to take me there.

*   *   *

Fai Tung flew to Atlanta at the summons of Shandian's new executive director, and went directly through the huge building to the penthouse floor.

When he entered the huge office, he made an immediate bow. *"Chin yuan liang, Bofu."*

"Speak English, Tung." The old man standing behind the desk gestured to a second man seated before him. "Our friend the emir does not comprehend Chinese."

"As you wish, Uncle." Fai eyed the Muslim's white robes, but smiled and bowed again. "Greetings, esteemed one. I have brought the latest information on the Colorado project."

"Good, good. Come and sit down, nephew. We have much to discuss."

Shuzhi studied his brother's firstborn without expression. Having failed to produce a son of his own, he'd taken Tung from China at an early age and groomed him as his successor. "You are still eating too much, I see."

"A failing of mine, as well." The emir turned slightly in his chair, and Fai Tung noted the impressive girth only vaguely disguised by the flowing djellaba. "I find American cuisine quite delectable."

Tung grinned. Outside of tong business, eating was his favorite occupation. "Then, we must dine together, my uncle's friend."

"The emir's faction was most disappointed by the loss of the SOAR technology," Shuzhi said.

"SOAR?" Tung gave the emir a startled glance. "Forgive me, I was not aware there were other bidders for the bio-core prototype."

"Chang Yu-Wei swindled both our governments before he drowned off the Florida Keys during Hurricane Deanna." Shuzhi thoughtfully stroked his chin.

"A pity he took the prototype with him. I am certain we could have worked out a mutually agreeable arrangement with our new friends in the Middle East."

"It is enough that we are working together now to achieve our goals." The emir beamed. "Shandian Corporation has a formidable reputation for efficiency. We will all profit from this partnership." The dark glasses glittered as he looked at Tung. "Unless the vein has proven to be less than previously anticipated?"

That was Tung's cue. He removed a file from his briefcase and handed it to Shuzhi. "The ore analysis on the samples obtained from Hunter Mining. Nearly seventy-five percent of the ore is composed of pure rhodium."

"Seventy-five percent *pure*?"

The Muslim leaned farther toward Tung and removed his dark glasses. Nestled in the swollen folds on his face, small black eyes gleamed with greed. "Three-quarters pure rhodium, you say. There has never been such a find. How is it possible?"

Tung had no idea, but he wasn't about to tell the Muslim that. "A happy anomaly, emir, attributed to ancient volcanic activity in the region."

"Indeed. And the vein is consistent?"

"We have taken samples at three fracture points," Tung lied. "The results have been identical."

Shuzhi sat down and studied the reports in silence.

"How soon will you begin shipment?" The emir sounded eager.

"We have the ships docked and waiting for the trucks. Mining will begin immediately." Tung turned to address his uncle. "Weather presents the greatest hindrance, but Richmond assures me the ore can be moved."

"Ah, yes. Mr. Richmond, without whom we would not have such a marvelous opportunity for profit." Shuzhi handed the file to the emir. "You have the evidence to prove him responsible for Tremayne's death?"

"Of course." Tung looked aggrieved. "Exactly as you specified, Uncle."

"Good. I believe we will have need of it soon." Shuzhi made a casual gesture. "It has been suggested that when we begin manufacturing the ore that the American government may try to interfere. We will need Mr. Richmond's talents if such a thing occurs."

"He has indicated he plans to retire with his share of the profits," Tung said.

Shuzhi smiled. "I did not say he must be willing, my nephew."

Laney had held Joe's life in her hands too many times not to take it. Not if she was working for Richmond. He considered this, and several other inconsistencies, then went to her.

She remained huddled against the wall of the cave, her head resting against her arms. He was tempted to pick her up, hold her in his arms, but pulled her to her feet instead. She wouldn't look at him.

"Enough." He shook her once. "I want some answers. Now."

"Really?" She sounded dull, defeated. "Okay. Shoot. Excuse me, I mean, go ahead."

"Why did you chase off the cougars?"

She gave him a rather silly grin. "Because they were going to eat you, and I didn't want them to get indigestion."

"Why did you take care of me when I was sick?"

Laney yawned. "There was nothing good on television."

"There is no television in the cabin."

She nodded. "See?"

His hands tightened. "What were your instructions from Richmond?"

"I don't know any Richmond." She frowned. "I think I said that already, didn't I? About a million times?" She covered a huge yawn with one slim hand. "I beg your pardon."

"I need to know what's going on, Red."

"You need some therapy, pal." And then, to his complete astonishment, she sagged forward against him and started sliding to the cave floor.

"Laney?" He caught her, lifted her limp body up against his chest. Her small face was still, her eyes closed.

She'd fainted. Was she hurt? Had the cats gotten at her? Joe put her down on the first flat surface he could reach and tugged open her jacket. No blood that he could see. He patted her cheek. "Laney? Wake up. Talk to me."

"So . . . tired . . . " She snuggled against his hand, went still again, and started snoring.

She was *asleep.*

He picked her up again and carried her to his sleeping bag. "Okay, Red. Sleep now, questions later." He tucked her into the insulated envelope and zipped the side up until only her face showed above the edge. Then he pulled the bear hide up over her, sat down, and watched her breathe.

Poor Delaney will be so disappointed.

The image of Laney asleep, sitting on the floor beside the bed, still clutching the cloth she'd used to keep his fever down.

All you have to do is cooperate, and you won't get hurt.
She'd said that, holding his own penknife at his throat.

The genuine curiosity in her voice when she'd asked, *How do you know all that stuff?*

Joe watched her sleep for a while. He never got tired of seeing the firelight gleam in her hair, or the rosy glow it lent to her pale face. She'd lost weight, he saw now, weight she didn't need to lose.

Taking care of me. Being my hostage.

Soon Joe's own exhaustion had him nodding off. At last, cold and tired, he unzipped the sleeping bag, crawled in next to her, and pulled her into his arms. She wound herself around him, drawn to the warmth of his body.

That was fine with him. He'd get his answers later.

Pagent was waiting for them when Sean and Kerass got back to camp. He didn't look happy. "Kerass, you're needed down below." Sean waited until the other man left before speaking. "The cabin was deserted. I think Tremayne's still alive. He's probably got the girl."

"Who is she?"

"We don't know."

Pagent's hands fisted. "Where would he take her?"

"Out on the ridge, probably in one of the caves." Sean spat on the ground in disgust. "It would take a good month to search all of them."

"They'll run out of food" was Pagent's prediction. "I'll send a man to keep an eye on the cabin."

"I'll do it," Sean said.

Richmond's foreman shook his head. "Charles wants to talk to you about another job."

"Another one?" Sean's silver brows rose. "Who does he want dead now?"

"He didn't say. C'mon." Pagent walked with him back to the main office, passing Jill Hunter on the way. She kept her head down and didn't look at either of them.

"What's her problem?" Sean asked.

"Don't know." Pagent looked back over his shoulder. "Probably mad at Richmond again."

Sean whistled. "Girl has a death wish, doesn't she?"

Richmond met them just inside the office door. Diane was sitting behind the reception desk, filing her nails. "Matt, Sean, come back to the office. We need to talk. Diane?" The blonde lifted her gaze and smiled. "I'll be with you in just a moment, darling."

She waggled her fingers at him. "I'll be waiting."

Once inside the office, Richmond got right to business. "What did you find at the cabin?"

"The girl's gone." Sean looked from Pagent to Richmond. "From the looks of things, the man took her out of there. It may be Gareth Tremayne."

"Tremayne is supposed to be dead," Richmond said. Sean only shook his head. "Or it could have been a setup. Where are they now?"

"Probably hiding up in the caves."

"I see." Richmond remained silent for a moment. "This changes my plans. Sean, go and track down Tremayne and the girl, and take care of them. The other hit can wait."

That got Pagent's attention. "What other hit?"

"Hunter's daughter," Richmond said. "She's been getting curious about too many things lately. If she finds out about ten, she won't keep her mouth shut."

"We may have been able to cover up the old man's death, but the police are going to jump on this one," Pagent said, his voice harsh. "Two family members, both dead within weeks of each other? Can't do it. Look, she won't find out. I'll take care of it."

"Is that right?" Sean's expression turned ugly. "Trying to cut in on my profits, foreman?"

Richmond chuckled. "Sean, you do Tremayne and the woman, and be sure to bury them deep this time. Pagent, if you can't get Jill Hunter to shut up, Sean will have to get rid of her. Now, if you gentlemen will excuse me, my companion is waiting."

Outside at the reception desk, a hand reached for the lit intercom button, and switched it off.

The knock on her door surprised Jill, but not as much as the sight through the peephole of who'd made it.

She removed the chain lock and bolt, and opened the door a few inches.

"Jill." Pagent stood on the front porch, his hat in his hands. Snow fleeced his dark hair.

"Mr. Pagent." He might not be tall or handsome, but the force of his presence was undeniable. And the last thing she wanted to do was let that force in her house.

"We need to talk."

She considered making an excuse, but some bizarre impulse made her pull the door open and gesture for him to come in.

"Would you like some coffee?" she asked as she led him down the hall to the kitchen. "I was just getting ready to make some."

"No, thanks." He stood watching her as she prepared the coffeemaker. "You live by yourself, don't you?"

"No, there's a three-hundred-pound linebacker for the Broncos renting my spare bedroom. Of course I live alone."

"Dangerous."

She poured water into the machine and turned it on. "What? The linebacker?"

"Living by yourself up here. What happens if you get hurt?"

"I hopefully crawl to the phone and call 911 before I pass out. Why?"

Pagent didn't reply, so Jill took a covered dish from the refrigerator and placed it in the oven.

"What's that?"

"The world's worst tuna casserole." Jill set the oven temperature to reheat and removed a mug from the cabinet above it. "Dad made a bunch of them, and wouldn't you know it, I absolutely loathe tuna fish."

"Why are you eating it, then?"

"Dad didn't like to cook, so he always made huge batches of everything. After the funeral, I found all these casseroles in the freezer." She poured the coffee, trying to keep her hands from shaking. She failed. Hot liquid slopped over onto the counter. "I've been having one every week since he died."

His voice deepened. "How many more do you have to eat?"

Jill wiped up the spill. "This is the last one." If she kept busy, she wouldn't have to think about Dad or look at Pagent. "Would you prefer something besides coffee? I don't have any alcohol in the house, I'm afraid, but there's tea, soda, or juice."

Two hands rested on her shoulders, making Jill tense. "I'm fine."

That he was. But there was no way she was going to let Richmond's right-hand man into her bed. Or her heart. No matter how lonely she'd been since her father's death. Jill sidestepped him and swiveled around. "What did you need to talk to me about, Mr. Pagent?"

He moved closer. The way he liked to invade her personal space was really beginning to annoy her. He got close, close enough for her to smell him. The scent of his skin reminded her of how he drank his coffee—dark, potent, and as hot as a woman could make it.

I don't want to make him hot. Do I?

"Why are you afraid of me, Jillian?" As he spoke, his breath caressed her cheek.

God, the way he said her name. "Who said I was afraid of you?"

One of his slim hands stroked her arm. "You should be."

Jill was backed up against the counter, with no room to avoid Pagent. She panicked. "You can leave any time now."

"Or I could do anything I want to you. Have you thought about that?" He made her look at him, his hand under her chin now. His body settled against hers, using up the small spaces that were left between them. "Right here, right now. You could scream and no one would hear you."

"I can do more than scream, Mr. Pagent." Sounding calm and indifferent wasn't difficult. Resisting the urge to tug his mouth down to hers was. "What do you want?"

His head lowered. "I want you to give up these crazy ideas about keeping the mine open."

She opened her mouth to tell him what she thought of that, and flinched as his hand closed over it.

"You said it yourself, Jillian." His hips moved on hers, making her instantly, vividly aware of how much trouble she was in. "You live alone up here. All alone."

She jerked her head sharply to the left, dislodging his hand. "I can take care of myself, Pagent."

"And if you couldn't?" He traced one of her golden

brows with his fingertip. Then her nose. Then her lips. "There's no one to protect you. What do you think would happen if someone broke in here in the middle of the night?"

Jill couldn't think, period. "I would—I'd—"

"The middle of the night, you'd be sound asleep, wouldn't you?" His hand slid down, landing on her left breast. He massaged it slowly. "What if he came into your bedroom and tied you up to that pretty little brass bed you sleep in?"

She was so shocked she couldn't move. Couldn't breathe.

He bent lower, resting his mouth against her ear as his hips moved against hers again. "What if you couldn't stop him from doing whatever he wanted?"

He could do whatever he wanted. Right now. She closed her eyes for a moment. "Matt."

The sound of his name seemed to have the same effect on Pagent as a bucket of ice water. "Jesus Christ." Roughly he pushed himself away from her and strode across the room.

Bewildered, Jill took a half step after him before stopping herself. "Matt?"

"Stop meddling with things at the mine, Jillian." He stood in the doorway, but didn't look back at her. "If you don't, you're going to end up like your father."

That cleared her head. Instantly. "What are you talking about?"

"Do what I said, or I'm going to have to take care of you." Now he turned his head. "And you don't want that to happen."

He left her standing there. All Jill could think was, *Oh, yes, I do.*

*   *   *

Warmth enveloped Laney from head to toe. The luxurious sensation made her burrow deeper into her blankets. As she snuggled, her nose bumped into something hard. She frowned and tried to push it away, but it wouldn't budge. She must have rolled into the wall, she thought, and indulged in a lazy yawn.

Walls don't have hair on them.

She opened one eye and saw a wall of tanned skin covered with black hair, pocked by dozens of tiny, nearly healed wounds.

Joe. She glanced up through a tangle of red hair to find the man himself watching her. "Hi."

"Hi, yourself." One large hand smoothed the curls away from her face. "Feeling better?"

She was feeling plenty of things now. Joe's body, pressed against hers. The solid layer of muscle beneath his clothes. The soft tickle of his beard against the top of her head. The sudden spike of heat that resulted from all of the above.

"I didn't know I was feeling bad," she said, then winced at the throb in her foot and the twang of sore muscles. "Ugh. Correction. I do now. Ouch. What did you do, beat me with a club?"

The gunmetal eyes settled on a point just below her nose. "Go back to sleep, Red."

Gingerly she raised herself up on one elbow, and found she was curled up next to Joe in a sleeping bag. "What happened?"

"Exhaustion. You passed out."

"I what?" Her jaw dropped. "No way. I've never fainted before in my life."

"Then you do a damn good imitation." Joe caught her hand as she fumbled for the zipper. "No, stay put. The only place you're going is back to sleep."

Not if he wanted to stay dry, she wasn't. "Can't. I

have to go to the bathroom." She remembered where they were and sighed. "I mean, the nearest shrub."

"All right." Joe unzipped the sleeping bag and helped her to her feet, then steadied her when she landed on her cut foot and yelped. "Stand still, right there."

Joe retrieved her jacket and the snowshoes, and helped her put them on. "Go slow, now."

"I'm not running any marathons," she said, then yawned.

The temperature felt considerably warmer than the last time Laney had left the cave. She smiled as the air nipped at her face. "Looks like we're getting a break in the weather."

"Yeah." Joe studied the convex slope above them for a long moment, muttered something under his breath, then pointed to a cluster of nearby boulders and snow-crusted shrubs. "Over there."

Laney limped away, surprised and grateful when he didn't follow her.

After she'd taken care of that problem, she hobbled back to where he waited. The air was so still that the hollow crunch of the loosely packed ice crystals under her snowshoes seemed to echo throughout the ridge. She looked down and saw cracks in the surface hoar running out in every direction. Melting, she thought absently. "Any sign of the cougars?"

"No. They're long gone." Joe's eyes moved from the tree line up to the cornice at the top of the ridge.

"What if they come back?"

"I think we're okay. Typically they never come this far down the ridge, or anywhere near humans."

"Hmmmm. I don't *smell* very human," Laney said, sniffing at her sleeve. She didn't mind the cold, but being unable to wash or change into clean clothes was still a sore point. "Neither do you, for that matter."

"You're right," he said, astounding her with a grin. "That's probably why they attacked us. We smell like that old bear hide."

"I can see the commercial now." She smiled back. "Eau de Bigfoot. The cologne nine out of ten cougars find completely irresistible."

"Come on, smart-ass." Joe slid a supporting arm around her waist and guided her back toward the cave.

"Do we have to?" She was whining, but she didn't care. "I'm not tired."

"Time you gave me some answers."

"I've told you everything I know."

"Then you'll tell me again."

Back in the cave, Joe heated water for coffee over the fire as she limped to the sleeping bag and sat down.

"This is a waste of time, you know," Laney said.

"I have nothing better to do. I know your car didn't get stranded up here, Laney. I've scouted this area for miles around. No Escort—red or otherwise—is anywhere."

She folded her arms over her chest. "If I tell you, you won't believe me. I swear, you won't. Then you'll think I'm nuts. Which is actually a fair exchange, when I think about it—but no. You won't believe me."

He brought her a mug of black, steaming brew. "Try me."

"I'm serious."

He sat down beside her. "So am I."

"Okay." She set the coffee down beside her. "I was checking with the police on Neal's case—Neal's been missing ever since finding this dead senator—but there were no new leads, which took an entirely frustrating four hours to find out, and then my uncle picked me up—"

He frowned. "Who's Neal? Your boyfriend?"

She nearly corrected him, then decided an imaginary boyfriend just might come in handy. "Neal's the other bane of my existence. Anyway, my uncle asked me to come with him to see if a Bigfoot was living up here."

"Bigfoot."

"That would be you. Or what the locals call you. Don't look at me like that. You're the one who's been running around the ridge wearing a bearskin. The hair and beard don't help, you know, because when people see you, they're automatically going to assume you're—"

"What else?"

"Well . . . when we got to the cabin, my uncle checked the water, which was working, *thank God*, because I would have gone nuts without it, and then he helped me get a fire going. I haven't used a real fireplace before; it's not as easy as it looks, is it?"

"Cut to the chase, Red."

"Okay. Uncle Sean said he'd forgotten something and he had to go out to the car to get it. A half hour went by, and I got worried, so I opened the front door. That's when I found out my uncle and his car were gone. I spent the next three, no, four days cursing and burning my fingers on that wretched stove and trying to keep from going crazy. After that, I saw you outside, digging through my trash, and I thought you were a bear, and I shot you. End of story."

He gave her a thank-God look. "Why would he want to strand you here? Did you have an argument?"

"No, we never fight. I love my uncle. He's the closest thing I've ever had to a father." She traced idle patterns on her jeans with one fingernail. "Mine died when I was little."

"What about the rest of your family?"

"My mom was a nightclub singer. She took off for Vegas with her piano player when my sister and I were teenagers. Uncle Sean looked after us until we were old enough to head out on our own." She pictured Neal's face, and gnawed at her lower lip. "I think he was worried about me getting into it with the police over Neal." At Joe's frown, she shook her head. "Long story, has nothing to do with this."

"Your boyfriend in a lot of trouble?"

She didn't have to lie when she sighed and said, "Neal's *always* in trouble." Laney picked up her coffee and took a sip. And nearly blew the bitter mouthful back into the mug.

"Too hot?"

"I can't tell. It just killed my tongue."

"I don't have that kind of luck." Joe swallowed the rest of his—a feat that impressed Laney to no end, considering the taste—then regarded her with a skeptical expression. "So that's it? That's your story?"

"That's it."

"When you're not rescuing your boyfriend Neal, you go around helping your uncle track down suburban myths? The same uncle who dumps you in the middle of nowhere for no reason?"

"See?" She assumed a long-suffering expression and shook her head. "I knew it. I told you, you wouldn't believe me. But did you listen to me? No."

"And you've never heard of Charles Richmond, Shandian Corporation, or the Dream Mountain mine?"

"Nope." Honesty compelled her to admit, "Well, I have heard of the mine. It was in all the papers a couple of months ago, when the owner died."

"Great." Joe got up and started pacing back and forth.

Was he going to jump off the deep end again?

"Look, just forget about it, okay?" Laney rose and awkwardly hobbled toward him. "No offense, Joe, I really like your place, but . . . can we go back to the cabin now?"

"No. They'll be waiting for that."

More of his distrustful paranoid maniac stuff again. "Please. I've had enough of caves and killer cats and crude accommodations. I want four walls between me and Mother Nature. I want to change my clothes, and use a bathroom instead of a bush, and sleep in a real bed." When his expression didn't change, she stamped her good foot down hard. "Do you know what I get like when I can't have a bath every day?"

"A bath." He made a disgusted noise. "Just like a woman, to be worried about how you smell."

"Hey." She planted her hands on her hips. "I am a woman. Live with it."

The chilly gaze thawed a few degrees as Joe studied her, then he glanced toward the entrance to the cave. A faint line appeared between his black brows. "Okay. We'll head back to the cabin."

Joe knew going back to the cabin was risky, but with the shifts in temperature and build up of snow on the upper ridge, it was even more dangerous to stay in the cave. He'd done an intern year with the CAIC during his days with the Colorado Geological Survey, and knew the conditions and terrain were ideal. Loose rock covered the lee side, and if they stayed under the current conditions, the whole side of the ridge might come down with the snowpack, and seal them in for good.

As for Laney's story about Bigfoot and her uncle, it made little sense. At the same time, it was so ludicrous it might actually be true. She'd certainly delivered it without a hitch.

The part that bothered him was learning Little Red had a boyfriend. Who was this guy Neal, and why had he disappeared? How had he gotten mixed up with a dead senator? Joe had refrained from grilling her about him, unwilling to let her see how much it aggravated him. And it did, big time. But why?

Because she's mine.

Realizing that caused him no small amount of astonishment. Yet it was true, he'd begun thinking of her as his woman, his property, and learning another man had prior claim infuriated him.

If she's telling the truth this time.

Joe decided she was. He also knew the danger of emotions he had no right to indulge in. Both their lives were on the line, and Richmond was hunting for them. He'd let her have a bath at the cabin, get a change of clothes, then he'd whisk her back up to the cave before anyone at Dream Mountain got wind of their presence.

Laney was so eager to get back to the cabin she started for the cave entrance, but Joe caught her arm.

"Wait a minute." He retrieved a pack, two ski poles, and a long red cord that he tied around her waist.

"You don't have to put me on a leash." She tugged at the rope. "It's not like I can run anywhere. What are these arrow thingies on it for?"

"I don't have any transceivers." Which, given the weather conditions, worried him. Before she could ask, he shook his head. "Never mind. Just keep it on until we reach the cabin. And put those snowshoes on."

They started the long trek across the lee slope of the ridge toward the densely packed tree line. Knee-high drifts hampered him, but Joe stayed close to Laney. With every step, his tension increased. He glanced around.

Snowpack is too high, too loose. Temperature's rising. "What's the matter?" Picking up on his uneasiness,

Laney scanned the area around them. "Think the cougars will be back?"

"No." He put a hand on the small of her back and gave her a gentle push. "Don't stop. Keep heading for the trees."

Laney limped along willingly enough, until a strange sound made him pull her to a halt. The noise sounded exactly like brittle wood slowly splintering and cracking.

"What is that?"

Joe turned his head, and saw what he'd feared most.

A huge slab of snow had broken off from the slope above and was sliding down, crashing into trees, swallowing boulders, and creating a three-foot-high wall of white.

It was also headed directly at them.

He didn't think; he reacted. With one arm he grabbed Laney, slung her over his shoulder, and tried to run. For once, she didn't struggle.

"Oh, my God! Joe! *It's coming right at us!*"

The sound of the avalanche grew louder as he fought to get to the trees in time. The faint crackling swelled into a ferocious roar of smashing rock and grinding ice.

The outer clusters of pine and aspen, only a few hundred yards away now, began to shiver.

When the avalanche's front wave hit them, Joe clamped his arm tightly around Laney's waist and tried to shield her with his body. But the weight of the mammoth collapsed slab was too much, and the resulting centrifugal force wrenched her from his grip almost at once.

"Laney—"

As the snow and rock debris crashed over him, he automatically resorted to the training he'd received as a student. He tried to roll to the side, to get out from under the slab. When it became apparent he was too close to the center to escape, he clawed his way up, swimming through the snow to reach the surface. Already he could feel it fracturing, slowing, and settling as the front edge hit the timberline.

Where is she? Was she thrown clear?

When the avalanche halted, he found himself wedged between two tree trunks, buried in snow up to his armpits, his body battered but still in one piece. He shook the ice crystals from his eyes and looked for Laney.

Nothing but silent, ice-pocked snow stretched out around him.

"Red? Red!" He used the lower branches of the trees to pull himself out of the drift. "Laney! Can you hear me?"

No response.

Frantic now, Joe waded out into the unstable avalanche field, searching every inch around him, shouting her name over and over. "Laney? *Laney!* Goddamn it, answer me!"

An internal clock began ticking. If she was completely buried, he had less than five minutes to find her. She'd die of suffocation, or trauma from hitting something solid during the slide, or from simply being crushed by the gigantic blocks of snow.

The cord, she was wearing the cord, where is it?

He pawed the surface as he slogged through the massive slide, furiously scrabbling at anything that wasn't white. Ice crusts jammed under his fingernails, making them tear and bleed. He barely noticed it.

She's alive, damn it. She has to be. I can't lose her now, not like this. I'll find her.

She's alive. He found himself making bargains as he

continued to search. *When I find her, I'll tell her I believe her. She won't have to be afraid of me anymore. Then I can tell her the rest. How much I want her. How much I . . .*

His gaze zeroed in on a ragged inch of red a few yards to the left. A hoarse cry of relief left him as he lunged toward it. When his hand closed over the end, he held his breath and gave it a gentle tug. Something was still attached to the other end.

Laney. He'd found her.

He began scooping armfuls of snow and tossing them aside as he dug down into the snowpack. A foot in he found her small, limp hand and one of her feet. The temptation to pull her from the snow was strong, but he had no idea if she was injured. It took another minute to dig down to her face, which was still. Blood oozed from a shallow cut on her brow, turning the snow covering it into crimson slush.

When he touched her cheek, she took a ragged breath. Then another.

"Red." He thrust his hand in the snow to check her jugular. A weak beat pulsed slowly under his numb fingertips. "Thank God. Hold on, sweetheart. I'll get you out."

Ten minutes passed as he exhumed her from the snowy tomb and checked her for broken bones. He found a number of small lacerations but nothing more. It took another half hour to carry her through the drifts, into the trees, and back to the cabin. By the time they arrived, Joe didn't care if Richmond and every one of his hired goons were waiting. Laney had stopped shivering and was breathing even slower.

Hypothermia. Have to get her warmed up.

CHAPTER SEVEN

The electricity was still off, so Joe had no way of getting Laney into a warm bath. The stack of quilts she'd used the first night for him sat beside the fireplace. He'd use those, and himself. But first he had to get her naked and dry.

"Almost there, Red." Fabric ripped as he stripped her. He threw her torn clothes aside and used one of the quilts to wipe her down. She was still unconscious, her face dead-white. "I'm going warm you up, baby, just hold on."

After wrapping her up in another quilt and laying her gently on top of a couple more he tossed on the floor, he built a quick fire, then stripped off his own soaked garments. Once he was naked, he dropped to his knees, unwrapped the quilt and pulled her body up against his.

"Christ." The word exploded from him as her cool, bare skin collided with his.

She was too damn cold.

He checked her pulse, and blew out a breath of relief to feel it beating slow but steady. Automatically he began rubbing his big hands over her flesh as he watched her breasts rise and fall.

She's breathing regularly. She's going to be fine.

"Don't you ever do that to me again," he said against her hair, forcing warmth into her with his body and hands. "Come on, baby, let's get your blood going now."

Gradually her skin tone changed from alabaster to peach in color. Her stiff limbs relaxed and became more pliable. Even her breathing sounded better.

"That's my girl." Joe closed his eyes and pressed a quick kiss on the top of her head. "Pink and pretty as a rose, just the way I like you."

His voice must have penetrated her sleep, because Laney stirred.

"Mmmmm . . ." She made her first voluntary movement and tried to press closer, her fingers weakly clutching at him.

"Laney? Honey, can you hear me?"

She didn't respond. Then, to his disappointment, she slowly sagged, sliding back into unconsciousness.

"That's okay, Red." He rocked her, grateful for even that small sign. "You can talk when you wake up. You can talk yourself into laryngitis, if you want."

Her limp hand slid from his arm down between their bodies. What it landed on made every muscle in Joe's frame tense. His teeth clenched as beads of sweat instantly popped out on his forehead. Cautiously he reached down to move her hand.

"Not tonight, sweetheart—ah—" His breath hissed between his teeth when Laney's fingers reflexively curled around him. It didn't help that he got instantly hard, either. "Ah, don't do that."

She shifted against him and murmured something. Which was fine. The problem was, she wouldn't let go.

"Damn it." He tried prying her hand open. She only gripped him tighter. "Laney, sweetheart, you're killing me here."

She smiled a little in her sleep and made an "Mmm-mmm-mmm" sound when he tried to slide her hand off. She let him move her hand only so far, then pulled back, refusing to release him.

Joe wasn't a saint. He couldn't help closing his hand over hers, and holding it there. "God." Couldn't stop from moving his hips once, twice, then a third time. "That feels good."

On the last stroke, Laney's hand tightened, giving his erect penis a gentle squeeze.

"Jesus," he said through gritted teeth, fighting the need to roll her on her back and thrust his painfully engorged shaft into her body. Even in this position, all he had to do was reach down, guide himself into that tight, damp place, and take what he needed.

No, he wouldn't do that. Not until she was awake and warm and wanting him to. But the strength and will required to drag her hand away was beyond him. He wanted it, needed it too much to push her away.

"Forgive me, baby, but I need this, I need you." Slowly he began to thrust against her soft, slim fingers. "I won't take any more than your touch tonight, I swear." He looked down at her, smiled a little, and eased his free hand between her thighs. "Maybe just this much more."

Laney arched her hips, unconsciously welcoming him as he used his fingers to stroke her.

It was an insane promise to keep. Pushing himself into the silky cradle of her hand, feeling her melt and pulse against his fingers; all of it made him hungry to take more. "I wish I was inside you, like this," he said, panting as the sweet friction they created together began to work its magic. He was covered in sweat, she was trembling and moaning softly. "I know I could make it good for you, Red. I'd love you for as long as we could stand it. Would you like that? Do you like this?"

She made a sound that could have been "yes." Then she murmured his name as her breathing changed and quickened. She moaned, lifting her hips, pushing against his hand. Her fingers tightened around his penis.

He couldn't take much more. "Come for me, Laney."

She tensed, then he felt her convulse around his fingers. As if she'd heard every word. Joe held her tightly, groaned, and poured himself into her palm.

For a long time after that, he simply held her, vaguely stunned by the intimacy of sharing what had always been a simple, solitary act of relief. Belated guilt slowly built inside him, until he let her go and went about cleaning away the physical traces of his impulsive act.

It was wrong. She didn't know what you were doing. No, she knew. She'd climaxed, he'd felt it. And the way she wouldn't let go of him, stroking him like that—*No, she had to know.*

He gazed down at her sleeping face. "Could you feel how much I needed you? How good it was for me to touch you?"

Laney made no response. Joe cursed himself, then edged back into the pile of quilts with her. He stretched out on his back, pulling her to rest on top of him.

"There." His broad palms stroked over the smooth lines of her back. She stirred, nuzzling him with her nose and cheek. "That's it. Come back to me, baby."

She moved on top of him, shifting her weight and spreading her legs over his hips. The natural motion made her breasts drag across his chest, but that wasn't what made him groan. She'd managed to settle the most vulnerable portion of her anatomy almost right where it belonged—her sleek folds nestled against his penis, which reacted as if he'd never spilled himself over her fingers at all.

"Red . . ." He reached down, cupped her bottom, and with another groan shifted her again.

The access road to Nightmare Ridge was free of ice and snow, having been salted and cleared by Richmond's transport contractor. Sean was nearly at the cabin when he noticed the melting slush and the dripping icicles. About the same time he heard the avalanche.

Sweet Mother of God, does he still have her up on the ridge?

He slammed on his brakes without thinking, and sent the SUV into a wild skid. It ended when the rear end slammed into a deep bank and nearly rolled the car onto its side. The force of the vehicle righting itself caused his head to smash into the inner door frame, and a string of Gaelic curses erupted from his tight lips.

Sean didn't wait for his ears to stop ringing, but grabbed his binoculars from the glove compartment and wrenched open the door. The rear end was hopelessly mired down in the soft snowbank. Slowly the huge rumble died away, but he still raised the lenses to his eyes to search the lee slope above the cabin for any sign of his niece.

"Irish."

He spun around, his hand going into his jacket to pull the pistol he had holstered there out. The two anonymous-looking goons standing three feet away wore dark suits, sunglasses, and held twin, no-nonsense .38's pointed at his chest.

Not Richmond's. Slowly he eased his empty hand back out of the jacket. "What do you want?"

"Come with us."

A limousine stood, motor running, just around the curve. The two men marched Sean toward it without further comment. When they were a yard away, one of the tinted back windows slid silently down.

"Hello, Irish."

"You." Sean's eyes widened, then he spat on the ground and started to swear.

The door opened out. "Get in."

He didn't move an inch, not even when one of the suits prodded him with his gun. "You heard the slide. I've got to go to the cabin. Laney could be in trouble."

"Get in the car."

His frustrations straining his temper to near boiling, Sean strode over, ducked his head, and climbed in the back of the long black car, slamming the door behind him. The two gunmen went around and got in the front.

"Here." A lean brown hand offered a tumbler with two inches of malt whiskey. "Warm yourself."

Sean tossed back the mellow alcohol with two swallows, grunting as the heat seeped into his veins. He glanced back through the window toward the cabin. "I've got to make sure she's all right. Even you can understand that, you ice-veined bastard."

"She's fine." The man beside him took the empty glass and stowed it in a small compartment between them. The dome light overhead made his short copper hair glow. "You worry too much, Irish."

"I've got good reason to, thanks to you, Kalen. Richmond sent me to take them both out."

"Did he." One side of Kalen Grady's mouth curled. "Well, well. Charles is finally getting nervous."

"Knowing Tremayne's loose?" Sean snorted. "He'd be crazy not to be. It doesn't matter. I'm moving her back to the city. Now."

"With what?" Amusement tinted Kalen Grady's otherwise flat voice, but there was no humor in his dark eyes. "Your car isn't going anywhere. Do you think Tremayne is going to hand her over, just like that? He thinks she's Richmond's hired gun."

"What the hell are you talking about? Why would he . . ." Sean's voice trailed off and he clapped a hand over his eyes. "Mother of God. *Delaney*."

A phone rang, and Kalen answered it with a "yes." He listened, gave the caller instructions to continue the surveillance, then hung up. "They're both in the cabin now. Laney is in good hands."

Sean was too angry to notice the barely perceptible hesitation between "is" and "in." "You send in whatever man you've got watching them and take her out, Kalen."

"I can't move them, not now. Neither can you. We have other problems to deal with, Irish." He removed a folded page of newspaper from his jacket and handed it to Sean. "J.R. jumped bail two days ago."

His hand trembled as he saw the image of the headlined murder scene. Neal, standing over the body of the dead senator. "Oh, no."

"Some clerk leaked the still, and now the security tapes have been stolen from evidence. This changes everything. We have to wrap up this Hunter Hardrock mess quickly. Understand me?"

"Yeah." Sean put down the newspaper and rested his head back against the seat. "Tell me what you want me to do."

* * *

The dream was strange and unlike any Laney had ever had before.

It started out scary, with her body being hammered and tossed in some airless, blinding storm. Pounding forces knocked the breath from her lungs, wrapped her in ice, and dragged her down into some kind of bizarre white coffin. She was so cold and weak from lack of air she couldn't force the lid to open. Snow filled her mouth. That was when Laney knew the end had finally come, and began to pray. Yet she didn't beg God to save her.

She prayed for Joe. Prayed he would survive the storm. That God would watch over the man she loved, and protect him from whatever was tormenting him, real or imagined.

Then something big and dark had wrenched away the coffin's lid and touched her. A deep voice spoke to her.

I'll get you out.

She wanted to reach up and take the hand, but she was so paralyzed by the cold, she couldn't feel or move her body anymore.

He knew. *I'm going to get you warm, baby, just hold on.*

Something started chipping away at the icy shroud around her, and warmth slowly seeped back into her numbed limbs.

His voice got angry. *Don't you ever do that to me again.*

She tried to touch him herself, but it was too much: she didn't have the strength to hold on. Deep inside Laney cried out with frustration, with the powerless state she'd been reduced to. Then her hand closed over something thick and hard, and the feel of it made her sigh with satisfaction.

He tried to take her hand away, and she resisted. Then he must have felt the pleasure, too.

Oh, God, that feels good.

Joe needed her. She needed this. *I need to touch him. I won't take any more than your touch tonight, I swear.*

Then the dream had moved into a world in soft focus, where she could feel the glide of hot, smooth flesh against her fingers. Something was stroking her, too, something that eased the emptiness and made her move. She rode the twin sensations, reaching for the delight that hovered so near.

Joe was touching her.

She nearly woke when she realized that. But her need had grown and become too intense to escape. She shattered under his touch. Heard him groan. Felt him pulse against her palm, spilling over her fingers.

Oh, Joe, it's so beautiful.

She dissolved into the pleasure.

When Laney came out of the darkness, she discovered she was on the floor of the cabin, near something very hot. She moved instinctively toward the source of the heat, and felt the floor beneath her rumble something low and absolutely obscene.

Floors don't talk or swear. I must still be dreaming.

She lifted her head, yawned, and tried to plump her pillow. Her pillow didn't budge, but it did let out a sound that could have been a groan.

Laney went still as she remembered the terrifying crack and subsequent surge of snow that had swept her from Joe's arms and into the white darkness. Was she hallucinating? Was she . . . She opened her eyes, too afraid not to know what was happening to her.

Four things became immediately apparent to her. She was naked. She was lying on top of Joe. Joe was naked. She wasn't going to think about the fourth thing, which was firmly nestled between her thighs.

She met a distinctly disgruntled gaze. "Hi."

"Hi, yourself."

"I guess we made it."

"Yeah, we did." Joe's expression turned guilty, then he rolled her off to one side and released a tense, heavy sigh.

"I . . . see." Reaction set in with the loss of his warmth, and Laney began to tremble. "We got caught in that avalanche. There was so much ice and snow, and I thought—I thought we were going to die." Tears spilled over her lashes as she remembered everything.

Joe swore, and flung an arm up over his eyes. "Don't cry now."

Laney tried to stop, but it was impossible. That horrible, suffocating sensation, the ice filling her nose and mouth as she struggled to free herself. No wonder she'd dreamed she'd been in a coffin.

"I'm sorry. It's just . . . I couldn't get out, couldn't breathe. I thought I was buried alive. What am I saying?" She started sobbing. "God, I *was* buried alive!"

"Shhhh." He pulled her into his side. His rough hands stroked slowly over her hair and back as he soothed her. "You're fine, sweetheart. I dug you out in time. We made it. We're okay."

In spite of the generous heat radiating from his body, Laney's teeth chattered. Without thinking she crawled on top of him again, desperate to sink into his warmth.

Then she knew what she needed, what she wanted, what she had to have. There was no question he wanted the same, from the feel of his penis throbbing against her. She moved her hands up his chest, looked down at him, and moved her hips into a better position.

"Make love to me."

The large hands stilled, tensed, then once again tried to set her aside.

"Joe." She pressed her mouth to his throat. His skin tasted faintly salty against her tongue. "Don't you want me?"

"You'd better hear this first."

Laney listened as he told her in bald terms what had happened, then tried to think of what to say.

So the dream wasn't a dream at all. Thank God. Joe looked directly at her, unashamed of what he'd done. That gave her the courage to tell him how she really felt.

"I only wish I'd been awake." Then with a surge of brazen confidence, she brushed her lips over his. "Didn't you like it?"

"Like it?" He rolled over, taking her with him, until he was on top of her. "I loved it."

"Then don't feel guilty." Now Laney took the last, terrifying plunge as she lifted her fingers to his mouth. "All I can think about is how much I want to touch you, make love with you. Would you let me do that?"

He laughed once. "Baby, I might let you breathe. *Might.*"

He kissed her. At the same time, his hands cupped her breasts, his fingers tugging at her nipples. His thighs spread hers apart, and the swollen head of his penis pushed an inch into her sleek, sensitive folds.

He tore his mouth from hers. "Say it again, Red. Say you want me."

Breathless, she complied. "I want you."

"Here?" He moved, and sank a little deeper into her

body. "Is this where you want me? Where you need me?"

He'd barely penetrated her, and she was ready to scream. Beyond words, all she could do was arch her back, and clutch him with frantic hands.

"Red." His mouth settled over hers again, and she grabbed onto his broad, flexing shoulders. "Hold on," he said against her lips. "I'm going to come into you now."

Laney felt him pull her hips up. Small moans of longing became mindless, urgent sounds of need as his thick shaft pushed in. Joe paused for a moment, gathering her up against his chest, then bent and gently used the edge of his teeth over her nipple. At the same time, he thrust the rest of the way into her body.

Laney cried out, not from the moment of sharp, burning pain, but from the way he fit into her, stretching the narrowness, filling every recess. Her nails dug into his shoulders as she trembled with the aftershocks.

Joe didn't have the same reaction. He froze and lifted his head to stare at her. "You're a virgin."

Laney, trying to adjust to a whole new world of sensations, managed a smile. "Was. *Was* a virgin."

He propped himself up on his elbows. "You should have told me. I could have—" The cords in his neck tightened when her small, accommodating movements lodged him even deeper. "Jesus, don't do that."

"This?" Awed by the effect it had on him, Laney pushed down again, and felt the jolt when he touched the edge of her womb. "Why? Doesn't that feel good?"

"It feels incredible." One of Joe's hands curled around her neck, and he brought her up for another extended, intense kiss. "But you're a rookie at this, sweetheart."

Men. "So teach me."

Laney grabbed him when he moved, thinking he meant to withdraw from her body. But Joe only pushed back into her, his movement tentative, as if testing their fit and her depth.

"I've never been with a virgin," he said, one of his hands repossessing her breast. His thumb swept over the hard, sensitive nipple, back and forth, mimicking the gentle movements he was making below. "You're so small, so tight. Tighter than your hand, even when you were squeezing me."

"I can tell you all about tight and being squeezed," she said.

That made him thrust deep inside her, then he went still. "Am I hurting you, baby? Tell me."

"No." Lost in a surge of new torment, Laney reached down to grab his waist, and lifted her hips. "Don't stop, I want more, I need more—"

"Christ, Red." His big body stilled, and every muscle seemed to turn to stone. Again, he cautiously withdrew from her. "You don't know what you're asking for."

"I do. You won't hurt me. Please." Laney wound her arms around him. She still felt a little sore, but the building ache of need was worse. "Oh, God, please, Joe, I can't stand it, I need you!"

"Laney." He buried himself in her, and began moving with hard, heavy strokes.

Distantly she heard her own sob of relief as Joe's powerful body worked over her. Sweat trickled between them, adding to the sounds of their bodies colliding. The forceful drive of his flesh into hers hurtled Laney past thought and reason, and she strained up, frantic now to leave the pain behind and take the pleasure.

"That's it, baby," Joe said, panting the words, his hands pinning her wrists to the bed. He changed the angle of his thrusts, riding her higher, rubbing the hard knot of her clitoris without stopping. "Come on, give me it. Give me all of it."

The world shattered around Laney as she screamed, body taut, vaginal muscles gripping his penis and holding it deep within. Her climax was so strong that she nearly fell back into the darkness.

Joe wouldn't let her.

"Look at me. Look!" His gunmetal eyes narrowed as he forced himself into her one last time. "This time you're mine, all the way, *you're mine.*"

Dark delight and agony blended in his expression as he stiffened. His jaw clenched, and he released a deep, primal sound. His semen jetted into her body. Joe shuddered, then his head sagged against her shoulder.

"Oh, Joe." Tears streaked her face as Laney pulled him down to her.

The morning after the dangerous encounter with Pagent, Jill found herself searching for excuses not to go back to the mine. She'd just decided to call in sick when the phone rang.

"Hello," Jill said, trying her best to sound raspy.

"Miss Jill? This is Tom Clark's wife, Iris. I was hoping you could—— you could—" The woman on the other end of the line burst into tears.

"Mrs. Clark?" Thinking there had been a cave-in, Jill paled. "Please, try to stop crying and tell me what's wrong."

The older woman's sobs subsided, and she told Jill what had happened when Tom and the other men had reported for work that morning.

"Tom would throw a fit if he knew I was calling, but please, Miss Jill, is there anything you can do to help us out?"

"I'll try, Iris."

After she hung up the phone, Jill forgot about ducking Matt Pagent. After what the miner's wife had told her, nothing short of a National Guard Division could have kept her away from Charles Richmond.

She drove directly from the house to the site. In the parking lot, a couple of Richmond's flunkies gave her the usual leers and whistles. She wished briefly she had her father's service revolver handy, then stalked into the business trailer.

Once inside, she threw her scarf, jacket, and gloves on the first available surface. Which was the desk Matt Pagent was sitting behind.

"Good morning, Jillian." He picked up the articles as if nothing was wrong, and hung them on the coatrack by the desk. "I didn't expect you to come in today."

"Neither did I," she said, wishing she was a man for once, just so she could punch him out. "Things change."

She started down the corridor toward Richmond's office. Pagent followed, and when he saw what she intended, stepped deliberately in her way.

"I thought you were going to take my advice."

"You thought wrong." Jill went around him, and without bothering to knock or announce herself, strode into Richmond's office. "Mr. Richmond. I need to speak with you."

"Good morning, Ms. Hunter. Matt, get the door, will you?" On the phone, Charles gave Jill a benign smile, pointed to the seat in front of his desk, then went back to his call.

The door closed, but she knew Pagent had stepped

inside. It didn't matter. Jill reached over the desk, and pulled the phone from Richmond's hands. "He'll have to call you back," she said to the unknown caller, then hung up the phone. "Mr. Richmond, I said I need to speak to you *now*."

"Well, Ms. Hunter." More astonished than angry, Charles sat back in his chair. "This must be important."

"I got a very interesting phone call this morning. One of the men's wives informed me that as of six a.m. this morning, Hunter Hardrock laid off the last twenty-seven men on the payroll."

"It was closer to seven a.m., I think, but yes. That's correct."

"You laid off all of them." Jill wanted to be sure. "All twenty-seven."

"That's accurate. I can have the figure verified, if you like."

"We still *need* every one of those twenty-seven miners." She let her gaze drift over his immaculate suit. "Unless you plan to pull the equipment out of the shafts by yourself."

"I have other employees transferring in from one of my divisions to handle the equipment teardown, Ms. Hunter. It had to be done. Now, if you'll excuse me—"

"*Had* to be done?" Jill's control snapped. "How the hell could you do this? It's nearly Christmas, those men and their families were *counting* on those final paychecks!"

The intelligent brows arched. "I assure you, they were all given severance pay."

"Which was what? A half-week straight time? You're a real humanitarian son of a bitch, aren't you?"

Charles sighed. "Matt. If you don't mind."

Hard hands clamped around Jill's waist. "Let's go, Jillian."

She tried to turn around and hit him, but Pagent was strong and fast. He hauled her out of the office before she could blink. However, Jill was strong, too. Before Pagent could do more than kick Richmond's door shut, she twisted free. A hiss of frustration left her when Pagent caught her hand before it connected with his face.

"Temper, temper."

"Did you know about this last night?" He nodded. "Yet you didn't say a word. What a good company man you are, you slime. Let go of me." She couldn't bear his touch or her automatic reaction to it. Not knowing he'd been a party to this.

"I will, as soon as you settle down and go back to playing Sweet Suzy Secretary."

Despite the debts she owed on her father's behalf, nothing could convince her to work another millisecond for Charles Richmond. She'd rather take her chances in the unemployment lines. "I quit."

"Good." Pagent looked immensely pleased, and released her hand.

"You're glad." Why did that hurt so much? "You don't care that I'm quitting at all."

"Of course not." He sounded amused. "You're a nice kid, Jillian, but you're out of your league here."

He thought of her as a kid. A *nice* kid. That cut to the bone. "Right. I'll type up my resignation immediately."

"Don't bother. Just go." He let his gaze drift down to her shoes, then up to her nose. "Unless you'd like to be *my* secretary?"

Jill did slap him then, and the sound cracked loudly between them. A dull red mark spread over one lean cheek, but he simply stood there, watching her with a serene gaze.

"I'm clearing out my desk first."

"Whatever you want." He turned his back to her and went for Richmond's door. "Just make it fast."

The hell she would, Jill thought as she stalked off to her tiny office. This was the last chance she had to stop Richmond and save the mine. If she could just prove there were ore-producing veins waiting to be worked. . . .

Jill cleared her personal belongings from the small desk and piled them into a cardboard box. She had few regrets. She'd never liked playing secretary and was happy to be done with it. Absently she looked over the employee termination sheets, and noticed two names had been crossed off, one near the top, the other at the bottom. Butler. Upton.

"Oggie and Webb?" She checked the latest payroll, and saw Richmond had approved severance checks for everyone but those two men. "This has to be a mistake, that miserly cretin wouldn't keep them on."

The two older men would need those last checks, too. And Jill would make sure they got them.

Setting aside the box, she pulled an employee file, picked up her phone, and dialed Oggie's home number.

"Mrs. Butler? Hi, it's Jill Hunter from Dream Mountain." She listened for a moment. "Yes, I was sorry to hear about the layoffs, too. Is Mr. Butler there? No? But wasn't he . . ." Her frown deepened as she listened. "I see. Sorry for the mix-up. Thank you. I will. Take care." Jill slowly replaced the receiver and stared at it for a long time. Then she went to her closet, and swiftly removed the gear she would need to go down into the mine.

*   *   *

Oggie and Webb had managed to drag out the final four stoper drills, and were now faced with disassembling the last of the big drifter units. The hard work was made even more difficult when the mine lights began flickering steadily.

"Can't take up the conveyor assembly if we can't see the frigging thing!" Webb said when they took their meal break in the main shaft.

"You got your hat." Oggie hadn't felt good about the job since they'd started on it. "Use it."

"Goddamn cheap bastard, like to see him try to work under these conditions—" Webb stopped and stared as the lift began to descend. "Someone's heading down. How much you want to bet it's that big-mouthed jackass Kerass?"

"Don't want to take your money." Oggie dusted his hands off and closed his lunch tin. He watched the skip descend, then raked a hand over his gray hair when he saw who occupied it. "Well, I'll be. It's not Kerass, it's Miss Jill."

Jillian Hunter had often come down into the mine when Big Ben was alive, and all the men liked her. She had some odd ideas, but then, her daddy had sent her to college to get them. She'd also been the best mine engineer Oggie had ever worked for.

"Miss Jill." He reached out to catch the latch on the cage when the skip stopped. "What are you doing down here?"

"Checking on you guys, Mr. Butler." The fair-haired girl was dressed to work, and hoisted a tool pack from the floor of the skip. "What does that idiot hayshaker have you two doing down here?"

"Clearing stope nine, Miss Jill." Webb put the lunch

he hadn't felt like eating aside and tipped his hat to her. "Good to see you down here again."

"It's the last time, I'm afraid." Her pretty eyes got a little brighter. "I just quit." She cleared her throat, then eyed the entrance to the tunnel. "Mind if I take a look before I go?"

"No, ma'am, not at all."

The two older men flanked her as they walked into the deep passage. Jill made a disgusted sound when she saw the string lights blinking on and off, then produced a powerful flashlight.

"I don't understand why he has you working down here. We've got twice this amount of equipment on the upper stopes, just waiting to be moved out." She directed the light beam toward the rock face and began a foot-by-foot inspection. "Unless there's something else . . ."

She spent several minutes studying the gouged wall, then rolled her eyes and looked up at the tunnel ceiling. Something caught her eye, and she frowned. Slowly she brought the flashlight up to illuminate the rock above them. "What is . . . I don't believe it."

Oggie peered up, and saw the edge of the neat bundle tucked into a man-made crevice. Webb did the same, and choked back a startled cry. "Son of a bitch. Son of a *bitch*."

"I want both of you out of here now." Jill's voice never wavered as she lifted a hand and carefully touched the protruding end. She started muttering under her breath. "Wedged in really tight, I can't move it. Three. No, four. Enough to take out the whole section." She turned on the men and flung her hand toward the main shaft. "Didn't you hear me? There could be more of them. Get the hell out of here!"

"No, Miss Jill. We're not leaving you." Oggie turned

to his whey-faced partner. "Webb, get a tram cart in here. I'll get the handpicks."

"Mr. Butler, I'm the mine manager—"

"Miss Jill, with all due respect, you just quit." The old man's stern face softened. "Let us help you."

The trio had to work carefully to remove the bundle of dynamite that had been planted in the ceiling of the shaft. Once it was out of the rock, Jill examined it.

"They were going to use a remote." After disabling the trigger mechanism, she gingerly placed the explosives in the tram. "Why would Richmond want to deliberately cave in this tunnel?"

"Lazy," Webb said as he carefully pushed the tram back out toward the skip. "Didn't want to backfill it the right way." He came back, shaking his head. "Must be crazy, sending us down here to work with that mother overhead."

Jill swallowed a surge of bile. "No, Mr. Upton. I think he meant to detonate the explosives while you and Mr. Butler were working in the tunnel."

"Has to be that pair they took down to ten." Oggie pulled out a bandanna and wiped the sweat from his face. "They brought some Chinese fellahs down there last week. Caught me and Webb watching them. Maybe we weren't supposed to see them."

"We weren't working ten." Jill recalled how upset her father had been, just after the original excavation. "Dad said there was nothing down there but unstable shale. Thought it might be the original tailings pit from the Grey Lady operation, back a hundred years ago."

"Something is down there," Oggie said. "Tremayne got himself killed just after he had a look. We ought to do the same."

"Get ourselves killed," Webb said with a grumble. "That's what we'll do."

Jill silently agreed, but went with the men down the shaft to the next level. The sight of the new equipment piled around the entrance to the lower tunnel made her lips thin.

"He's hit something." She strode into the tunnel, leading the two miners down until her light hit a stretch of glittering rock. She pulled a sample punch from her pack and had the miners help her drill it into the rock face.

The resulting foot-long specimen gleamed with a peculiar silvery light.

"I'll be damned." The unmistakable feel and texture nearly made Jill drop the tube. She aimed her flashlight up, and revealed an ancient pair of timbers.

"Ain't silver," Webb said in a nervous tone. "Ain't nickel, either. Tremayne had a chunk of it in his locker."

"Smelter matte. That's why Richmond killed him." Jill inspected the length and height of the vein, and took other surface samples. "He should have listened to him instead."

"Smelter matte all the way down here?"

"Very old smelter matte, Mr. Butler. Back in the nineteenth century, no one was interested in the by-products of smelting. They probably thought it was nickel sulfide, or iron."

"Why'd they shovel it back down here?"

"They used a chute." Jill pointed to the timbers. "The old mines sometimes resorted to a crude form of the flotation method. They kept the heavy nickel and silver, and funneled the waste back down into the ground. This stope intersects the bottom of Grey Lady's funnel shaft. This collected here since the old operation began. A good twenty years."

"But what is it?"

"Nearly pure rhodium. Probably two or three tons of it." She carefully packed up the tube and her sample containers. "Equal to the entire world's annual production."

"He'd kill us for that," Oggie said.

"Why?" Webb wanted to know.

"Rhodium is worth double its weight in gold. There's been an increased demand for it ever since the invention of the catalytic converter, but I'll guess the Chinese want it for their new space program." She laughed bitterly. "Richmond must have sold them on the idea of a vein. Lord, he thinks he's struck it rich."

Oggie eyed the wall. "There isn't a vein?"

"No. Rhodium is a by-product. What we have here are two decades' worth of nineteenth-century ignorance. They smelted the nickel and threw away the rhodium." Jill measured the mock vein with a practiced eye. "He hasn't even bothered to sink sample cores. The Chinese just bought themselves a red herring."

"Whatever he's sold, we got to stop him, Miss Jill. This ain't right."

"I don't know what I can do, other than go to the authorities. And all that will do is prove Richmond is defrauding the Chinese." Jill sighed and propped herself against the far wall. "It won't keep the mine open, or get the men their jobs back."

Oggie's face took on a savage pleasure. "It will if we can prove he killed your daddy, Miss Jill."

CHAPTER EIGHT

"You're leaving."

"I'm staying."

"I'm not arguing with you about this."

"Fine. Don't argue. I'm still staying."

Joe pulled on a pair of trousers he'd found in the closet and turned around. And promptly forgot about persuading her to see things his way.

Laney sat in the middle of the bed, the edge of the sheet tucked around her breasts. With the sunlight streaming over her bright hair and porcelain skin, she looked like a very small, thoroughly ravished angel.

He cursed himself and zipped up his trousers. "You're going."

"No, I'm not." She slid to the edge and onto her feet, wrapping herself up with the sheet. The dusky circles of her nipples showed plainly through the material. "Besides, how can I? It's not like I can walk back to Denver."

He wanted to cup those small, hard breasts in his hands and fondle them. For a month. Joe dragged his gaze away from her. He had to find a shirt. Not play with her nipples. "I'll find a way to get you out of here."

"In case you haven't noticed, we have no phone. No

electricity. No vehicle. And you aren't leaving me here by myself." Laney went to her suitcase and pulled out a pair of jeans and a long-sleeved flannel shirt. "Where you go, I go. Just think of me as your shadow. That's how close I'll be."

He left the room, unable to stand watching her dress without putting his mouth on her.

In the kitchen, as he awkwardly put together a meal for them, Joe thought about what had happened the night before. Laney had been a more than willing lover—passionate, insatiably curious, and altogether willing to do whatever would please him.

He'd done a lot to her, too, considering the fact she'd never been with a man before. Somehow knowing he was the first had driven him crazy. He hadn't been able to stop touching her, kissing her, teaching her. She'd picked up everything—and pretty damn fast, at that.

Remembering exactly what she'd learned made him swear. All he had to do was think about having her, and he got hard again. That was no good. He had no business treating her as though they'd been lovers for years instead of hours.

It felt like it, taking her last night. Felt as though we'd never been apart, even when we first came together.

That was when he knew what he had to do, and went to retrieve what he needed from his pack. He'd just finished and returned to the kitchen when she emerged from the bedroom.

"How about I make the coffee? And what's that smell?" Laney came up behind him and looked around him at the pan on the top of the stove. "Oh."

"Coffee's ready." He handed her a mug.

"Were those, um . . . pancakes?"

"Were?" He gazed down at the now dark brown,

rapidly solidifying contents of the frying pan, and cursed. "Eggs. They're eggs."

"You know, I'm not really *that* hungry." Laney gently took the handle of the pan from him and carried it into the utility room. When she came back, the pan was gone, and she had a big box of cereal in her hands. "How do cornflakes sound?"

"About as good as those eggs looked."

"Scratch the cornflakes." She went to the cold pantry and started rooting around.

Joe gave up, sat down at the table, and watched her emerge to start preparing their meal. "You really are a cook, aren't you?"

"Uh-huh." Deftly she sliced up some potatoes and onions and tossed them into a clean pan. "I have my own diner. D'Arlen's Place, in the heart of Denver."

He'd heard of it. She was that good. "D'Arlen's, huh?"

"No wisecracks about my name. I got enough of that at school."

"How did you end up owning a restaurant?"

"Frustration." While the potato mixture fried, she made several slices of toast and something with cheese and herbs in a smaller pot. "I started out in a chain franchise as a short-order cook, and hated it. Frozen ingredients, sauces from mixes, prepackaged entrées." She gave a small shudder. "One weekend my boss called in sick, so I decided to stop by the farmer's market and make a few changes to the menu. The customers loved it. We were packed, both mornings."

"And you got a raise."

"No. I got fired." She laughed as she stirred the contents of the pot. "They don't call them franchises because they want originality with their food prep. That's when I decided to open my own place."

She went on to tell him all about her diner. Joe listened as he ate what she'd made—something she called Irish Rarebit—as she described how quickly she'd made a success of her business.

"I didn't have an empty chair in the place, until a new homeless shelter opened up down the block. They never had enough on hand to serve meals to everyone who showed up. Some ended up at my place, begging for scraps." She sipped her coffee and made a face. "I couldn't turn those poor people away, and my paying customers resented them hanging around the diner. Then I came up with a solution that made everyone happy."

"You donated food to the shelter."

"No, I got all the local grocery store and restaurant owners together and formed a food bank. Then I spent a couple of nights over at the shelter, teaching the volunteers and the homeless how to cook." She carefully set down her coffee mug. "They're good people, Joe. They find jobs and housing for the homeless. Arrange medical and psychiatric treatment, too."

"I don't need to go to a homeless shelter, Red. Or a shrink."

"It's a great place, Joe. There are plenty of guys there who served during the Vietnam and Gulf wars, came home mixed-up, and would still be out on the street. But they're trying to make a new life, a better life for themselves. With the right kind of"—she yawned—"excuse me, treatment, they're able to deal better with all those horrible things they went through. The shelter gives them a real chance for a fresh start."

That endless babbling on she'd done about wars and veterans and the homeless and mentally ill—it finally made sense. She thought he was some kind of crazy veteran.

He scrubbed a hand over his beard. "Red, I hate to disappoint you, but I've never been in the military."

She frowned, puzzled. "Oh. You were a mercenary?"

"No. I'm a geologist."

"Okay." She got up and began clearing the table. "All I'm asking is you think about it, okay? You can stay with me when we get back to Denver, so don't worry about that. I can always use plenty of help at the diner. Robert, my night manager, is really a nice guy, I bet you two will hit it off right away. What do you think?"

She thought he was crazy, homeless, and in need of a job. And planned to take care of all that. For a moment Joe simply sat processing this, until she turned around and gave him an uncertain look.

"Don't be mad. I know it's hard to accept help from someone else, but you don't want to live in a cave for the rest of your life, do you? The bears might come back."

He held out his hand. "Come here." When she did, he sat her on his lap. "If I was an unemployed, homeless, schizophrenic ex-mercenary, you really would take me in, wouldn't you?"

"Of course I would." Her fingers brushed his cheek. "And you're not schizophrenic, Joe." She paused. "Are you?"

"No." Unexpected jealousy rose inside him. "You do this a lot? Help out other guys who are down on their luck?"

"No, of course not. I mean, I do help run the food bank, and I taught cooking classes for five years, but I leave the rest of that stuff to the shelter people. You're different. I lo—" She quickly looked away. "I *care* about what happens to you."

She was in love with him, and afraid to tell him.

Laney misinterpreted his reaction. "Joe? Don't be angry. Everyone goes through bad times. Let me do this for you."

Innocent and generous and completely unaware of what she'd just told him about herself. Joe felt his heart ache as he fingered the untidy red curls around her face. He didn't know what he'd ever done to deserve her, but letting her go was going to be the hardest thing he'd ever do.

"Honey, I'm not who you think I am. My name is Gareth Tremayne. I'm a freelance geologist, specializing in hardrock mining exploration. Richmond Corporation hired me eight months ago when they acquired Hunter Hardrock Mining, and assigned me to the Dream Mountain operation."

"You are?" Her eyes blinked sleepily, while doubt flitted across her expressive features. "But if you're a mining geologist, why are you living in a cave?"

"I found out Charles Richmond had defrauded the former owner, and possibly murdered him. I also found evidence that Richmond plans to illegally export rhodium ore as low-grade nickel to a Chinese corporation called Shandian. When Richmond found out what I knew, he tried to have me killed. Twice. The last time, I let him think he succeeded, escaped to the ridge, and I've been here ever since."

"Why did you stay up here? Why didn't you go to the police?"

"Because I didn't have enough evidence to prove what Richmond was doing." Joe paused, taking her hands in his. "And because I killed someone."

Her drowsy eyes went wide. "You killed who?"

"Her name was Susan Brona. She was Richmond's secretary. And my lover." He set her down on her feet and got up to pace the length of the kitchen. "I told her about what was happening on Dream Mountain, and she encouraged me to collect the evidence. Said she'd help me prove what Charles was doing. I came home one night, and she was waiting for me." He looked blindly out the window. "With a gun."

Laney made a hurt sound. "God, Joe."

"I thought she loved me, tried to talk her out of it." He propped his fists on the windowsill. "She laughed. Said she'd show Richmond she could do more than screw men he wanted information on. I got hold of the gun, but she struggled. It went off between us. She died a few minutes later."

He glanced at her. All the color had drained from her face. And he hadn't told her the rest of it yet.

"There's another thing. Before she died, Susan said Richmond had planned to use a contract killer named Delaney to take care of me."

"*Delaney?*" She backed up and bumped into the table. "No, that's not possible." She shook her head, then came to him, her hands curled in fists at her sides. "You thought I was the one she was talking about. The one who was going to murder you. That's why you've been saying all this stuff about me working for Richmond and asking me how I kill people, right? You really meant it. You thought I could do that?"

"Yeah. That's what I thought."

She hit him on the arm, then yelped and shook her bruised knuckles. "All this time, you assumed I was some kind of hit woman? Trying to murder you? And you didn't tell me?"

"Settle down, Red." He caught her other fist before it landed. "It was an understandable mistake. You just happen to have the same first name as Richmond's hired gun."

For a split second her expression grew bleak, then she shook her head again.

"That's not all I have." She jerked away from him and stalked to the doorway. "Maybe he's offering good money for you, *Gareth*. Maybe I'll see if he has a job opening. I mean, how hard can it be? I could kill you with my bare hands right now. A gun would make it much easier. Point, shoot, problem taken care of."

This was taking longer than he'd planned. A glance at her coffee cup revealed she'd only drank a quarter of the bitter brew. Joe followed her into the living room, where she flopped into a chair and stared into the fire.

He knelt beside her. "We both messed up, Red."

"*You* messed up." Her small nose lifted. "*I* was being sympathetic and helpful. *I* was the one who nearly gave myself a hernia dragging you in here and stayed up for three days taking care of you. *I* was the one who had to put up with being held at gunpoint, dragged barefoot through the snow, oh, I almost forgot, chased off a pair of starving cougars just to save your life. A total waste of time, if you ask me."

She needed an extra push, and he knew just how to do it. Without another word he lifted her out of the chair and up into his arms. She flung her arms around his neck as her scowl turned into an "oh" of surprise. Especially when he carried her back into the bedroom.

"What are you doing?" she asked on the way.

"You need to rest."

"I'm not tired."

He pushed the door open with his shoulder. "You will be."

"Oh really? That's it. I'm done being sympathetic

and helpful," she said. "Never again. I'm going to be cynical and selfish. From now on. Leona Helmsley is going to look like Mother Theresa, compared to me." She yelped as he dropped her on the unmade bed. Once she struggled into a sitting position, she swiped impatiently at the hair in her face. "Did I mention how much I dislike being manhandled?"

As he had no plans of doing anything but manhandling her, Joe began unbuttoning his shirt.

She watched his fingers for a moment, then folded her arms and tried to look tough. "Whoa. Hold on. Uh-uh. Sorry. You're not going to sidetrack me by getting naked."

Oh, yes, he was. Joe tossed his shirt to the floor, toed his shoes off, then unbuttoned the top of his trousers.

"Joe. Wait. Stop taking your clothes off." Laney ran the tip of her tongue over her lips. "I'm serious. Joe, I *mean it*."

With one smooth movement he stripped off his trousers and briefs, kicked them out of the way, then started for the bed.

Her gaze went south, then north. "You can't. I mean, I won't." Her head fell back as he leaned over her, and his hands went to the hem of her blouse. "You're not listening to me. Why aren't you listening to me?"

"I'm busy sidetracking you." He tugged it up and over her face, then left it there, trapping her arms above her head. She gave a small shriek when his open mouth landed on her right breast. He sucked her nipple, tugging on it then stroking it with his tongue. At the same time he dealt with the button and zip at her waist. When he lifted his head, he briefly admired the rosiness left behind by his mouth. Two more tugs sent her jeans and panties sailing over his shoulder.

"I'm really ticked off at you," Laney said, and yelped again as he started on her other breast. "Joe, my arms. Joe!"

The taste of her made him groan. He'd never get enough of it. Never. He used his weight to press her deeper into the mattress, and settled himself between her thighs. As he nudged her, he found her damp and ready for his penetration. He'd never felt anything half as good as the way she flowered open for him.

"Joe, I want to touch you."

There was that. He freed her arms, then brought one of her hands down between them. A feral hiss left him when her cool fingers curled around his shaft. "Tell me now you don't want this, Laney. Tell me you don't want me inside you. If you do, I can stop."

"I can't," she said, and tightened her grip.

The helpless way she arched under him was going to make him a liar. "Then show me what you need, baby. Put me inside you."

It took a moment for her to guide him. She was still endearingly inexpert. She bit her lip, then looked at him for approval. "Like this?"

"Yeah," he said, his voice low and hoarse, his attention locked at the place where their bodies joined. "Just like that."

He kissed her, enjoying the way she opened there for him, too. He cupped her face, slanting it to allow him better access. While he was kissing her, he finished what she had started with a long, powerful thrust of his hips.

Her back bowed and her lips tore from his on a cry.

"Yes, sweetheart. Feel me inside you? God, you're so hot, so wet for me." He'd wanted to go slow with her, but there was no hope of that now. He thrust over and over into her, not stopping when he sent her over the first peak. She bit his shoulder to muffle her cry. "Yeah, that's what I want. Again, baby." He reached down for the top of her sex, and the pulsing spot he wanted. "Give it to me again."

With fingers and shaft, he stroked her to a second orgasm, then a third. As she shuddered beneath him that last time, Joe finally gave in to the screaming demands of his own body, and poured himself into her.

When he lifted his face from her breast, Laney gave him a sleepy smile, then closed her eyes and sighed. A moment later she was fast asleep.

Joe got up and tucked the quilt around her damp body, then rapidly dressed. Between the sedative and exhaustion, she'd undoubtedly sleep for the rest of the day. By then it would be all over.

"With all due respect, Mr. Richmond, you have been deceived."

Matt Pagent, who had been leaning on the closed office door, straightened. "How?"

"Yes, gentlemen." Charles himself didn't allow a hint of the rage he felt to show as he regarded Fai's operatives. Or the disgust at the strong smell of the cologne both of them evidently had bathed in. "Do be so good as to explain this supposed deception."

"We took photos of the couple on Nightmare Ridge and had them verified through Shandian." One of the Chinese men produced a envelope of photographs, which Pagent took from him and examined. Wordlessly he handed them to Charles.

"Open that window, Matt, if you would." Charles also studied the startling images of a dark, bearded man and a much smaller, red-haired woman fighting off two mountain lions in the snow. "Who are they?"

"We don't know who the woman is. The man has been identified as Gareth Tremayne."

Pagent strode around the desk and peered at the photographs again, then met Charles's gaze and nodded. Intent on the subject at hand, neither man noticed the slight scuffling sound outside the half-open window.

So Tremayne *had* survived the avalanche intact. "Irish didn't attend to the matter personally, or Gareth would be dead." Charles studied the grim photos for another moment, then placed them on his desk. "I assume the cougars didn't kill them, either."

"No." Dark, almond-shaped eyes didn't blink. "They escaped without injury."

The door to the office burst open, and a big, angry man strode in. "Charles. We need to talk. Now."

"Sean, do come in." Charles watched Pagent replace the gun he'd pulled from his jacket, then nodded toward an empty chair. "Were you successful?"

"They weren't at the cabin. That's not the problem we have to deal with." Sean ignored the chair and swiveled to address Fai's men. "I got word from Denver. Seems Mr. Fai has made an offer to the state attorney to provide evidence that nails you for Tremayne's death."

Pagent put a hand inside his jacket, and waited.

Both of the Chinese reacted in minute ways to Sean's statement, Charles noticed. He smiled. "These gentlemen were just telling me that Gareth Tremayne is still alive."

Sean folded his arms and gave the Chinese a feral grin. "If that's right, Mr. Fai is going to have a lot of egg fu yung on his face."

"This man lies." One of Fai's men rose to his feet

and regarded Sean with disgust. "Who are you to accuse our employer of duplicity in this matter?"

"Forgive me for not making introductions. Mr. Ho, Mr. Chin, meet Mr. Sean Delaney."

"You can call me Irish," Sean said, and pulled a pistol from his jacket. "You want me to take these gentlemen for another tour of the mine, Charles?"

Richmond was tempted, but decided to play Fai Tung's treachery to his advantage. "No, thank you, Sean. I don't believe that will be necessary." To the Chinese, he said, "I'm sure you both are eager to prove Mr. Fai's innocence."

Both men exchanged a significant look, smiled tentatively, and nodded.

"I'll have one of my men accompany you to Nightmare Ridge." Charles picked up his phone, then paused to add, "Make sure you kill both Tremayne *and* the woman, and we'll consider the matter settled." He spoke into the receiver. "Kerass, come to the office." He listened, then frowned. "I see. No, I need you to take our guests to Nightmare Ridge. I'll have Sean attend to it."

After Kerass escorted the Chinese out, Charles turned to Matt Pagent. "Have you taken care of the problem with Hunter's daughter?"

"Yeah. She quit an hour ago. Packed her things and left."

"Excellent." Charles consulted his watch, then smiled. "It's time to tie up the last of the loose ends. Get ready to detonate the charges on stope nine."

Pagent nodded, and left. Sean stopped pacing as soon as the door closed.

"You've got to shut down the deal with the Chinese, Charles."

"I don't see why." Charles wondered if Diane

would be much longer in town. "Kerass will ensure I get photographs of the Chinese killing Tremayne and the woman."

"Kerass is a fool, they could plant evidence implicating you in front of his nose." Sean thrust his hands into his pockets. "They won't stop until they've got you to take the fall for something. Let me do them, at least then you'd be sure they're dead."

"I'm afraid I need you to deal with a more immediate problem here. Jill Hunter was seen going down in the mine with Webb and Butler."

Sean frowned. "Pagent said she was gone."

"Pagent has apparently developed a soft spot for Ms. Hunter, unfortunately for him. Wait until he enters the main shaft, then detonate the charges. Make sure none of them come out of that hole alive."

Cold now from the icy air seeping in through the window, Charles turned to close it. Faint depressions in the soft slush outside made him scan the deserted site for a moment, then he slammed the panel shut.

Laney rolled over, reaching for Joe, and opened her eyes when she didn't feel him there. Tender spots all over her body ached pleasantly, but the dryness of her mouth made her struggle to her feet.

Why am I so groggy? She looked around the room, confused. *Where's Joe?*

Once she'd dragged herself from the bed and dressed, Laney went to the bathroom. Rinsing out her mouth and splashing her face with cold water helped a little, but she still felt tired. That bothered her, until she realized what must have caused it.

"He didn't." She stared at her reflection, saw the telltale dilation of her own pupils. "Richmond won't have to pay anyone. I'll murder him for free."

Her quick, angry search of the cabin produced no Joe, no gun, and every indication he'd drugged her with her own sleeping pills and left her there to go to the mine.

"Good thing you took the shotgun, you jerk." Laney dumped the coffee he'd drugged down the sink and started a fresh pot. "This time I would have used the cartridges."

The sound of something trudging outside the cabin made her head snap up. *So he's come back to crawl into bed with me and pretend nothing happened, has he?* She eyed the coffeepot. *I should dump that over his head.*

She went to the back door to open it and vent her spleen, saw who was walking past it, and whirled away.

All three men were wearing gloves and openly carrying pistols. They were coming for her and Joe. And when they didn't find Joe—

Without thinking, she grabbed the coffeepot. As the front door opened, she ran into the cold pantry, closed the doors, and held her breath. The image of three different men, all wearing ski masks, came back to her. She began to shake.

Panic attack. No. I can't do this now. My life depends on me staying calm and quiet.

The holdup at her diner had been so unexpected and terrifying that Laney had nearly closed the restaurant for good.

She'd never even heard them as they forced their way in through the back delivery door. One minute she was stacking clean utensils in her storage racks, the next she was struggling to free herself from a brutal arm around her throat.

Get the tape, before she starts screaming.

Another man had slapped a piece of duct tape over

Laney's mouth, while a third ransacked the cash till drawer.

Did I set the alarm? Laney couldn't remember, and tried to see the keypad by the front door, but one of the men blocked her.

Got a couple of hundred in twenties. He'd pocketed the cash and yanked the drawer out. *And lookie here, a wad of fifties.* Coins flew as he tossed the drawer aside and removed the rest of the cash. *She does real good for herself, doesn't she? I liked that class she taught at the shelter.* He chuckled. *Maybe all she's selling ain't just burgers and fries.*

Laney kept trying to free herself, but the man's obscene laugh made her go still. *They're from the shelter. They're not just here for the money.* She'd looked away, but not before they'd seen her reaction.

Yeah, I bet you like putting out some special side services, don't you, bitch? The man went on to describe some of the acts he thought her capable of.

Shut your hole and hand me that tape. The one holding Laney jerked her around, and bound her wrists behind her back. *Where can we stick her?*

The one who'd made the filthy suggestions rubbed his crotch with a handful of fifties. *Right on this.*

We ain't got time for that. Come on, we'll put her in the back.

They'd dragged her back into cold storage.

How about here? One of the men opened the door to the walk-in freezer.

It was midnight, and Laney's morning manager wouldn't be in for another five hours. If they put her in there, she'd die. Laney yelled behind the tape as she shook her head and fought to free herself.

Yeah, that'll work. The man holding her pushed her

into the unit. Laney stumbled against a stack of plastic ice-cream containers and landed on her knees.

Gimme a couple minutes. One of the men came in after her, and hauled her up by her hair. *How about I take that gag off you, slut, and you show me what you can do with my meat?*

Let's go, man, before someone else comes in and finds us.

The would-be rapist got angry. *So what? We can shoot anyone who gets in our way.*

I'm not taking a murder rap just because you got a hard-on.

Yeah, yeah. He let go of her, and she sagged to the floor. *Another time, babe. Let me give you something to remember me by.* The he'd kicked her in the back, hard. Something snapped. Laney had screamed behind the gag, and tears streamed from her eyes as she huddled, writhing in agony.

The third one gave her a nervous glance. *What if they don't find her?*

Then they can thaw her out in the spring. Come on, let's go.

They'd shut the door, and the lights automatically went off. Laney remembered lying there in the dark, the agony of her back making her sob, the cold slowly leeching the warmth from her limbs.

If I set the alarm, the police would have been here by now. I'm going to die.

She tried to get up so she could keep herself warm by moving around, but the pain in her back was so bad she couldn't do it. Eventually she lost consciousness.

Later she found out she *had* set the alarm, but the security company had delayed calling the police while trying to reach her by telephone. A squad car was dispatched, and the officers who responded had found her in time. She spent the next month in the hospital while the doctors repaired the two fractured vertebrae in her spine. Another six on crutches.

She had survived the worst of all possible odds.

Still, for that seemingly endless period, Laney had been convinced she would die, alone in the dark. It made her stop teaching at the shelter. It made her afraid to be in closed-in places. And the fear had never gotten any better. Now here she was, alone in a small, cramped space, waiting for three men to come for her—

Cut it out! Laney heard footsteps getting closer and froze. Her heart pounded wildly as she held her breath.

"Look in the bedroom," she heard one of them whisper in a heavily accented voice. The Chinese Joe had told her about. *Is he alive? Did they kill him? What am I going to do if he's gone?* "I'll check the kitchen."

You're not tied up this time, you can defend yourself. Laney looked down, reached for a square can, then awkwardly tapped a handful of its contents into her free hand. *Let them come. I'm not going to die without a fight.*

Fai Tung mourned the fact his uncle had insisted he remain in Atlanta until the transport of the rhodium from Dream Mountain was completed. He missed his thrice-daily meals at the Golden Dragon, among other, more basic comforts.

"My operative is due to report to me this morning," he'd told Shuzhi. "All former Hunter employees have been dismissed, and the equipment is in place. Richmond is ready to begin production."

Shandian's executive director had regarded his nephew, then gave a slight nod, his version of enthusiastic praise. "Fortuitous times are upon us, my brother's son."

Now waiting in the temporary office his uncle had assigned him, Fai Tung studied the nearly incomprehensible reports from Peking on the orbiter project. The rhodium from Dream Mountain, once shipped back to China and further refined, would provide the material necessary for the high-temperature thermal emitters.

The scientists involved had even found a way to disguise the weaponry as benign, data-gathering apparatus so that the satellite strongly resembled the Hubble Space Telescope. So convincing was the facade that even the Chinese government had been fooled into believing the project was nothing more than a routine scientific endeavor.

The phone on his desk chimed, and Fai put the reports aside to answer it. "A call for you from Denver, Mr. Fai."

As usual, his caller wasted no time with honorifics. "My contact in Washington came into possession of some unexpected intelligence. It seems the CID sent a man in to infiltrate Richmond's operation here in Denver. He must be trying to gather evidence against Shandian."

Fai listened to the details, his round face impassive. When the seriousness of the situation became apparent, he thought immediately of his uncle. "We cannot allow this to interfere with the transportation of the ore. I will speak to the director. Wait and do nothing."

He went at once to his uncle, who confirmed the operative's discovery.

"We received the same information from our contacts in Washington. The undercover agent works for the American military, who are very interested in putting a halt to our orbiter project."

Fai, still disturbed by the revelation, spoke without thinking. "It seems an impossible situation."

"You have your operative in place, do you not? Why is it *impossible* for us to gain the upper hand?" Shuzhi handed a folder to his nephew. "Here is the information you will make available to the Denver State Attorney's office. While they take Richmond to Denver and charge him with first-degree murder, we will begin moving the ore out through the east audit, as originally planned."

"The moment I contact the authorities, Richmond will learn of our duplicity. He could request immunity in return for testifying against the tong."

Shuzhi reigned in a sigh. "The man will do nothing. The moment Richmond attempts to betray us, he signs his own death warrant. The attorney we send to represent him will remind him of this if he has forgotten. Make the call, my nephew." His face turned grim. "And assure this time Gareth Tremayne dies and remains dead."

The door to the cold pantry slowly slid open to reveal a Chinese man who looked in, then smiled. "I have found the woman," he called out as he leveled his pistol at her chest.

"Care for a drink?" Laney tossed hot coffee into his face, making the man yell and stagger backward. She shoved him aside and ran for the utility room. A heavy hand grabbed her hair and used it to yank her back.

An American looked down at her. "Silly bitch, where do you think you're going?"

The other man had struck his head against the counter and was now lying unconscious on the floor.

She still had a chance.

"Nowhere with you." Laney threw the handful of cayenne pepper she was holding into his eyes. The American bellowed in agony as he let go of her and clapped his hands over his face.

Laney wasted no time, but ran for the door. An explosion of splintered wood stopped her just as she reached for the knob.

"Stay where you are." A second Chinese man came after her, and pulled her back into the kitchen. "What did you do to him?" He pointed to the American, who was on his knees howling and rubbing furiously at his eyes.

"I just put a little spice in his life." Laney didn't flinch when the assassin's gun pressed into her chest. "Would you like some, too?"

"Ho. Get up." The Chinese man made a sound of disgust. "Where is Tremayne?"

Joe was still alive. "Even if I knew, I wouldn't tell you." The gun jabbed her, but she didn't move. "Go ahead, get it over with."

She couldn't help recoiling when the gun went off. Then to her astonishment, the second Chinese man reeled back. The gun dropped from his hand as a dark stain spread over the upper right panel of his coat. She looked over her shoulder, and saw another man standing in the doorway of the utility room. He was pointing a rifle at them.

"Get their guns," the stranger said in a voice of authority. "Bring them to me."

She got the guns, then looked at the strange man. "Who are you?"

"Matt Pagent. I'm an undercover agent with the Federal Bureau of Investigation."

She brought the weapons to him, and he gave her

an approving nod. "Good work. Stay here." He walked slowly into the kitchen. "Stay down, you sorry bastards. It's all over."

The American she'd nearly blinded looked up through streaming eyes. "You son of a bitch."

"Shut up, Kerass. Chin, sit down on the floor before you pass out." Pagent kept his eyes on the assassins as he addressed Laney. "Ma'am, I need you to call 911, now."

"There's no phone in the house."

Pagent made a short, chopping gesture with his rifle. "Kerass, face-down on the floor. Move it." When Kerass complied, the FBI agent looked quickly back at Laney. "Have you got anything I can use to tie them up?"

"Yeah. I think I do."

Laney got her spare panty hose from the bedroom, and Pagent tied up all three of the men. Once they were immobilized, she helped him temporarily bandage the Chinese assassin's shoulder wound.

"Where's Gareth Tremayne?" Pagent asked as she washed her hands in the sink.

"I don't know. I think he might have gone over to the mine to confront someone named Richmond."

Pagent swore under his breath. "Damn fool. He's going to get himself killed."

"Thanks for the reassurance," Laney said. "Do you have a radio, or some way we can contact the authorities?"

"Not here." Pagent shouldered his rifle. "I've got to get back to the mine to stop Irish from killing Tremayne. I'll need you to baby-sit these three for me until I can call in some help."

"Don't worry about Irish, Pagent," Kerass said.

"He's going to be busy doing your girlfriend." Then he laughed.

Laney's eyes went wide as she saw Pagent grab the bigger man by the throat and haul him up off the floor.

"*What* did you say?"

The American made some strangled sounds.

"Mr. Pagent, if you want him to talk, you'd better stop choking him like that," Laney said.

Pagent's grip eased just enough to let Kerass draw in one breath. "What about Jill Hunter?"

"Richmond . . . sent Irish . . . to blow stope nine . . ." Kerass worked up a nasty grin. "She's down there . . . with the two old geezers . . ."

Kerass might have said more, but the now furious FBI agent knocked him out with one solid punch to the jaw.

"Thank you." Laney was glad Pagent had hit the cretin. That saved her own knuckles. When the FBI agent gave her one of the pistols, she tried to hand it back. "I'm not going to need it."

"If Richmond sends reinforcements, you might." Pagent pressed the gun into her hands, then picked up his rifle. "I'm going back to Dream Mountain now. If one of them moves on you, don't hesitate. Shoot them."

"I'd be happy to," Laney said. "But I'm going with you."

Sean stepped out of the skip and secured the latch that would prevent it from descending back into the shaft. The short warm weather spell had faded away, and the drop in temperature made him pull up his hood and huddle under his down jacket.

All he had to do was tell Richmond the job was done, and then he could get Laney.

Richmond's mistress intercepted his path on the way to the business trailer. When she saw his face under the hood, she smiled.

"Mr. Delaney. What a nice surprise. I thought you were out . . . hunting."

"A little too cold for that, Ms. Beck." Sean had never liked the woman, but managed a polite smile. What was she doing back at the mine? "I'd have thought you'd be staying down in Denver."

"Charles asked me to run a little errand for him." She stroked her glove over the fur coat she wore. "He's been so generous to me, how could I refuse?"

Richmond met them in the reception area. "Hello, darling." He kissed Diane's cheek, then took her coat. "Ready to head back to the city?"

"Desperately ready," she said, and tapped a painted fingernail playfully on his chin.

"Did you take care of my man in Denver?"

"He gave me everything you need." She patted her purse. "I can tell you all about it, if you're finished here?"

Charles glanced at the big Irishman. "That depends on Sean."

"Pagent must have blown the charge," Sean said, shifting his weight from one foot to the other. "I couldn't get the skip down past eight."

"That can't be possible." Charles looked past Sean toward the shaft. "We would have heard it go off."

The Irishman never blinked. "That far underground? I doubt it."

"Darling, perhaps I'd better do this now." Diane opened her purse and handed Charles a large white envelope. "Mr. Donnelly is an excellent investigator. Of course, he came highly recommended."

"I expect Pagent is working for the government."

Charles ripped open the end and removed several documents, which he flipped through. "Or perhaps not."

The Irishman tried to see what Richmond was reading. "You think Pagent is a plant?"

"I did, but I was wrong." Charles folded the documents, handed them to Diane, then swiftly pulled a gun from his breast pocket. "Now that I know you are."

Diane stepped behind Charles, her expression rich with satisfaction. "Mr. Donnelly confirmed the other information you requested. It appears Mr. Fai has transferred over a half million dollars to a Swiss account bearing the name Sean Patrick Delaney."

"It's a setup!" The Irishman exploded. "I'm not working for the government or the blasted Chinese, Charles!"

Richmond lowered the gun until it nearly pointed at the ground, then fired. Sean yelled and stumbled backward, until he collided with a wall and slid to the floor. Blood oozed from a neat hole in his thigh.

"Now, Sean, I want you to tell me exactly what Mr. Fai has planned, and give me the access numbers to that bank account."

"Go to hell."

"Most assuredly I will." Richmond aimed at the uninjured leg. "But not before I make you into a paraplegic."

Before the Irishman could say anything, a muffled explosion went off. The business trailer shook for a moment. Richmond hurried over to the door and yanked it open. Clouds of smoke rose from the main shaft.

Diane joined him. "My God, Charles, what was that?"

"Dynamite." He went back to Sean and grabbed the front of his jacket. "You set the charges to blow on nine?"

Sean produced a painful smirk. "Try . . . lower . . ."

He lost consciousness.

Charles swore, then drove his foot viciously into Sean's side.

Diane clutched at his arm. "Charles. *Charles*. What did he do? What is it?"

"The bastard blew stope ten. Where the god-damned rhodium is." Richmond landed one last kick, then pushed his mistress away. "I have to go down there and see how much damage there is. Watch him."

Charles didn't listen to Diane's protests as he grabbed a miner's hat and hurried out of the trailer. Sean could have been lying, trying to add another layer to the deception. The only way to be sure was to go down and check the stopes himself.

He released the latch on the skip carriage and started down. On the way, he covered his mouth with a handkerchief as smoke and granite dust drifted into his face. It got thicker the lower he went, so he tied the handkerchief on and peered over the edge. The shaft walls had sustained a multitude of stress cracks. They'd have to be shored up before the first ounce of rhodium could be removed.

More delays. Fai would pay extra for it.

The sound and splash of rushing water made Charles halt the skip just above stope seven. Aiming the beam from his hat over the side, he saw what was rising rapidly from the very bottom of the shaft, and swore.

CHAPTER NINE

From her observation post in the equipment shed, Jill saw Richmond climb into one of the skips, and begin lowering himself down into the shaft.

"My God, he's insane."

She didn't hesitate, but grabbed her gear and ran from the shed to the unoccupied skip.

"Richmond! *Charles!* Stop!"

There was no answer. Dense clouds of smoke and dust still clogged the shaft, so Jill put on her goggles and a filter mask. She bent over the side of the carriage, and saw the other skip had halted below her at seven.

"Richmond!" All she could make out was the top of his head. "You have to get out of here. Head for the top!"

Richmond's face appeared. The cloth covering his mouth and nose was black, as was his hair and the rest of his face. "I can't, the motor's not working. Help me!"

Jill increased her drop speed, until at last she'd reached his skip and stopped level with it.

"Okay." She opened the gate to her carriage, then his, and reached out her hand. "Come on, grab on to me."

Richmond made as if to grab on, then jerked Jill forward. He punched her in the face with his fist. She cried out, sank to her knees, then fell over to the floor of her skip.

"Take a nice nap, you interfering bitch."

Richmond reached for the switch on her skip, then swore when it jerked and began to rise on its own. Someone topside had activated the return. He took out his gun and shot at the floor of the skip, but the resulting ricochet sent the bullet careening into the sides of the shaft. By the time the pinging whine had stopped, smoke made it impossible to see.

Let her go. He had to get down to his rhodium, make sure access wasn't blocked. Then he'd take care of Hunter's daughter personally, since none of the idiots working for him could be trusted.

Above the entrance to the shaft, three men stood waiting for the skip to return. Joe swore when he saw Jill crumpled on the floor of the carriage, blood trickling from her mouth.

Oggie and Webb helped him lift the unconscious woman from the skip, then Joe told them to take her back to the office. He pulled on a miner's hat and shouldered a thick coil of rope.

"You can't go down there, Tremayne." Oggie grabbed his arm. "That shaft is going to collapse, any minute."

"Richmond's still down there." Joe would have been happy to let him get himself buried in a cave-in, but Richmond was the only one who knew all the players in this game. The only one who could clear him of Susan's murder. "I'm getting him out."

The old miner didn't argue. "Before you go, listen to me. There's something you need to know about ten."

By the time Joe's skip reached Richmond's, he was knee-deep in icy water. The other skip was empty, and the partially collapsed entrance of stope ten beckoned.

"Crazy fool." Joe tied one end of the rope around his waist, and the other to the cage of the skip. "Richmond!"

He slogged through the rubble and water into the tunnel, and saw the silvery gleam of rhodium glitter beneath his feet. It was everywhere.

"Do you mind, Mr. Tremayne? You're standing on my billions." Richmond spoke from behind him.

Joe slowly turned around, and eyed the gun in his ex-employer's hand. "It's not yours. It belongs to Jill Hunter."

"A shame Ms. Hunter will never know that. She still thinks her beloved father died a pauper." Richmond's thin lips curved into a parody of a smile.

"But he wasn't a pauper, was he, Charles? He found out what you were going to do."

Richmond shrugged. "That's immaterial, isn't it? Hunter's dead, and the mine belongs to me now."

Joe clenched his fists around the wet rope. "So how did you pull it off, Charles? Making it look like he died from a massive coronary, I mean. Did you mess with his heart medication?"

"Now, Gareth, do you really think I'd confess to a crime like that? One I can assure you, I didn't commit."

"No, you wouldn't have the guts to do it personally, would you? Easier to pay someone else to do it for you. You know what's funny? It was all for nothing, Charles." Joe gestured to the floor of the stope. "There's no vein. The rhodium came from the Grey Lady's smelter. They didn't realize when they removed the nickel from the ore rock that they'd be throwing out the rhodium with the sludge. This whole section is nothing but an old tailings pit."

The other man smiled. "I know."

"Then why did you tell the Chinese it was a vein,

unless—" Joe paused, then shook his head. "You fool. Shandian's tong isn't going to fall for you swindling them."

"They'll have to." Charles looked around the stope. "They're greedy fools, easily dazzled by a few chunks of pretty metal and some promises. By the time Shandian realizes their mistake, I'll be enjoying the weather in the Caribbean."

"You're not going anywhere, Charles. I have all the evidence I need to convict you and the Chinese of violating about a dozen federal laws."

"But you don't have anything to prove you didn't kill Susan, do you?" The older man made a tsking sound. "Do you seriously think they'll listen to a homicidal maniac who's been hiding out in the mountains? No, I think they'll be more interested in hearing how you faked your own death to avoid a first-degree murder charge."

"I'll make them listen."

"I think you would, Gareth. Pity you'll never have the chance." Richmond made a motion with the gun. "Move back into the stope, if you would."

"The explosion must have punched a hole through that aquifer I warned you about." Joe glanced at the rising level of the water.

"Then you'd better hurry."

He spotted the end of a pickax sticking up a few feet ahead. Once he got hold of it, he let Richmond draw closer.

"A little farther, Gareth."

"Sure." He turned and threw the heavy tool at Richmond, who staggered to one side to avoid it.

"An excellent attempt to turn this around, Gareth." Richmond raised his pistol. "If you were a different kind of man, I'd hire you to work for me."

"No thanks." The water was even with his hips now. "What are you waiting for? Shoot me."

"I think I'd prefer to watch you drown." Richmond backed up another step, and pulled a piece of chicken wire out of his way.

Joe knew where the panel of wire had come from, Oggie had warned him about it. "Charles. Don't move another inch."

"Spare me the last-minute theatrics, Gareth, please."

"I'm serious. Look behind you, under the water." When Richmond took another step back, Joe lunged toward him. "No!"

"Stay back." Charles fired a round into the wall beside Joe's head. "Stay where you are." He turned around, took another step, and instantly plunged into the water to his chest. He fought to free himself and shouted, "What is this? What's happening?"

Joe waded through the water as fast as he could and reached out. "Grab my hand. Do it!"

But Richmond was going down too fast. He was sucked under another foot, and just before water filled his mouth screamed, "Help me! Help—"

The scream became a gurgle, then his head disappeared under the water. Joe stopped a few feet away, spotting the bottomless shaft's yawning black edge.

The tunnel ceiling sagged in front of Joe, then fell. Several tons of rock spilled into the water, pouring into the entrance of the hidden pit. Joe staggered back, out of the way, and watched as the cave-in successfully sealed off the top of the pit.

Richmond was lost. As was Joe's last chance to prove himself innocent of Susan's murder.

*　　*　　*

Laney opened the door to the business trailer and waved to the astonished miners carrying the unconscious woman. "Come on, bring her inside."

"Who are you?" One of them asked as they brought Jill over to a sofa and carefully lowered her onto it.

"My name is Delaney Arlen." Laney took off her jacket and draped it over the other woman. "I'm a friend of Joe's."

"Joe?"

"I mean Gareth. Gareth Tremayne." She knelt down and saw the grime and blood from the woman's face. "What happened to her?"

One of the miners filled her in while the other went to get a first-aid kit. As she wiped Jill's face and treated the small cut Richmond's fist had made on her mouth, Laney got the rest of the story about what had been happening at the site.

Webb leaned over. "Is she going to be okay?"

"I think so." Laney had already checked for signs of a concussion, but the only damage was the cut and a bruised chin. "Depends on if she wakes up, or stays unconscious."

"I'm . . . just . . . dandy . . ." Jill pressed a hand to her head and groaned. "Lord. What hit me?"

"Richmond," Webb said.

"I should have known." She looked up at Laney. "Hi. Who are you, and whose side are you on?"

"I'm Delaney Arlen. One of the good guys, I promise." Laney scanned all three faces. "Have you seen Joe, I mean, Gareth?"

"He helped us get Miss Jill out of the skip, then went down after Richmond," Oggie told her.

"What?" both women cried.

Jill struggled to sit up. "The shaft's destabilized, and

there's water pouring into the stopes. They'll both be killed."

"No one else is going down that shaft," Webb said. "With all that water down there, the motor units are off line. Both skips are inoperable now."

Laney looked at the telephone on the reception desk. "We have to get the police out here. Fire rescue. Someone."

"Storm's blowing in, we won't be able to raise anyone soon." Oggie straightened. "I can use a chain hoist to climb down and get them out."

"The water's pouring in too fast. You'd never make it, Og." Jill gingerly touched her bruised cheek. "The only chance they have is to get through ten to the east shaft."

"Where is that?" Laney demanded.

"On the other side of the rise. About three hundred yards east of the camp perimeter."

"Call the cops." Laney flew out of the trailer before any of them could stop her.

"She'll get herself killed down there," Oggie said, and made to follow. Jill grabbed his sleeve.

"No, Og. You've got a wife to think about. You, too, Webb." Jill gestured at the desk. "Do what the girl said, and call the police."

Oggie went over and picked up the phone. After a moment he put the receiver back down. "Miss Jill. The line is dead."

Pagent found the last of Richmond's hirelings and knocked him out with a short, brutal blow to the neck. He dragged him into the storage shed and left him tied up there with the others. Once outside, he pulled a cell phone from his jacket.

It didn't work. "Out of range," he read from the display. Disgusted, he thrust it back in his pocket. The main power shed was only a few feet away, he'd tap into a phone line there.

When Pagent walked into the shed, he saw nothing but open panels and cut wiring, and cursed. He knew his first priority was to check in with his field supervisor, but what he really wanted to do was find Jill Hunter and get her off the mountain.

Patiently he found the telephone input/output panel and began to trace the clipped wires to their leads. As he worked, he wondered why Richmond had cut off the phones.

"Get away from there," a gravelly voice said behind him.

He turned and saw Oggie Butler holding a shovel the same way he would a broadsword. "Mr. Butler. Someone's cut the phone lines. I'm just putting them back on line."

"Sure you are. And I'm Santa Claus." Oggie made a threatening gesture with the shovel. "Back away now, boy, or I'll clobber you."

"Oggie. I'm going to take out my wallet now." Matt reached in to his back pocket and pulled out his ID. He tossed it over so that it landed close to the miner's left foot. "Take a look at that, will you?"

Butler bent down and snatched up the wallet, then flipped it open. "My God." He put down the shovel and slowly came forward to hand Matt his wallet. "Sorry, we thought you were working for Richmond."

"I was." Pagent's smile was grim. "But only to gather evidence to convict him."

Oggie nodded toward the panel. "Can you get that working?"

"I'm going to try. Where's Jill?"

"Back at the business trailer. Webb's watching out for her."

"You'd better go help him. And here." Pagent produced his spare pistol and placed it in the old man's work-scarred hands. "You might need this."

This is no place for a claustrophobic.

Laney looked over the edge of the bottomless black hole. No light except for some tiny little ones strung along the shaft. Tons of rock all around her. If she got lost, she'd never find her way out. Going down there would be facing her worst fear.

For Joe, she would face anything.

In spite of her determination, the moment the skip jerked and started to descend, Laney yelped and grabbed the nearest handhold. She reached up to switch on the light on the helmet she'd taken from the rack outside the shaft, and forced herself to let go of the rail.

He's still alive. I'd know it if he was dead.

The shaft on this side of the mining operation was rough with uneven rock and sagging timbers shoring up the different horizontal tunnels. The strings of lights along the walls flickered wildly, then went out altogether, plunging Laney into complete darkness.

I can do this. She leaned over the side of the skip and cupped a hand to her mouth. "Joe?"

The faint echo of her voice was all the answer she got.

The deeper she got, the louder the sounds of trickling water became. The woman back at the trailer had been right, there was almost no time left. Laney could feel it.

A deep, menacing rumble shook the earth, making the skip shudder. Laney grabbed on to the rails again.

No, don't collapse on me now. "Joe? Can you hear me? It's Laney! I'm here. Are you all right? Answer me, please!"

She stopped and listened. There was something. A faint, low sound that could have been "here." Maybe it was just an echo—

Then she heard it again.

". . . here . . . here . . ."

"Joe! I'm coming down the east shaft! Follow the sound of my voice!"

Water rushed in the sides of the skip carriage, and Laney clumsily switched it to halt. Before her was the entrance to the lowest tunnel, which was starting to crumble in front of her eyes.

"Joe! Hurry!"

Splashing water. A male curse. Then silence.

Small falling rocks hit Laney on the head as she stepped out of the skip and into the rising, icy water. Using the light from her miner's helmet, she hurried into the stope and started turning her head from side to side to direct the light.

"Joe? Joe!"

The water was above her waist now, and she couldn't find him. What if he'd fallen under the water? What if she found him unconscious? She'd never be able to pull him out of here in time.

Then I'll just sit with him and wait for it to be over.

Angry at herself for giving up before she'd even tried, Laney yelled, "Joe? Where are you? Talk to me! Do you think I like splashing around in caves or mine shafts or whatever this is? The things I do for you. Joe! Joe!"

There was a distant sound of splashing, then Joe called her name. Laney hurried in the direction it came from, then stumbled back when a huge boulder crashed into the water just in front of her.

"Jesus. Joe? When we get out of here, you have got to get another job. Why don't you try something safer, like working for the bomb squad?"

"Sounds like Laney." The voice was faint but only too familiar. "Laney?" There was a choking, spluttering sound. "Laney? That you?"

"Who else would be crazy enough to come down here? Of course it's me." The water was turning her legs to lead. "I'm coming, hold on, Joe!"

She kept talking to him as she waded in. She crossed another fifteen feet before she saw him, on the bottom of the tunnel, wedged in between two huge stones. His head was nearly submerged.

"Joe." She raced toward him, tripped on something beneath the water, and fell hard on her hands and knees. The icy dunking made her shriek with frustration as she struggled back up on her feet. Finally she got to him, and pushed against one of the two rocks pinning Joe down. It didn't budge. She tried the other, without success.

"Laney." Joe spit out water and dragged in air. "Can't do it. My leg's trapped." The water had nearly covered his face.

"Not for long." She turned to the other, smaller stone, and pit her weight against it. It moved slightly. "I can do this." But try as she might, she couldn't shift it off Joe's leg.

"Too heavy, honey." He shook his head. "I need you to get out of here now."

"No. I'm not leaving you like this." A piece of floating timber bumped into her, and she pushed it away. Then immediately grabbed at it. "Joe, which one of these is on top of your leg?" He nodded at the smaller stone. "Can you feel a space under the rock?"

He went under then came back up and blinked the

water from his eyes. "Yeah." He eyed the timber. "Let me have one end."

Together they maneuvered one end of the wood between the tunnel floor and the rock.

"Ready? One, two, three . . . now!"

Laney pushed as hard as she could on the other end, using leverage to move the rock up and most the weight off Joe's leg. At the same time, Joe wrenched his body to the side, and dragged himself backward. The timber splintered in half, sending Laney back into the water.

Joe stood and helped her up. "Easy, honey. Find your feet." When she did, he pulled her into his arms. "Are you hurt?"

She shook her head.

"Good." Cold lips pressed a dozen kisses all over her face. Then he shook her and started yelling. "Are you insane? I'm going to strangle whoever let you near this shaft. What were you thinking, coming down here?"

"Gee, I thought I'd try to mine something. See if I could find some diamonds. What's a little claustrophobia, right?" She slapped the front of his soaked jacket. "What do you think I'm doing down here, you numskull?" She looked down at the increasingly rapid flow of water coming from the west end of the stope. "Let's yell at each other later, okay? We've got to get out of here."

He kissed her once, hard. "When we get out of here, I'm going to make sure you don't sit down for a week."

Laney didn't care about that now. Nor did it matter that she was getting wet or loud rumbles reverberated through the shaft. Joe was alive. She'd found him. They were together.

As they waded out of the stope, Laney looked back. "What about Richmond?"

"He's dead." Joe helped her into the skip, then got in and slammed his fist into the switch panel. With a lurch the skip began to rise. "Along with whatever proof I could get to clear my name."

"We'll find a way," Laney told him, then staggered into his arms again when the skip whined to a halt halfway up the shaft. "What's wrong?"

"Motor burned out." Joe tried unsuccessfully to get the skip to move, then eyed the distance to the narrow opening overhead. "We're going to have to go up the cable."

"Great." Laney looked at her palms. "That was the one thing I failed in P.E. every year. Climbing the rope."

Joe turned around. "Get on my back. I'll carry you."

"I'm too heavy. We'll fall." Laney gulped and wiped a trembling hand across her face. "You go on without me. Maybe you can get this thing to work when you're at the top."

"The motor unit is down there, under four feet of water." Joe whipped the coil of wet rope off his shoulder and, before Laney could protest, tied it around their waists. "You're going with me."

Laney was too terrified by the renewed shaking of the earth to protest any further.

"Hold on to my neck." Joe reached up, grasped the cable with both hands, and pulled. Laney held as still as she could and watched in awe as he continued to pull them up out of the skip, hand over hand, by the cable suspending it. "Here we go."

It seemed to take forever, there in the dark, Joe climbing the cable foot by foot. Laney held on to him with numb fingers.

"Is Jill all right?"

"She's got some bruises and a bit of a headache, but otherwise she was fine when I left her." Laney squeezed her arms tighter. "Two of the miners stayed with her."

The rumblings got louder, but sunlight and snow fell on their faces. Another three or four yards, and they would be at the top of the shaft. The rope binding Laney to Joe's body creaked with every movement.

"Joe, if something happens—"

He made a harsh sound in his throat. "Don't, Laney."

"I have to. I love you. I want you to know that."

Below them, there was a tearing sound, then the cable undulated and cracked as the skip tore free and fell to the bottom of the shaft. Joe's hand slipped an inch. They swayed back and forth.

Laney closed her eyes tightly and buried her face against Joe's back. "Oh, my God."

"Almost there, baby. Trust me. We're almost there."

The tremendous physical strain was taking its toll. Joe's arms were trembling, his breath labored. He reached up again, and swore when his hand slid down.

Laney saw why as a shaft of light fell over them. "You're bleeding. Joe, your hands are bleeding!"

"It's steel cable, honey." He wiped the blood from his hand onto the front of his jacket and reached again.

Aghast, Laney fumbled for the knot in the rope. "I can't do this to you."

"Laney." Unable to grab her hands, Joe went still. "Either we get out of here together, or I let go." The sides of the shaft began raining chunks of rock down into the rising water. "Are you with me?"

She let go of the rope and nodded against his back.

Slowly, pausing every foot to wipe the blood from his torn hands, Joe pulled them up the cable. At last he grabbed the bottom of the skip's suspension frame, then with one final huge pull hauled them both up and out of the shaft. They fell into the snow, Laney on top of Joe, and for a moment just lay there, panting.

"You're right," he said when he caught his breath. "I need to get another job."

"At least." She looked over, and saw the damage the cable had done. "Joe, your hands."

He glanced at the deep gashes in his palms, then thrust them in the snow. "It's okay. Couple of stitches and I'll be good as new."

When the flow of blood had stopped, he reached down to untie the rope around them. "How about you?" He ran his injured hands over her. "Are you hurt?"

"I'm okay. Well, no. My heart's never going to be the same," Laney said, and wiped at her eyes. "I really thought we weren't going to make it. And I haven't told you everything. My uncle—"

"I know about your uncle, Laney," Joe said, and touched her cheek with his fingertips. "You told me yourself you had two last names. Arlen for your father, and Delaney for your mother's brother, right?"

She nodded, her head bowed.

"You must have known he was Richmond's hit man when I told you about Susan. Why didn't you tell me then?"

Laney got angry. "My uncle isn't a killer. I'd know if he was. For God's sake, Joe, he's the closest thing I have to a father."

"Let's go to the mill, we can get some dry clothes there." Joe tossed the rope aside and helped her up. "Then we'll find Uncle Sean, and straighten this whole mess out."

*　　*　　*

On their way to the mill, Laney filled him in on what had happened at the cabin after he'd left her.

"So Pagent is a Fed. Figures." Joe smiled. "With the way this operation has played out, I won't be surprised to hear those two old boys are undercover State Department agents."

"Everyone seems to have a secret identity but me," Laney said, holding herself with her arms as her teeth chattered.

"In here." Joe opened the side door to the mill, and led Laney back to the miners' locker room. He bolted the door from the inside, ignored the racks of coveralls worn by the mill workers and guided Laney to the shower room.

"Why did you lock the door?"

"We need a little privacy." Without preamble he turned on one of the showers, the heat from the spray creating billows of steam. Joe began peeling his saturated clothes off. "Strip."

"I'm tired of being wet," Laney said, stepping back from the spray. She was so cold he could see a faint bluish tinge to her lips. "Can't we just dry off with some of those towels over there?"

"Would you for once not argue with me, woman?" Naked, Joe strode over to her and stripped her down. "This will warm you up fast. Trust me."

She let him pull her under the shower, then at once shrieked and leapt out from under it. Snow flew from her curls as she shook her head. "Ow, Joe! It's too hot!"

"You'll get used to it." He held her in place, letting the heated water pour over both of them. A few minutes later she relaxed against him. "There. Better now?"

She let her head fall back so the water soaked her hair. "Mmmmm."

The movement exposed her throat and breasts. Joe

admired the view as he lifted his hands to wash the blood from them.

Laney groaned when she saw them. "Oh, they're awful." She cradled his hands with hers. "Do they hurt? How do they feel?"

A groove appeared in his cheek. "Let me see." He cupped her breasts with his hands. "They feel just fine."

"That's not what I meant and you know it." Laney tugged at his hands. "Now I know why you locked the door."

"You know something?" He bent down, pressing his brow against hers. "Leaving you this morning was the hardest thing I've ever done."

Laney pulled back, her smile fading. "Drugging me, however, didn't present a problem."

"You wouldn't listen to me." Joe lifted his hand to her wet face. "It doesn't matter. Whatever proof exists about Susan's death is buried along with Richmond at the bottom of that shaft."

"There's got to be a way," Laney said, and slid her arms around his waist. "I know you didn't murder that woman. You couldn't have done it. You're not capable of it. I'll tell them about everything, and they'll listen to me."

"Sweetheart, I don't think they're going to take your word for it." He smiled. "I'm just glad we got out of there alive."

"I was so scared." She shuddered. "We could have been killed so easily."

"We made it. That's what counts." He licked beads of water from her lips, and threaded his fingers through her wet curls. With his other hand, he urged her closer, until she pressed full-length against him. "Kiss me, Laney."

Joe groaned as she gave him her mouth without hesitation. A heartbeat later he took her down, dragging her with him onto the wet tile floor. Once he had her pinned under him, her breasts pressed flat against his chest, he moved his legs between hers and lifted his head.

"Let me take you," he told her in a hoarse voice.

"Where do you want to go?" Her hands slid up his back, her nails leaving a tingling trail. She smiled when he moved against her. "Ah, there. Yeah. I'd like to go there."

He stared down at her, conscious only of the beautiful longing in her eyes. There was only one thing left to say.

"I can't protect you, Laney," he said. "Any more than I could at the cabin. You could end up with a baby. My baby."

She gave him a brilliant smile. "I'd like that, too."

His hands trapped her against the tile as he bent over her and began working his way down the front of her body, using his mouth on her. Water poured over them as he licked and bit and nuzzled from her nipples to the indentation of her navel. He gently spread her thighs with his hand, and cupped her, pushing one finger slowly into her. That made her moan and roll her hips. With his other hand he parted and exposed her to his eyes.

"There you are, sweetheart." Gently he stroked her pulsing clitoris, and listened to the sounds she made. "So pretty and pink." Unable to resist, he took his hand away and pressed his mouth against her, using his tongue on the small nub. He added another finger to the one moving in and out of her, and felt the soft liquid heat of her drench him.

Just before she went over the edge, Joe pulled himself up and over her, bringing her thighs up with him.

"I felt it the moment I saw you," he said as he found her mouth, and began to enter her. "Just watching you from the window made me hard. I wanted to smash the glass, climb in, and put my hands on you." His penis throbbed as he sank into her an inch at a time. She shivered and clutched at him. "I almost did."

"I felt it, too," she said, and released a sigh as he seated himself deep inside her body. "In the shower, when I was washing you. I wasn't really shy. I wanted to touch you."

"It was worth waiting for." He traced the shape of her ear with the tip of his tongue. Deliberately he teased himself and her, moving slowly, keeping his strokes shallow. "Wasn't it?"

"Joe." She dug her nails into his shoulders, pushing up against him. "Don't make me wait. Please."

He outlined her bottom lip with the rough edge of his thumb, his voice lowering to a whisper as he pushed into her again. "I want you to remember this. Remember me."

He took her slowly, enjoying the way she twisted under him and pleaded against his mouth, holding her at the brink until at last she cried out and shuddered with her orgasm.

Something broke loose in him then. He kissed her wildly, demanded everything, his palms kneading her breasts, stroking down the sides of her body, circling over her hips. At last he cupped her buttocks and thrust into her, over and over, as deeply as he could. His climax slammed over him, and he held himself in her, knowing now he would never forget.

CHAPTER TEN

"You're not going to prison."

"Laney, there's nothing you can do about it."

"Ha. Just you wait and see. I am a resourceful woman. You have no idea."

Laney finished towel-drying her hair and buttoned up the front of the mill worker's coveralls. It was a little too large, so she rolled up the sleeves and pant legs.

Joe was already dressed, and sat on one of the benches, watching her. "Richmond planted evidence at my apartment implicating me. Like I said, sweetheart, the police won't take your word for it."

"Then we'll leave the country."

"Laney."

"I'm serious." She yanked down the collar into place. "Do you think for one minute I'm going to have this baby by myself? Ho, no, pal. Nine months of carrying all that weight around is bad enough. But handling midnight feedings and colic and teething pains? Absolutely not, not on my own. No, if I'm going to be a mommy, *you're* going to be a daddy. A daddy who changes diapers—even the really stinky ones, I might add—"

"Laney." He gave her a bemused smile. "You don't know that you're pregnant."

"Maybe I'm not. You certainly did your best to get me that way, I think. But if I'm not, well, then, we'll keep trying until I am." She found some boots, walked over to him, and handed him the largest pair. "In Brazil."

"We're not running away together, Laney. What about your restaurant?"

She considered that for a moment. "I'll sell it. That will give us plenty of money to set up one in Rio."

"What about Neal?"

She grabbed a clean white towel, tore a strip from it, and started wrapping one of his hands. "Neal will survive without me. She always has."

"She?"

"I'll tell you all about it on the plane trip. Now, let me take care of this other hand."

After she'd bandaged his palms and neatly tied off the ends, she rummaged through the lockers until she found two jackets for them to wear. "Let's go over to the business trailer. I want to make sure Jill is okay before we head to the airport."

"We're not going to South America, Laney."

"Do you have to argue with me about everything?" She stamped her foot. "My sister is missing, my uncle is an assassin, and the man I love has been framed for murder. America has lost its charms. Let's go."

She headed out for the business trailer, not bothering to hide her relief when Joe followed. "You know I'm right."

"You're something. And, I suspect, exactly like your uncle."

"I don't strand people in the mountains." Laney sniffed, and looked around. "That guy Pagent should be here somewhere. Just don't confess who you are, because—"

"Laney." The FBI agent met them at the door of the business trailer. "I've disabled the hired guns. Someone cut the phone lines, but I've managed to rewire the panel. I'll call in to get reinforcements. Richmond?"

Joe simply shook his head.

"Good," Pagent said. "Saves me from having to shoot the son of a bitch myself."

Laney's eyes went to the man with the injured leg propped in a chair beside Jill Hunter. "Uncle Sean! What happened to you?"

"I got myself shot, darlin'."

Pagent slammed the door to the trailer shut. "Oh, yeah, I forgot about Uncle Sean."

Laney stomped over to where Sean sat and folded her arms. "So, all this time you've been running around with cretins like Charles Richmond and killing people, and telling me and Neal you were an entrepreneur. A professional assassin, what is Father Patrick going to say about that? You'll be saying Hail Marys and Our Fathers until they're ready to give you your Last Rites. And about stranding me at the cabin—which I did not appreciate, one bit—how could you do that? I was scared out of my wits, thinking something had happened to you, not that I wouldn't mind you getting caught in an avalanche now. And that's another thing—"

"Laney, please." A spasm of pain made the Irishman grimace. "I'm happy to see you, too."

She tapped her foot. "Start talking, Uncle Sean."

Joe took the rifle from Pagent. "One less hit man won't break this case, right?"

"Forget about it, Joe." Laney never looked away from her beloved uncle's face. "If anyone shoots him, it's going to be me."

"Or me," Oggie Butler said, producing the gun Pagent had given him.

"Gareth, Mr. Butler, don't." Jill, who was huddled beneath two jackets now, sat up with a groan. "Let the police handle it."

Pagent didn't move. "He killed Susan Brona for Richmond."

"I didn't kill Susan," Sean said in a weary voice.

"No he didn't. I did. It was an accident," Joe said.

"But he was going to kill you, Jillian." Pagent held out his hand. "On second thought, Tremayne, give me back my rifle."

"Be my guest." Joe handed the weapon back to Matt. "Why don't you start with the left leg, work your way up?"

Pagent leveled the business end of the rifle at Sean's groin. "I prefer the direct approach."

"Uh, boyo, don't go making a serious mistake now. You're a bit mixed up." Sean went to remove something from his jacket, then froze when Pagent slipped his finger over the rifle's trigger. "May I take something out to show you?"

"Nice and slow," Pagent said.

"Here." Sean produced a bloodstained wallet, and tossed it at Pagent's feet. "That should satisfy you, FBI man."

Pagent knelt, never taking his eyes from Sean, and picked up the wallet to flip it open. His rifle sagged as he studied the ID inside.

"I'll be a son of a bitch. You're army. CID." He looked up at Sean. "Why wasn't my department notified you were working this case?"

"Seems our bosses could step up communication," Sean said. "I've been working on this from the Chinese angle, following the paper trail from Shandian Corporation. Appears you got started on the same thing, just from the other end."

"Yeah, I did. I was assigned to join Richmond Corp, watch Charles, and gather evidence for the grand jury." Pagent walked over and handed Sean the wallet. "My apologies, Colonel Delaney."

"*Colonel* Delaney?" Laney kicked his chair. "Uncle Sean, what's this all about? You retired from the army ten years ago!"

"Well, actually, darlin', no, I didn't." Sean grimaced as he shifted in his chair. "I just went into a different division."

"Covert operations," Pagent said.

The big Irishman gave him a dirty look. "I'll be thanking you not to give these *civilians* chapter and verse, Special Agent Pagent."

"I sure as hell want the chapter and verse. I want the whole blasted *book*," Laney said. "Uncle Sean, you knew what was going on up here? And you brought me to the cabin, and left me there, and never said a *word*?"

"General Grady's fault, darlin'. He needed to locate Tremayne, draw him out from the ridge, and you were elected. I didn't agree to it, I had no idea," Sean tacked on hastily when Joe made a low, ominous sound. "I've been trying to get you out of here for two weeks now."

"So you told me the story about Bigfoot and left me there, like a walking bull's-eye." Laney kicked his chair again. "Forgive me if I don't shower you with my gratitude."

"I got shot, didn't I?" Sean pointed to his leg. "That's punishment enough, darlin'."

"I disagree."

A blonde woman in a gorgeous dark fur coat

stepped out from around the corner, and trained the gun she held on Pagent.

"Put the rifle down, Matt. Nice and slow. Very good." She looked at Joe and Laney. "You two, over there."

"Diane." Pagent laid his rifle on the floor of the trailer. "Richmond's dead."

"I'd break out the champagne, but there's no time." Richmond's mistress backed up to the reception desk, while never taking her eyes from Pagent. "Mr. Delaney and I are going on a little trip."

"I'm not going anywhere with this bum leg, blondie," Sean said.

"That's kidnapping, Diane. Give me the gun." Pagent took a step toward her. "Don't make it any worse for you than it is now."

"Tung dislikes being subpoenaed." The blonde eyed the distance between her and the telephone. There was no way she could use it and keep her gun on the rest of them. "You"—she pointed to Laney— "come over here and pick up the phone."

"Fai got to you, didn't he?" Joe asked, thrusting his hands in his pockets and shuffling his feet. "How much money did he offer to pay you to sell out Richmond?"

"Oh, I'm already on the tong's payroll, Gareth. I have been for years." Diane allowed a sneer to curl her upper lip. "Mr. Fai isn't much of a lay, but he is very, very generous."

Laney swallowed hard when she realized that Joe was inching toward the blonde.

"Not generous enough to cover twenty to life, Diane." Pagent exchanged a brief glance with Joe, then took another, cautious step toward her. "Which is exactly what you're looking at if you don't put down the gun."

"By the time the police get here, I'll be on a plane halfway to Shanghai." Diane adjusted her grip on the gun. "Much as I will miss Rodeo Drive, I'm sure I'll find plenty of things to amuse me over there, and I'm very fond of Chinese silk." She jerked the pistol in a threatening gesture toward Pagent. "Stay where you are, Matt, or I'll be happy to make a new opening for the Bureau."

"You'll be shot the minute you step on Chinese soil. If you even make it that far." Joe gave her a slow, insulting smile. "The tong doesn't like employees who fail. Especially American female employees."

"I haven't failed." The blonde's face flushed with anger. "I did everything Fai wanted. I even let him and that pig Richmond paw me on a regular basis, just to get the information the tong wanted. He won't forget that."

"Neither will you, which is why you're a dead woman. Now, give me the weapon." Pagent came toward her, drawing her attention to him.

At the same time Joe lunged across the remaining space and knocked the gun from Diane's hand as he tackled her. It fired. Jill screamed. The bullet lodged into a wall, barely missing Pagent's face by inches.

"It's over." Joe pinned the squirming woman beneath him. "It's all over."

Within the hour the FBI and the Denver police had descended on Dream Mountain. Diane Beck was taken into custody, along with two of the three men found tied up in the cabin on Nightmare Ridge. Due to the their gunshot wounds, the injured Asian and Sean Delaney were flown out by helicopter.

Laney walked beside her uncle's gurney to the medevac chopper, holding his hand the entire way.

"Laney." Sean's face was pale and tired. The noise from the whirring helicopter blades overhead was deafening; she had to bend over to hear the rest. "Do you forgive me for letting them use you?"

She placed her mouth next to his ear. "No. I'm going to ride you about this unholy mess every day for the rest of your life, old man. That will be another thirty, forty years. Got it?"

"Got it. Love you, too, darlin'." Her uncle gave her one last, carefree grin, then closed his eyes as the attendants transferred him into the back of the enormous flying ambulance.

Laney stood watching until the helicopter disappeared over the ridge, then returned to the business trailer, which had become the authorities' central command post.

"Can't pump the water out before the top layers start to freeze," one of the FBI agents was saying to Jillian Hunter as they looked over a schematic of the underground mine. "No one is getting down below the second level until the ground thaws."

"Good." Jill folded up the map and saw Laney. "Hey, how are you doing?"

"Okay." Laney rubbed her cold arms with her hands. "I think I'll make some more coffee, if that's okay?"

"Good idea. These guys tend to drink it like water." Jill came around the desk. "So do I."

Back in the lounge area, Jill admired Laney's economical movements as she filled and began heating the two huge drip machines. "You're an old hand at this, I see."

"I must do it a hundred times a day, back at my

place in Denver." She looked through the window at the men gathered around the entrance to the shaft. "Have you seen Joe—I mean, Gareth?"

"He and Pagent are over at the mill with some of the investigators. Apparently Richmond had stowed some new equipment in one of the storerooms, hiding it until he got rid of the rest of us." Jill put out Styrofoam cups, cream, and sugar. "When they're done here, the police want us to go back with them to Denver to give our statements."

"I don't know about you," Laney said with a rueful look, "but I'm ready."

"Yeah." Jill's mouth thinned as she glanced toward the mill. "There's nothing I can do here."

Matt Pagent and Joe stayed behind with the FBI team, while Laney, Jill, and the miners went to the city with the police. No one had much to say on the trip. Jill Hunter sat and stared silently at the scenery. Laney laid her head back against the seat and closed her eyes.

Joe, I love you.

When they arrived in Denver, the rest of the day was devoted to giving their statements. Laney insisted Jill spend the night at her apartment above the diner.

"No use driving back up to the ridge. Like you said, there's nothing you can do up there now. Come on." Laney wasn't eager to face her empty apartment anyway. "I'll make you one of my famous hamburgers."

A squad car dropped them off in front of D'Arlen's Place just as Laney's night manager Robert was preparing to close.

"Good Lord, girl, we just filed a missing-person's report on you!" The formerly homeless ex-Marine gave her an enthusiastic hug. "Where the heck have you been?"

"Long story, Robert. I'll fill you in tomorrow. Mind

if I borrow your keys? Mine are back at Uncle Sean's cabin." She took the key ring and glanced at the phone. "Any word from Neal?"

"No word yet." Robert's broad face went gentle with sympathy. "Sorry, Laney."

"Don't worry, we'll track her down. Thanks for holding the fort while I was gone, Robert." She walked him out, then came back to find Jill admiring the classic fifties-style interior. "Well, what do you think?"

"The decor is amazing, and with such detail. Right down to the doo-wop songs on the jukebox."

"Plenty of my older customers helped me out by telling me stories about their old neighborhood diners." Laney hugged herself and gazed around with pride. "Yeah, I think I did pretty good, if I say so myself."

"You may, as long as you make me one of those hamburgers you've been talking about."

"Sure." Laney chuckled, and waved Jill back to the kitchen. "Come on, you've got to see my grill."

Jill not only saw, but helped prepare their meal. She carefully watched Laney add the secret ingredients to the ground sirloin before she molded it into patties.

"I know the dark green chopped stuff is chives, but was that brown stuff some kind of paprika?"

"Nope." Laney placed the patties on her broiler. "A dash of unsweetened cocoa."

"Chocolate hamburgers?"

Laney grinned at Jill's expression. "Wait 'til you taste it."

A half hour later, Jill sat back in the red vinyl booth and sighed with pleasure.

"Teach me to make these. I'm begging you. Matt will go crazy for them." A shadow passed over her features, and she toyed with a french fry.

"You're worried about him, aren't you?"

"Guess it shows, huh?" Morosely she bit off the end of the fry. "It was one thing, thinking he was one of Richmond's goons. But an FBI agent?" She shrugged. "They're so committed to their work, I'm sure he doesn't have time for anything else."

"Anything else being—oh." Laney looked up and had enough sense to keep her voice neutral. "You're in love with him."

Jill nodded. "Desperately, hopelessly in love with him."

"You should tell him, Jill. How is he going to know if you don't say anything? Men aren't psychics." She smiled at a point past Jill's shoulder. "It would be a much better world if they were, but—look, just tell him."

"When? I'll probably never see him again. Besides, he spent most of his time on Dream Mountain trying to get rid of me."

"That was my job."

Jill jerked around, her jaw sagging as she took in the sight of Matt Pagent standing only a foot away from her. "How long have you been there?"

"Long enough. Come here."

Laney quietly picked up their dishes and took them back into the kitchen. From the muffled sounds in the diner, she might as well stay there and clean up.

She'd finished when the couple appeared in the doorway, arms around each other. Jill's lips were as rosy as her cheeks.

"Laney, you're going to be the first to know," she said, and smiled up at Matt. "We're getting married."

It didn't take a genius to figure that out. Laney congratulated them anyway, giving Jill a hug and Matt a stern warning to take better care of her.

"I will. I talked to my department chief this afternoon, I've been approved for a transfer to the Denver office."

Laney regarded Jill. "Are you going to try to reopen the mine and get to that rhodium deposit?"

"No, it's too dangerous. Now that I can prove Richmond defrauded my father, I can reclaim the money he stole from our accounts, and use it to hire back the men. We'll seal the Dream Mountain shafts, then go looking for a better, more stable site to work farther along the ore bed."

"Tremayne will help," Matt said. "He knows this country better than anyone."

Given that opening, Laney looked eagerly at Pagent. "Is he okay? They're not going to charge him with Susan's murder, are they?"

"No. My investigation and your uncle's statement cleared him of Susan Brona's murder. He's got to appear at a press conference tomorrow at the state attorney's office, then he's a free man."

Sheer elation shot through Laney's veins. "This press conference, is it open to the public?"

"Yes. Ten a.m., if you plan to go."

Laney planned to do a lot of things. "I'll be there. Have you got a place to stay, Matt?"

He nodded. "My hotel is just down the street."

Jill blushed. "I was hoping you wouldn't mind, but I'm going to spend the night with Matt. " She gazed up at her fiancé with visible adoration. "We have a lot to talk about."

Laney privately doubted they'd be doing any talking at all. "Then get going, why don't you?" She grinned. "I'll see you tomorrow at the press conference."

*   *   *

Laney hardly slept that night, expecting the phone to ring at any moment. It didn't. By the time dawn filtered through the windows of her apartment, she'd convinced herself that Joe was never going to call.

No, I'm not giving up that easy. I'll go to the press conference, like I told Matt.

She dressed, brushed her curly hair into reasonable order, and covered the shadows under her eyes with a light application of makeup.

Her morning shift manager was just as surprised and happy to see her as Robert had been. Laney left her diner in capable hands, and headed out in her Jeep to track down the man she loved.

Driving through morning rush-hour traffic set Laney's nerves on edge. By the time she'd reached the capital building, she was ready to pull her hair out. She signed in at the lobby desk and was directed to the state attorney's conference room. Hordes of television, radio, and newspaper reporters crowded the large room, so many that there was standing room only.

A line of men filed into the room from a back entrance, and took their places along the conference table. Laney stood on tiptoe to catch a glimpse of Joe.

"Oh, my God." She spotted him. He'd shaved off his beard, and the stark planes of his face made her blink. With a beard, he'd been handsome, but without it, Gareth Tremayne was simply, undeniably gorgeous.

What if he doesn't want me?

The State Attorney was the first at the podium. "Good morning, ladies and gentlemen. After a two-year investigation, I'm pleased to announce that the state of Denver, along with several other governmental branches, is prepared to hand down a total of one hundred fifty indictments against Shandian Corporation, with charges ranging from racketeering to first-degree murder."

The reporters began shouting questions, which the attorney ignored. Instead he held up one hand. "Because this is an ongoing and active investigation, I can't release much information. What can be made public will be in my press statement, to be handed out immediately after this conference. I would now like to turn the podium over to this gentleman"—he pointed to Joe—"who has an important statement to make."

Joe walked up to the podium, and scanned the crowd. "My name is Gareth Joseph Tremayne. I was declared dead six months ago, lost in an avalanche at the Dream Mountain mine site." The corner of his mouth hitched. "But as you can see, I am very much alive."

The reporters fell silent for a moment. One of them waved a notebook in the air. "Hey. You're the one the police suspect murdered a Denver woman, aren't you?"

"Yes, I was the prime suspect in the death of Susan Brona. I didn't kill her. All charges have been dropped—" Joe focused on someone, then got an odd look on his face. His voice dropped to a near whisper. "Kathy?"

Laney felt her heart shatter when she turned like everyone else and saw the lovely, petite brunette pushing through the crowd. Those pieces splintered into dust when her gaze dropped to the brunette's protruding stomach, clearly outlined under the maternity smock she wore.

"Gareth. Thank God." The woman got through the reporters at the same time Joe came around the table. She flung herself into his arms, and Laney could see tears running down the beautiful face. Joe lifted his head and met her eyes from across the room. He held on to the woman in his arms, then said something to another, fair-haired man standing close by.

"Must be the wife," a reporter near her said, and that was all Laney had to hear.

Before she got halfway to the door, the man Joe had spoken to stepped in her way. Through dull eyes she recognized his very famous face. "Excuse me."

Luke Fleming grinned down at her. "You're Delaney Arlen, right?"

"That's me." She tried to go around him again, but he caught her arm. "I'm sorry, I really have to leave now."

"Gareth wants to talk to you."

She bet he did. Like telling her how he'd forgotten to mention that he had a wife. Still, she could make a show of some dignity. "Tell *Gareth* I hope it's a boy, and to be happy."

Luke's green eyes narrowed. "Wait, Ms. Arlen, you're a little confused—"

"I have to go." She pulled free of his hand, and ran out of the conference room.

Her footsteps echoed as she raced toward the elevators. Alarmed people got out of her way, which was a good thing. The tears in her eyes made it nearly impossible to see clearly.

The elevator was empty, for which she was grateful. Uncontrollable sobs shook her, and she pressed the lobby button before burying her face in her hands. The doors began to close.

Oh, Joe, how could you do this to me? Why didn't you tell me?

Something stopped the doors from closing, and Laney half turned away, ashamed to be seen in such a wretched state.

"Where the hell do you think you're going?"

Laney's hands fell away, and she cringed as Joe entered the elevator and punched the stop button. "I'm sorry, I didn't mean to embarrass you. I had no idea she would be there, and you didn't tell me who she was, and—and—and I'm leaving, right now."

"Why?"

"Go back to your wife. I'm sure she'll understand—"

"What wife?"

"You know." Laney closed her eyes wearily. "The pregnant one with the dark hair and beautiful belly? Kathy?"

"I don't have a pregnant wife. I don't have any wife. *Yet.*" Joe sounded furious—and something else. "Laney, Kathryn isn't my wife. She's my little sister."

"She's not? I mean, she is?" The vise around Laney's throat eased.

"Don't you believe me?"

She nodded slowly. Suddenly, everything changed. Color returned to the world. The pieces of her heart slowly merged back together. She could feel again.

She could love him.

"As soon as I saw you, I asked Luke—Kathy's husband—to bring you up so you could meet her. Then you were running away. Now I see why." Joe gently pried her arms apart and drew her into his. "Baby, I'm sorry. She thought I was dead, and the FBI flew her in as soon as they got word. She came here from the airport as soon as her plane touched down."

"You dreamed about her, when you were sick." Laney couldn't press herself close enough to him. "The way you said her name, I thought . . . and after everything my uncle did, well . . . God, I'm an idiot."

"It doesn't matter." Joe gathered her against him. "I'm in love with you, not your uncle."

"What?" Laney backed away. "You're in love with me? But you never said—"

"I know. And I've said a lot of things to you that weren't true." Joe came toward her, his expression intent. "Sort of makes us even, doesn't it?"

Laney still couldn't quite believe he loved her. "You love me. Really? You never told me, why didn't you tell me? And here all this time, I thought your heart was made out of stone, and you were just using me for sex, and once we left Nightmare Ridge I thought for sure it was over, because you didn't call me, not one single solitary time, and then—"

"Laney." He gently placed his fingers against her lips to stop the flow of words. "I love you. And you're right, I did have a heart of stone." He gently took her hand and placed it against the front of his jacket. "You brought it back to life. And if you ever run away from me again, you'll break it into a million pieces." Joe gently tilted her face up to his. "Sweetheart, I love you. Don't ever leave me like that again."

Just before his mouth touched hers, Laney made the first of many vows. "I won't."

Epilogue

A week after the press conference in Denver, Diane Beck's testimony before a grand jury resulted in more arraignments. Fai Tung and Fai Shuzhi were arrested in Atlanta while attempting to board a private Learjet bound for Beijing.

Matt and Jill Pagent watched the report on the evening news as they sat in Ben Hunter's enormous armchair.

"That witch." Jill wriggled to a more comfortable spot on her husband's lap. Something occurred to her that made her look at Matt. "Don't tell me she's getting immunity for turning state's evidence."

"A little." He nipped at the side of her neck.

"You're kidding, right? Stop that. I'm serious, Matt." Jill tugged away, angry now. "It's not fair to let that shrew get off while everyone else goes to prison."

"That's the way it goes, honey. Don't worry, Diane is still going to do time." He pushed a lock of her hair out of his way. "By the time she gets out, she'll be an unattractive, *middle-aged* shrew."

"I guess I'll take your word for it." Jill began to relax and enjoy the feel of her husband's mouth on her skin. "We finished backfilling the last of the Dream Mountain site today. Know what that means?"

Matt grinned. "We can finally have our honeymoon?"

"Yep." Jill bounced on his lap. "So, where are you taking me? Hawaii? New York? Paris?"

He stood, swinging her up against his chest. "Let's start out with that brass bed down the hall."

Halfway across the country, another couple were well into the second week of their honeymoon on Paradise Island. At that moment they were both lying on chaise lounges beside the enormous pool behind Luke's house.

"It's so beautiful here," Laney said as she propped her chin on her hands to watch the sunset. "All the white sand and the dragonflies and beautiful flowers." She sighed. "Paradise."

"It's warm." Joe ran one of his tanned hands down the length of her naked back. Since they were alone on Paradise Island, Laney didn't have to bother with a swimsuit. Her pale flesh had gradually acquired a soft golden tone, and she'd put on a few pounds, which only made her look more delicious. His fingers spread over the curve of her backside and gently kneaded. "And getting hotter by the minute."

"Mmmmm." Laney lifted her hips, relishing his skillful touch. "A shame we have to go back to all that ice and snow. I could live here forever."

"No problem." Joe slid his hand down, following the tender crease to stroke her between her thighs. "I'll keep you warm."

"We promised Mike we'd check in today," Laney said, a dimple appearing beside her smile.

Joe rolled off the lounge and bent to pick Laney up from hers. "Mike can wait."

"It'll only take a minute, then"—she reached up and nibbled at his jaw—"I'll do whatever you want me to."

She would, too. Laney's sensual generosity still regularly astonished Joe. Since they'd come to the island, they'd devoted the better part of every day to making love.

"Okay." Reluctantly he set her down on her feet. "We check in with Mike. Then I get to molest you."

Mike Anderson, a friend of Luke's who ran a food-service company some fifty miles away on Marathon Key, also kept Joe and Laney in touch with the rest of the world—via ham radio.

When Joe contacted him, Mike immediately related the news about Diane Beck, and the indictments being handed down against various members of the Shandian Corporation.

"That's the good news. Now for the great news," Mike said. "Is Laney there, over?"

"Yeah, she's here, over." Joe squeezed his wife's waist.

"Luke just called from the hospital, said he wanted you two to be the first to hear this. Kathy's had the baby—a boy, eight pounds, six ounces. Luke's a blithering idiot, mother and son are doing fine. Congratulations, kids, you've got a nephew, over."

Laney shrieked and hugged Joe before snatching the microphone from his hand. "Mike, this is Laney. Tell Luke and Kathy we're so happy for them. Tell me about the baby—is he chubby or skinny? What color is his hair? Was Kathy's labor long? What did they name him—"

Joe grabbed the mike. "I'm gagging her, right now, I promise, over."

Laney smacked him, then started to chuckle.

"Keep tickling her, that works too. To answer your questions, Laney—chubby, blond hair, twenty-one hours, and Joseph Lucas Fleming." Mike gave one of his deep laughs. "Luke mentioned he's got feet like his uncle. Maybe he'll end up being Little Bigfoot, over?"

"Over my dead body, over," Joe said, then they all laughed together.

Once he'd thanked Mike and signed off, he pulled Laney down onto his lap. "How does it feel to be an aunt?"

"Pretty neat. I never thought I'd get a chance." Laney's mouth turned down at the corners as she thought of Neal. "My sister isn't exactly the maternal type. I just wish I could tell her about the baby . . . ."

Joe recalled how much he'd resented the mysterious "Neal." Funny how they'd both gotten jealous over each other's sisters. "She's safe, honey. That's what counts."

After witnessing the murder of an important Senator, Neala Delaney had been placed in the Federal Witness Protection Program. Just in time, too, as they learned when Matt Pagent had called them with updates on the case. Key evidence had mysteriously disappeared, and now Neal's testimony was the only proof the District Attorney could use to convict the killer.

"I can't believe he put a contract out on my sister." Laney shuddered. According to Matt, there was a million dollar bounty for the nightclub singer. Dead *or* alive. "I may never see her again."

"Sean said he'd watch over her, and once the case goes to trial, it will be over. Don't give up hope, sweetheart."

"I won't. I know Neal can take care of herself." Laney briskly wiped the tears from her face before sliding to her feet. "We'll have to head over to the mainland and see the baby tomorrow. Want to go for a swim before I start dinner?"

"I'd rather pick up where we left off," Joe said, and lifted her in his arms again.

"I'm all yours. Oh, one more thing—you have to tell Luke and Kathy to pick another nickname for Joseph. We're going to being using that one."

"Huh?" He stopped. "For what?"

Laney patted her stomach. "For our Little Bigfoot, silly."

Where is Neala Delaney?

The sultry nightclub singer has gotten herself
into a predicament that might be too much even
for a girl with her street smarts. Can this confirmed
city slicker get along with rough-around-the-edges
ranch owner Will Ryder long enough to come up
with a plan to vanquish Shandian Corporation
for good? Or will the sparks that fly between
them prove too distracting?

Turn the page to see their first explosive
meeting in a preview of Gena Hale's
next contemporary romance, *Sun Valley*.

Coming March 2002 from Onyx Books.

And if you missed the story of
Kathy Tremayne and Dr. Luke Fleming,
don't forget to pick up a copy of
Paradise Island, also from Onyx Books.

A flash of red caught Will Ryder's eye two seconds before he saw the car he was about to plow into. His boot slammed on the brake pedal, and the truck went into a skid.

"Goddamn it!"

His day had already gone from wrecked to ruined. After the phone call from Grady, his foreman had dragged in two battered, sullen hands. They'd admitted, after some prodding, how they'd gotten drunk the night before and beaten the hell out of each other. Firing them had forced Will to cancel the rest of the crew's days off until he could hire replacements. More phone calls made him even later leaving the ranch for town.

Now this fool was going to get them both killed.

Melting snow kept the roads slick and anything trying to stop on it susceptible to fishtailing, so Will had plenty of practice coming out of a skid. Once he'd managed to stop without smashing into the car or rolling into the drainage ditch, he threw the truck into "park" and shut off the engine.

A woman wearing a red coat stood to one side of the car. No, not a coat—a *dress.*

A very tight, glittery, low-cut red dress.

For a moment, all he could do was stare. She was

wearing a dress. A cocktail dress. In Montana. In February.

The obviously deranged woman sauntered over to his truck. She carried a large suitcase and a coat folded over her arm.

Here comes trouble, his Dad would have said, *looking for a place to happen.*

Will climbed out of the truck and slammed the door. "Lady, what do you think you're doing?"

She halted midstride, and looked bewildered. "You mean, besides turning into a frozen entree?"

He swore as he strode over to the car. "You don't park in the middle of a highway."

"I didn't park. I broke down." She gave him a singularly adorable smile.

"Why didn't you put on the emergency flashers?" Without waiting for an answer, Will reached in and flipped them on to avoid a repeat of what he'd just been through. "You've got to get this heap off the road. Now."

"I'm sorry, I didn't think of the flashers. I would have moved the car to the shoulder if I could have, but it's too much for me." The tall, dark traffic-stopper shaded her eyes with one hand to have a better look at him. "Could you . . . ?" she made a small, helpless gesture.

Once Will pushed the car off the road and safely onto the shoulder, most of his temper had evaporated. He turned to deal with the owner and got his first good look at her face.

Whoever she was, she was a beauty. Long, curly sable hair spilled around an elegant face. Flashing dark eyes met his, while her full red lips curved. The smile did a better job than the dress, but only because he refused to look below her collarbone.

Like something out of a movie. God, she's gorgeous.

"You okay? Any bumps or bruises?"

"Oh, no. I'm peachy." She flashed the megawatt smile again. "Just peachy."

Her skin was exactly that color—light, rosy gold—and maybe just as smooth. Realizing how much he wanted to touch her and find out made him knot his hand into a fist. "What's wrong with the car?"

"Silly me." She rolled her eyes. "I ran out of gas. You're a Godsend, you know; I was praying someone would stop and pick me up before I had to be defrosted in a microwave." She put down the case, turning her back on him in the process. Which was when he discovered her dress was backless to the waist. The sight of all that smooth exposed skin made his teeth clench all over again.

She'd get picked up, all right. Then beaten up, raped, and probably murdered.

"Put your coat on." He took it from her, and their arms brushed. Touching her was a mistake. Her skin *was* soft, and smooth, and sent a jolt of heat straight to his groin.

She shrugged back into her coat. "I would have walked to the nearest gas station, but I'm afraid I'm a little lost, too."

"Either you're lost, or you're not. There's no little about it." He moved in closer, watching the way her expression changed. Wary, he thought. About time she realized how vulnerable she was, out here alone, dressed like that. "Where were you headed?"

"Civilization, assuming it still exists out here." She looked down as he began buttoning up her coat, then peeped up through her long, curly lashes. "You're not lost, I hope?"

He finished the job, then pushed his Stetson back on his head. "Lady, I live here."

"Really." She drew the word out as she scanned their surroundings. Her dark curls danced as she shook her head. "My condolences."

His temper returned in full force as he moved away from her and pulled out his cell phone. "Have you got Triple-A?"

She glanced at his truck. "Um, to be honest, this isn't exactly my car."

He stopped dialing. "What?"

"I sort of borrowed it."

"You stole the car? Dressed like that?"

"I did not *steal* it. I borrowed it—from a couple of friends." She looked down at her buttoned-up coat. "And what's wrong with the way I'm dressed?"

"Nothing, if you like getting frostbite."

Her chin went up at that. "I'm from Colorado."

"Colorado. Right." He redialed the garage, and told his mechanic to send a wrecker out for the car. Ms. Survivor was practically shaking out of her thin coat by the time he finished the call. "Here." He shrugged out of his sheepskin-lined parka, draped it over her shoulders, and gave her a push toward his pickup. "Get in my truck."

As Will opened the passenger door, she pulled his parka closer around herself before stepping up. Her thin, high-heeled shoes slipped on the running board, and he grabbed her from behind to keep her from falling.

"Easy does it, Calamity." He'd felt the way she'd recoiled when he put his hands on her, felt the way she was trembling now. *Not as tough as you want me to think you are.* Once she was settled, he buckled her in. "Sit tight."

He went around, got in behind the wheel, and started the engine. His passenger still shivered violently, so he turned the heat on high and adjusted the vents for her. His movements made her jump a little.

"Thanks." She eyed him, gnawed at her lower lip, then looked out at the road.

Will could almost smell her fear. It should have made him back off; instead it aroused an instant, nameless response inside him—one that was so primitive and possessive it bordered on predatory.

He performed another, slower inspection. This close, he could smell her skin—no perfume, just her—warm and spicy, the way purple sage smelled in full bloom during the summer. And her skin was so clear that he could see the delicate blue veins at her wrists and temples.

The heated air from the vents fluttered through her hair, and a stray curl got caught between her lips. Before she could smooth it back, Will reached over and gently pulled it free. Her hair should have been coarse, stiff with hair spray and whatever else females put on their heads these days. Instead, it felt like silk. As he released the curl, he wondered how the rest of it would feel, filling his hands.

Bet she'd do more than jump.

Unlike most of the women he knew, she wore plenty of makeup—gleaming lipstick to match the dress, rose blush on her narrow cheekbones, black liner around her dark eyes. All very skillfully applied, but he didn't like it. He wanted to see what was underneath it. Would she be just as stunning after a dunk in a trough and a good scrub to get all that goop off her skin?

She'd be wet. Wet and mad and ready for taming and why the hell am I even thinking about it?

She shifted a little further away and broke the spell.

What was the matter with him? No matter how nicely she was packaged, the woman was trouble. Probably a car thief. Definitely the only car thief in America who wore a cocktail dress to work.